UNLEASHED

Books in this series:

The world reeled in terror and catastrophe.
Humanity seemed to have gone mad.
Then came the greatest horror—the forces of evil were . . .

UNLEASHED

by Leon Orr

Southern Publishing Association, Nashville, Tennessee

Copyright © 1979 by
Southern Publishing Association

This book was
Edited by Gerald Wheeler
Designed by Mark O'Connor
Cover illustration by Marcus Hamilton

Type set: 10/11 Times Roman

Printed in U.S.A.

Library of Congress Cataloging in Publication Data

Orr, Leon.
   Unleashed.

   I. Title.
PZ4.07624Un   [PS3565.R72]   813'.5'4   79-13290
ISBN 0-8127-0230-1

CONTENTS

Chapter 1

PRESIDENT-ELECT

President-elect McGrath stood gazing out of her office window, vaguely conscious of the snarled traffic in the streets below. A freezing rain glazed the first snowfall of the season. Taxis skidded down the Washington streets, and pedestrians cautiously inched along the sidewalks. It was quitting time for the tens of thousands of government employees who spilled from the office buildings into the gray dusk and clustered, shivering, at each bus stop or headed for the nearest subway station.

"Rasmussen, without your support I could never have won, and without your counsel I would never attempt to govern this nation. But, as valuable as your advice is to me, I wouldn't want to keep you away from your family over Christmas. Why not fly home tonight and stay till after New Year's Day?"

The elderly man seated in the office easy chair stroked his gray goatee before responding. "You are always kind, my dear lady, but I could not enjoy the holidays while you struggled alone with all the decisions that need to be made before you take office. You have decided to stay in Washington, haven't you?"

"We have worked hard for months and need a rest." She turned to face him. "A short break would clear our minds to cope with national problems more effectively. I think I'll ask my secretary to reschedule my appointments for a later date and spend the weekend with my daughter in Virginia. Why don't you join your family in Wisconsin—at least for the weekend?"

He smiled. "If you insist. But please call me if you come to any decision about our Middle East involvement or how we should cope with the threatened famine."

"Naturally I will. You know I always consult you on major decisions. However, I hope to set aside these grim realities and have a few days of inward peace."

Rasmussen reluctantly left the office. He had long aspired to a position of power, but his reputation for chicanery, his advanced age, and his known interest in spiritualism had made a political career unlikely.

Arlene McGrath, however, possessed certain intangible qualities that inspired confidence, and though she had won the election by a narrow margin, she would soon be in a position to catapult him to fame. The middle-aged widow was remarkably responsive to his suggestions, and Rasmussen determined to keep her dependent upon him. He had no doubt that he was much more capable of governing the nation than she was. They both knew that only his shrewd maneuvering of certain power groups had won her the election, and he didn't intend to let her forget that.

After Rasmussen's footsteps faded into silence, Arlene McGrath left a note for her secretary, locked the office, and headed toward the elevator. Her Secret Service guards silently followed her. Snowy-haired Senator Rice waited for her to descend.

"Leaving Washington for the holidays, Senator?" she asked him.

"Definitely." He took her hands in his. "How about you?"

"I'm just going a few miles to my daughter's home in

Virginia. But at least I'll be out of the office for a few days."

He laughed heartily. "By all means enjoy this Christmas. It will probably be your last chance for at least four years."

Senator Rice had unsuccessfully tried for his party's nomination for President on two occasions. But any bitterness he once might have felt had gradually dimmed, replaced by a sort of gratitude that he did not have to face responsibility for the spiraling series of events that had plunged the United States into disrepute at home and abroad.

As Arlene McGrath stepped out into the cold rain her car came up. "Where to?" the Secret Service agent and driver asked.

"Washington Cathedral."

As the limousine inched along the treacherous streets, an overwhelming sense of inadequacy flooded her. True, Rasmussen seemed to possess an uncanny wisdom, and she felt fortunate to have his services, but she would, nevertheless, be responsible for all the final decisions. What if conditions failed to improve during her administration? Could they possibly get worse? Would history books portray her as the woman of the era or the greatest failure of all time? Then the thought occurred to her that if she didn't succeed in bringing peace and ecological balance, there would be no history books.

Arlene McGrath had had little experience in private, personal prayer, but she felt that if ever she needed God's guidance, it was now. And where would she more likely find Him than at the cathedral? Surely God, having guided man's evolution so far, would not abandon him now. And if God was as powerful as He was reputed to be, would He not hear the prayer of Arlene McGrath and give her miraculous skill to govern the nation? From Sunday School days she vaguely remembered a story about King Solomon's request for wis-

dom when he ascended the throne. Praying would be awkward at first, she suspected, but hopefully God would understand, even if her words were inadequate. And if it became
known that she had gone to the cathedral to pray for wisdom,
perhaps was even photographed on her knees, wouldn't that
appeal to a nation desperately turning once again to religion?

Chapter 2

NEW YEAR'S EVE

Duane glanced for the second time in five minutes at the large decorator clock on the marble fireplace. Half an hour till midnight. His eyes smarted from the tobacco smoke. A waiter, noticing his empty glass, rushed over with his tray.

"What will you have, Mr. Manning?" he asked, his wilted smile betraying his weariness.

"Nothing more, thank you." Just then the hostess, Mrs. Shapasian, grabbed his arm. "Oh, Duane! I have never heard our piano sound so good! Your Chopin was magnificent. Did you get enough to eat to replenish all that energy you used up?"

He tried to flash a smile suitably charming for the occasion. "More than enough, thank you. Your caterer is exceptional."

Mrs. Shapasian then darted off to attend to her other guests. Duane headed slowly toward the glass doors that opened onto the terrace. Two middle-aged men vehemently argued in front of the exit doors. How, he wondered, could he get to the doors without becoming involved in the argument? He rarely took a stand on any political issue. Soon a new President would try her hand at bringing peace and, Duane sincerely hoped, would be more successful than her predecessor. Suddenly one of the men knocked his glass of red wine onto the white carpet. Duane slipped out of the room unnoticed.

The biting Massachusetts cold was a welcome contrast to the stale air inside. The bare trees cast shadows on the glazed snow, which reflected the floodlights illuminating the terrace. In the distance, evergreens decked in multicolored lights still celebrated Christmas.

Once Christmas had been a joyous season as Duane's mother, excited as a child, shopped and wrapped gifts in lavish ways that sometimes belied their meager contents. Together they would decorate the tree with assorted lights, balls, chains, icicles, and angels accumulated over the years. The finished tree generally evidenced more exuberance than artistry.

This year Duane and his father had celebrated alone. It had been a struggle for Duane to decide to go home for the holidays, and he had gone more to cheer up his father than to enjoy himself. His father attempted to make things festive, and Duane tried to show his appreciation. But both felt a deep loneliness that revealed itself in fleeting expressions rather than in words. Two days after Christmas Duane returned to Worcester, wondering whether he would ever visit home again.

The voices of the guests droned on inside. Duane did not consider himself especially religious, but it seemed that New Year's Eve should be a time for something more serious than cocktail conversation. Just then the door opened and Gina rushed out, her long black hair flowing down her slim figure. Her hand squeezed his. "Duane! You'll catch pneumonia. I've been looking all over for you. Have you been out here all the time?"

"Not long. Just came out for some fresh air."

"It's almost midnight, and you don't want to miss the celebration."

Reluctantly he followed her inside, where someone thrust a horn into his hand. Presently the clock struck twelve, and bedlam broke loose. Ten minutes later everyone breathlessly reassured one another that it was the best New Year's party ever. Someone proposed a dance. While they cleared the spacious living room of all furniture except the grand piano, Duane found Mrs. Shapasian, thanked her for inviting him, and excused himself for leaving early on grounds that he was playing a recital in two days and needed to get as much rest as possible.

The Shapasian home was in Boylston, a town small enough to still allow private automobiles. He had parked his tired economy-sized car at the street end of the winding driveway partly because he had felt that its rusting body looked conspicuous on the immaculately tended grounds, but primarily because he wanted to make sure that no other car would block it.

The seven miles to Worcester sped by while Duane mulled over the details of his upcoming recital. Soon he arrived at the new multitiered parking lot and drove to his rented stall on tier six. Since the recent prohibition of private cars on the streets of cities of over a quarter of a million inhabitants, such parking lots had cropped up everywhere. Duane wondered whether he should keep the car at all, since the rent on the parking stall was almost as high as that on his studio apartment. And the price of gasoline itself was prohibitive.

As he walked the half block to the bus stop, Duane hoped the authorities had relaxed the midnight-to-five curfew for New Year's Eve. He was confident they had when he found a group of people waiting for the bus. Most of them appeared to be partygoers with the beginnings of hangovers. One woman with a slipping eyelash and streaked mascara giggled to herself. A paunchy middle-aged man clung to the lamppost. The others had sullen, leave-me-alone expressions.

The bus arrived with only three empty seats. Duane helped the drunk man to one of them and stood by to keep him from tumbling into the aisle. Several standees swayed as the bus lurched to its frequent stops. The drunk managed to mumble his destination, and Duane offered to help him home, as the man's stop was only three blocks beyond Duane's.

The trip from the bus to the upstairs flat where the man lived should have taken five minutes. Instead, it required about twenty, and Duane fervently wished for a policeman to help him steady the man's buckling knees. With great relief Duane delivered him to a cursing, frowsy wife more interested in berating her husband than in thanking Duane for bringing him home.

The walk from the flat to Duane's apartment took him past Tony's corner grocery. He paused to admire some ripe persimmons in the window, thinking he might wander over in the morning to buy one for breakfast. Then he remembered that tomorrow would be a holiday.

Until recently Tony had stayed open seven days a week by paying a nominal fine for violating the blue laws. But now the fines for being open on Sundays and holidays were so heavy that no one could make enough profit by staying open to offset them. Repeaters who felt they were justified in refusing to obey an unjust law found themselves serving long jail sentences.

Duane missed the convenience of being able to drop in at Tony's for small purchases between trips to the supermarket. He chided himself for not having had the foresight to replenish his nearly empty refrigerator. As he wondered whether the stalk of brown-flecked bananas hanging above the persimmons would survive till Monday, the shrill blast of a police whistle startled him. He glanced in the direction of the sound and saw an overweight policeman hurrying toward him. Unsure whether the man had blown the whistle at him or not, he just waited. The officer arrived, puffing too hard to talk for a few seconds, but soon recovered his breath sufficiently to demand Duane's identification card.

Duane reached for his wallet. It wasn't there. Then he tried the inside pocket of his overcoat. Not there either. Futilely he examined every pocket while protesting helplessly that he must have been robbed on the bus. He remembered the other standees bumping him a few times. His story failed to impress the officer, whose face had a weary, here-we-go-again expression as he took out his pad.

"Your name?"

"Duane Manning."

"Address?"

"704 Jensen Street."

"Age?"

"Twenty-three."

"Occupation?"

"Student."

"Why are you out after curfew?"

"I thought that on New Year's Eve the curfew would be relaxed."

The policeman frowned. "If you had bothered to read the newspapers, you would have known that it went into effect at 1:30. It is almost two o'clock now. Come with me."

Silently he followed the officer to a police cruiser a few blocks away. At the station he waited with other offenders for what seemed like hours. Finally someone asked him for a detailed account of his evening activities. Then the desk sergeant called Mrs. Shapasian to verify his story, which she did, adding an unsolicited testimonial as to the excellence of his character and sending her regrets that he was in trouble.

Since Duane knew neither the name of the drunk man nor his house number, the police could not check that part of his story. Shoving a piece of paper toward him, the sergeant announced gruffly, mechanically, "This application form mailed with ten dollars will entitle you to a new identification card. However, if you lose that one, it will be harder to replace. We do not intend to let unauthorized individuals wander about our streets after curfew. The law *will be enforced*. People often complain that we now have a police state. When freedom is abused, it must be replaced with whatever is necessary to maintain order."

Duane thanked the officer, who directed him to the police cruiser, which took him home. When he finally dropped into bed it was four o'clock.

Chapter 3

MRS. SCHWAB

Sunday evening most of the culturally elite in the small town of Hudson gathered at the art gallery for the third in the season's series of events sponsored by the Women's Literary League. Those who arrived early wandered around, glancing perfunctorily at the few dozen paintings and art objects, mostly by local artists, that they had viewed each previous visit to the gallery.

Backstage Duane tried to calm the trembling of his knees and hands by deep breathing and positive thinking. Too much deep breathing could make a person dizzy, while positive thinking seemed to work in inverse proportion to the proximity of the performance. The poorly heated room in which he paced seemed to be a storage area for cast-off furniture. He tried to warm his cold hands by keeping them in his pockets. A restroom opened off a nearby hallway, but the lavatory ran only cold water, which did nothing to improve the condition of his stiff fingers.

When the time came to begin, Duane cracked the door to the stage and peeked out to see whether he had an audience yet. About a hundred people had found seats, and probably another thirty still wandered around looking at the paintings and ceramics.

Then Mrs. Corcoran Schwab arose and cleared her throat. Those still standing quickly took their seats. Around

17

forty-five years of age, short in stature, Mrs. Schwab had a commanding air that well qualified her for the presidency of the Women's Literary League in addition to numerous other civic responsibilities. Her freshly coiffed blond hair, the matching diamond earrings and necklace, the chic black dress that minimized her ample girth, the firm set of her chin, and the directness of her gaze attested to a forcefulness that wealth had enhanced. Even her husband, an executive at W. J. Thornton Company, generally acceded to her wishes.

In a resonant voice she announced, "Ladies and gentlemen. We are delighted that so many of you are here for what promises to be a most rewarding evening. Our artist, a graduate student at Thornton School of Music, in Worcester, has already performed extensively in the United States and Canada. Some of you may have heard his exciting performance last season with the Worcester Symphony Orchestra. Those wishing to meet him are invited to the green room, where refreshments will be served following the recital. And now I am pleased to present our artist, Duane Manning."

During the applause that followed, Mrs. Schwab returned to her seat on the front row, flanked by her husband and eight-year-old son. When Duane walked to the center of the platform and bowed, she beamed with vicarious satisfaction. She could never forget that she had been destined to be an opera prima donna till marriage interfered. But the adulation denied her would come to her pianist son. Patting his arm, she dreamed of the day Spencer would also bow before a rapt audience—not in some little art gallery, but in large concert halls around the world.

Her son's thoughts, however, were far from music. They rambled from football to his favorite TV program, which he was missing because of this miserable recital, to how he would get even with Randy, who had called him a sissy in front of the whole third grade, and finally to how he could manage to get away from his mother after the recital to make sure he got to the cookies before they were all gone.

Soon Spencer noticed that a lock of the pianist's wavy brown hair had slipped down over one eye. The boy wondered how soon the rest would follow. Just as another lock seemed ready to slide to join it, the piece ended, and the pianist smoothed the errant lock into place as he rose to acknowledge the applause.

Many hours later—or so it seemed to Spencer—he hurried to the green room, where well-wishers filed by to congratulate Duane. Most balanced a cup of coffee and cookies in one hand while shaking hands with the other. The boy's mother insisted that he also shake hands with the musician, and he reluctantly complied. Then, in his hurry to escape, he backed into someone's coffee, spilling it on the floor and on himself. He let out a wail of pain as the hot liquid ran down his neck. His mother hurried him off.

Soon Mrs. Schwab returned with Spencer, patting him proudly. "This young man is going to be an artist like you. He plays very well for only three years of lessons."

"I'm glad to hear that," Duane said politely. "Do you enjoy practicing, young man?"

Spencer grimaced.

"I hear that you give lessons as well as concertize," Mrs. Schwab resumed. "What is your fee?"

Duane sensed that he was being considered as a teacher for Spencer. He gave an evasive answer and hurried to add that he had about as many students as he could handle with his performing, studies, and fellowship duties at the Thornton School of Music.

Mrs. Schwab didn't appear too disappointed. "Spencer has an adequate teacher for now. But when he gets a little more advanced, he'll need to make a change. I hope you'll still be in the area, because I think you would make an

excellent teacher. You could inspire him as his present
teacher cannot.''

"Possibly. Maybe in a few years I could help him."
Duane smiled, silently hoping to avoid further contact with
the domineering matron.

The Schwabs saw him to his car after everyone else had
left. Mr. Schwab handed him the check that was his fee for
the recital and thanked him for the performance. As Duane
started the motor, Mrs. Schwab called, "We'll keep in touch
with you."

He sensed it was more than a mere pleasantry.

Chapter 4

LAUREL

Thornton School of Music was only five years old. W. J.
Thornton, multimillionaire, whose visual-aids plant was in
Worcester County, had endowed it. Mr. Thornton's cellist
wife was the daughter of Emil Sokoloff, famed conductor
who, with his orchestra, had perished in the Atlantic Ocean
when their chartered plane disappeared en route to London.
As a memorial to his father-in-law and to fill the need for a
music school in central Massachusetts, Thornton had given
the land and had invited other companies in the area to join
him in supporting the venture. The school was small but
apparently on sound financial footing.

Madame Isolde Wolfinger, a former operatic soprano,
served as one of the voice teachers. A handsome woman in
spite of her girth and unruly blond hair, she had had to leave
the stage many years before because of high blood pressure.
Considering how she taught, along with trying to run the
private and professional lives of her students as well, it was
hard to imagine that her singing could have been any more
strenuous. She never sat while teaching but demonstrated for
her students constantly. Drumming her interpretation of the
rhythm and tempo into the shoulders of the accompanist, she
shouted warnings and encouragements in a mixture of En-
glish and German.

Unable to play the piano, she was constantly dependent

21

upon the services of an accompanist. Duane accompanied her lessons fifteen hours each week in return for free tuition at the school.

On the second day of the term after semester break, Duane entered Madame Wolfinger's studio to find her interrogating a young woman. The girl was rather tall, with fair skin, and her golden brown hair rested in loose waves on her slender shoulders.

Madame motioned for Duane to take his place at the piano. "Duane, ve haff another zoprahno—Laurel Lambert."

The flush in her cheeks and her reluctance to say more than was necessary to answer Madame's questions revealed the girl's nervousness.

Laurel nodded when the voice teacher asked, "You studied many years, ja?" Then, "Vat you bring to zing for me?"

The girl produced the Schumann cycle, "Woman's Love and Life," and sang two songs. Madame was pleased with her voice but not with her previous training or her German pronunciation. After demonstrating some exercises to achieve relaxation and proper support, she sang the pieces Laurel had brought. In spite of her sixty years the woman had not lost her voice.

"You go now. I vill hear them again next veek. Und get zome help mit der Churman." She waved as Laurel backed out of the studio, then said to Duane, "She vill zing very gut zomeday. You vill zee."

Laurel found her way to the lunchroom and stopped at one of the vending machines for a carton of milk. Six long tables were crowded into the small, smoke-filled room. Most were completely occupied, but she managed to find a seat where four young men were heatedly discussing President McGrath's inaugural address. They didn't seem to notice her as she bowed her head in a short prayer before opening her lunch sack.

"I think the speech was nothing but a series of inanities." The speaker emptied the bowl of his pipe into the ashtray.

"What did you expect of a woman President, anyway?" asked the scrawny one.

"She won't be running the country," a third interjected. "It's that rascal Rasmussen who dictates her every move."

The fourth student rose and started loading the empty dishes onto his tray. The others, still oblivious to Laurel's presence, continued their discussion as they headed toward the door.

In a few minutes Duane came by with his tray and asked if he might join her. She smiled. "Are you a new freshman?" he inquired.

"No. I'm a junior transfer student."

He placed his dishes on the table and pushed the tray to one side. "Where have you been attending school?"

"I had two years at Atlantic Union College, but it was a private school that had to close for financial reasons."

He thought a moment. "Say, isn't that the college in Lancaster operated by Seventh-day Adventists?"

The girl nodded.

"I played there once. Strange. I thought the school appeared to be quite stable."

"It operated for over a century. But they wouldn't accept government money because they didn't want the strings attached. As tuition rates continued to rise, fewer and fewer students could afford to attend. They couldn't maintain a faculty on the reduced income."

"Too bad. I hear quite a few private schools have closed lately."

She toyed with her food. "My parents taught there. When the college closed, they retired."

He leaned back and studied her a moment. "Oh? What did they teach?"

"Dad taught biology, and Mom taught French. They're on a farm now." The girl laughed pleasantly, and her blue eyes crinkled in the corners. "A more impractical couple you couldn't find anywhere."

"Do you have a place in town here?"

"No, I commute. It's only twenty miles. A regional commuter train passes within a mile of the farm." She laughed again. "The walk twice a day should improve my breathing so that I'll sound more like Madame Wolfinger wants me to."

Laurel glanced at the wall clock and gathered up her music. Then saying a quick goodbye to Duane, she went in a futile search for an available practice room. She hesitated to occupy either of two vacant rooms, since they had music left open on the pianos. After making the rounds of the practice rooms several times, she decided that the ten-minute interval one could be away from a practice room without forfeiting it had been exceeded, so she timidly went into one and began to sing.

Almost immediately a petite brunette entered and announced, "This room is taken."

"Sorry," Laurel replied. "Is this your music?"

"Yes, it is."

"Then you must be Gina. I'm Laurel." Her smile brought only a halfhearted nod. "How does one get a practice room around here?"

"Come early and stake out a claim like everyone else."

Since Gina's frosty tone did not encourage further conversation, Laurel picked up her things and left. She felt terribly lonely as she made her way to the library and wondered whether she would turn out to be a misfit at Thornton.

Chapter 5

RASMUSSEN

Rasmussen shuffled to the window and pressed the button that opened the scarlet velvet drapes to admit the pale afternoon rays of a March sun. The midnight-blue tapestry covering the walls of Rasmussen's White House conference room seemed to swallow the wan light. The aging man dropped wearily into a leather recliner, which sighed beneath his slight form. He tilted the chair back, squirmed a bit to find the most comfortable position, and closed his eyes.

The message just communicated by the spirits had been clear enough. But how was he to tell President McGrath that she was powerless to end the violence, disease, and hunger plaguing the nation? And how could he tell her that foreign relations would actually continue to get worse?

Rasmussen had confidently expected that his spirit-directed counsel to the new President would solve the nation's problems and bring him fame as the greatest statesman of all time. But the spirits offered no solution—only dire predictions. Already he detected rumblings of discontent throughout the nation because a spiritist was interfering in government policy.

He was angry with himself for accepting the responsibility of Presidential adviser, and he was becoming contemptuous of President McGrath for being so dependent upon him. And while he resented the people who criticized him, he much more detested the masses who seemed so oblivious to the nation's plight. At times he almost wished he were still in Wisconsin, practicing law.

Reluctantly Rasmussen opened his eyes, picked up the evening paper on the table by his chair, and fumbled with the lamp switch. Then he drew his reading glasses from his pocket and scanned the headlines:

"Over 20,000 Perish in Ecuador." Skipping the story, he decided, "Suppose we'll have to send relief. I'll check on that this evening." His eye moved down the front page.

"More Cattle Die in Texas." "So, they claim disease has already killed hundreds of thousands. We'd better find the cause quick. In the meantime we had better check on the quarantine situation." He turned the page.

"Another Crop Failure Predicted for Midwest." "Unless, contrary to predictions," he thought, "the drought breaks, we'll have a real food shortage this year. Many of the farmers who went bankrupt last fall have gone into other employment. People are already hoarding food. God have mercy on the others."

"Rasmussen Linked With Labor Scandal," declared the headline on another page. "I thought I'd rate the front page on that one. Maybe this will all blow over sooner than I expected. I may not be loved in Washington circles, but at least I'm feared. Not many members of Congress or the courts would want to risk displeasing the spirits by humiliating me. Strange how no one will admit publicly to having anything to do with spiritism, while so many privately practice it."

He let the paper slip to the floor. "When Arlene calls, I'll suggest she have our ambassador to the Vatican propose that the pope join American Roman Catholics in a day of prayer for the ending of the drought. Then if it ends, we'll all be lucky. If not, that impostor can try to explain his lack of influence with Heaven. In either case my reputation will not suffer.''

The late afternoon sunlight reached his knees. Rasmussen had not slept well for many nights. The warmth of the sunlight made him drowsy. He switched off the light, settled deeper into the recliner, and closed his eyes. His head began to nod and his jaw dropped as he drifted into a deep sleep.

After a while he became aware of his phone ringing. His body seemed numb as he struggled out of the recliner. He stumbled over a chair in the darkness and bumped his thigh on the oak table in the center of the room while groping his way toward the desk and phone. When he picked up the phone his voice was husky.

"Rasmussen speaking. . . . Ah, yes, my dear Arlene, it's really me. . . . No, nothing is wrong. . . . The spirits haven't been too helpful yet, but I have two suggestions. . . . First, let our ambassador to the Vatican enlist the aid of the pope in proclaiming a day of prayer in early summer for the end of the drought, and second, start rationing food and storing up nonperishables right away. . . . But I believe in showing my faith by my works. . . . What scandal? . . , Oh, that! I'd rather explain it to you in person. . . . All right, I'll be right over. Good-bye.''

Flipping on the light, he staggered to the bathroom to wash his face in cold water. Glancing at his reflection in the mirror, he noted that the past few months had sallowed his complexion, etched the lines of his face deeper, and rounded his shoulders. He smoothed his goatee and combed his gray mane perfunctorily without thwarting the chaotic tendencies of his wiry locks. After straightening his tie and securing his false teeth, he felt satisfied that he looked presentable enough to visit the President.

Arlene McGrath seethed inwardly that her adviser should have been involved in a scandal so early in her administra-

tion. She had been aware of the promises he had made to
labor leaders in exchange for union support for her campaign.
If she blamed Rasmussen at all, it was for failing to take
proper precautions to keep the matter secret. Now she dared
not risk an investigation for fear of what it might uncover.
And relieving Rasmussen of his responsibility as her adviser
would be unthinkable, not because she really enjoyed having
him as confidant and friend, but because without him she was
helpless.

Rasmussen strode between guards who opened the door
to the office, then closed it after him. President McGrath
motioned toward a chair, and Rasmussen silently took a seat.
He stared at the ceiling. The President spoke first.

"What do you suggest we do about this labor mess?"

"Nothing." He didn't take his gaze off the ceiling.

"Why do you say that?"

A shrug. "What can we do that won't make things
worse? I predict no one will press for an investigation."

She thought a moment. "What about Senator Clark? You
know he's an honest man, and he's after your hide besides."

"I think you'll find that he won't be a problem." A faint
smile lurked at the corners of his mouth.

"He cannot be bribed or intimidated," she persisted,
"and he's quite a leader on Capitol Hill."

"True. The country could use more like him."

The President nervously fussed with her hair as if stall-
ing. "Word has come on good authority that he plans to see
you're ousted from your position as my personal adviser.
Don't you think you should pay him a visit and—uh—
attempt to persuade him not to bring charges?"

"No. I don't plan to go near him."

"Well, if you won't face him, I'll call him in and feel him
out. I'll try to learn how much he actually knows about the
affair."

Rasmussen's smile became more irritating. "Don't be in too much of a hurry."

"I'll try to convey the impression that I want to cooperate in every way to bring to light any improper deals," she persisted. "I'll set up an appointment for tomorrow morning."

"Could you wait till next week?"

"I'm afraid not."

"How about two days from now?" He leaned forward.

McGrath eyed him. "What's to be gained by waiting?"

"You can reduce the risk of exposure."

"Explain yourself. It had better be good."

"Just trust me this time, please, Arlene," he replied, with just a calculated hint of begging in his voice.

"All right." She picked up her desk calendar. "Today is Tuesday. I'll set up an appointment for Friday morning. Does that give you enough time to plan your defense?"

"Friday will be fine. Incidentally, my defense is already planned."

"Good." She turned away from him. Picking up the stack of letters on her desk, she glanced at the signatures.

He backed toward the door, reached for the handle, and said softly, "I'll be going now unless you have something else to discuss."

The President didn't seem to hear him. As he slipped out the door she continued to read a letter.

Thursday morning Arlene McGrath glanced at the newspaper headlines while having breakfast alone:

"Clark Dies on Senate Floor."

Chapter 6

GINA

Gina Schiavina was beautiful. No one ever questioned that fact. Selected beauty queen of her high school in her senior year, the following year she was runner-up in the Miss Massachusetts contest. With her delicate figure, fair skin, brown saucer eyes, and flowing black hair, Gina had mastered the art of appearing helpless and innocent around males. Her mother, who operated a charm school, had coached her well.

As a voice major at Thornton planning on an operatic career, Gina showed promise. Her acting ability was superb, and her voice, while not powerful enough to rise above the orchestra in loud passages, was clear and pleasing. Also she was quite intelligent, though she artfully concealed the fact.

She was recovering from the abrupt ending of a long affair with a married man whose wife had discovered it and had insisted the family move to another state. The affair was not common knowledge at the school, though probably no one would have been surprised to learn of it.

Her father, a successful businessman, had indulged her every whim, and she would not marry anyone who would not humor her as he had. Sinking into an upholstered chair in the student lounge as far as possible from the group of students watching TV, she began running through her mental file of bachelors: Adrian—too stuck on himself; Bob—too flabby; Chuck—too intellectual; Dick—a good possibility, but she wouldn't be seeing him for two weeks because the law school was on vacation.

Just then Laurel and Duane entered the lounge. The girl had observed them together quite a bit in the few weeks since the new term began. They were well suited to each other, she thought. Both were tall and lithe, though Duane was slightly stooped from too many hours on the piano bench. She considered both too serious about their studies and disgustingly old-fashioned in their outlook.

Gina admired Duane, though she considered him too unsophisticated. He had comforted her once when Madame's fury over an ill-prepared voice lesson had reduced her to tears. Madame had told her the road to stardom was "Verk, verk, verk," and ordered her out of the studio till she had decided that time in the practice room was more important than before the mirror.

She had assumed that Duane was oblivious to women. That he should be spending time with a girl whose face was rather plain and who did nothing to camouflage the fact annoyed her. It would be a challenge to discover what kind of man he really was, and she relished that type of a challenge. She eyed him as the couple sat down on a sofa against the opposite wall, oblivious of anyone else in the lounge.

There was to be an orchestral concert at the school that evening. Duane asked Laurel whether she planned to attend.

"I really wish I could, but my parents would never approve of my walking the mile from the train to home late at night. It would be too dangerous."

"Yes, I suppose it would. But I'd be happy to drive you home. How about it?"

Her eyes widened. "That's very kind of you. Let me call home to let my folks know when to expect me."

While Laurel went to phone, Duane waited in the lounge. He attempted to ignore the noisy TV and picked up the morning paper. The headlines were as depressing as ever, and he laid it down.

Suddenly he sensed someone watching him, and for the first time he noticed Gina across the room. She smiled enigmatically and continued to gaze in a direct way that made him uncomfortable. He looked away and picked up the paper again. Two minutes later Laurel had not returned, and Gina still devoured him with her eyes. Rising, he headed for the door just as Laurel entered.

The concert ended at ten o'clock, and within fifteen minutes Duane and Laurel had arrived by bus at the parking lot. He apologized for the antiquity of his car and for the fact that it hadn't been washed recently. She laughingly suggested he might as well wait till April when the snow and slush would be gone.

As they drove along he began asking about her family. "Aren't your parents rather young to be retired?"

"Oh, they're not that youthful. They're in their late fifties. They finished their education before starting a family. I have a brother four years older."

"Oh? Where is he?"

"In medical school in California. This is his second year."

He glanced at her. "That's a heavy financial burden on your parents, isn't it?"

"Yes, it is. But my brother has a scholarship, and my tuition is less now than it was at Atlantic Union College. My church job of playing organ on Sunday helps a bit too. We get no income as yet from the farm."

"This farm of yours—what do you raise on it?"

She laughed. "It's really an apple orchard. We have five acres of apple trees. For our own use we have a corn-field and a vegetable garden. We were such amateurs that we didn't have much of a harvest last fall, but Dad is busy studying books on agriculture, and next year should be different."

The road was rather deserted. Few people could afford to drive much anymore. Duane was silent a moment, apparently wondering what to say next. "You once mentioned your dad's attempts at milking. Do you have a large herd?"

"Just one—a Jersey. She gives all the milk we can use. . . . I'm sure you'll meet Sheba, our black German Shepherd. She feels it her duty to announce every visitor. We have forty hens too. Mom sells eggs to all the neighbors."

"Are your parents happy with their new life?"

"They love it. They wonder why they didn't get out of the classroom long before. Dad has finally started writing the book he had planned for over ten years."

At this point Laurel indicated a right turn. "That's the house on the left—at the top of the hill. I see Mom has the outside lights on."

The house was a white two-story frame dwelling, apparently built around the middle of the century. A large sign in the front yard read, "Three Elms." As the car turned into the drive a dog ran to meet it, barking excitedly.

Laurel rolled down the glass and called, "Quiet, Sheba."

Immediately a happy whining and vigorous wagging replaced the barking. The dog almost knocked Duane off-balance as he opened the car door for Laurel. She invited him in for a few minutes to meet her parents.

Mrs. Lambert, a more mature version of Laurel, was still

up. Her gray hair framed skin still smooth except for small laugh wrinkles around her eyes. "Laurel's dad said to tell you he was sorry not to be able to wait up tonight to meet you," she told Duane. "Our days begin much earlier now that we have a cow. But he will look forward to meeting you another time. Would you like some hot chocolate to warm you up? I can have it ready in five minutes."

"Thank you, Mrs. Lambert. Maybe I could stay that long. The curfew is rigidly enforced in the city, you know."

"Oh, I forgot. Has it really reduced crime?"

"I don't know. The government seems finally serious about enforcing law and order."

Mrs. Lambert set a kettle to boil on the stove. "Isn't there a danger that they may go too far?"

"I suppose there is. But my mother was murdered a year ago for the few dollars in her purse."

"Oh," Laurel gasped. "I didn't know. We're so sorry."

"You must be lonely," Mrs. Lambert said later. "Feel free to visit us whenever you wish."

Driving back to the city, Duane continued to feel the warmth of the hot chocolate and Mrs. Lambert's kindness. He hoped Mr. Lambert would prove to be as pleasant. Laurel's references to her father depicted him as an intellectual trying desperately to be practical.

When Duane got home he found a note under his door:

"Dearest Duane,

"Forgive me for coming to your apartment. I would have called if you'd had a phone.

"Dad is inviting a few friends to join our family at our cabin on Mount Snow for the weekend. Would you be my guest?

"We could pick you up at noon on Friday. We'll return late Sunday night. If you don't own skis, they can

*be rented at the slopes. In case you don't enjoy skiing, we
have a piano at the cabin where you could practice
undisturbed while enjoying a glorious view.*

*"Please don't disappoint us, as we are really looking
forward to your company.*

"Your friend,
"Gina

*"PS. Concert Manager Phil Sumpsion will be there.
You might enjoy meeting him."*

Until he read the postscript Duane had little interest.
Now he wasn't sure how to reply.

"Surely it won't hurt to cultivate the friendship of Phil
Sumpsion," Duane mused. "His Boston office books concerts throughout New England. I can probably endure Gina
for a couple of days in the interest of my career."

Chapter 7

MOUNT SNOW

Duane felt trapped. The A-frame cabin offered no escape from Gina's gaze.

It was Saturday morning. After Duane announced that he planned to spend the day practicing, Gina decided she was not feeling well enough to join the rest of the group as they went skiing. She lay regally on the couch, occasionally glancing at the magazine in her hand while listening to Duane and making admiring comments, apparently unaware of the out-of-tune piano.

Finally Duane realized he was accomplishing nothing. He doubted that Gina knew the difference between practicing and just playing the piano, and he couldn't bring himself to start the note-by-note, phrase-by-phrase type of practice that he needed.

Not only was the weekend wasted as far as practicing was concerned, but he had seen nothing of Phil Sumpsion. When he asked about him Gina made some vague comment about a change of plans. Duane suspected the postscript about Sumpsion had been Gina's bait. He was angry with himself for being so gullible.

Finishing the passage he was working on, Duane stood up. His shoulders and neck ached from three hours of constant playing. He walked to the wall of glass that offered an unrestricted view of the valley. The noon sun shone warmly on the snow, causing it to drop in wet clumps from the branches of the dark-green hemlocks. A cluster of naked white birch leaned toward the cabin.

Spotting a neat stack of logs under a tarpaulin not far from the cabin and noting only two logs in the wood carrier by the fireplace, Duane suggested that he replenish it. Gina agreed to prepare a snack while he went after more wood.

The wet snow that clung to Duane's boots hinted that skiing was about over for the season. The spring that the skiers hoped would delay as long as possible couldn't come too soon for him. But in a way he envied the skiers and wished he could share the thrills of the slalom. Perhaps, he admitted to himself, his devotion to music had cost him too much.

The lunch Gina prepared was richer in calories than anything else. She only nibbled, as she was committed to a lifelong diet. As they ate they sat on the deacon's bench in front of the fire. Gina seemed remarkably vivacious for someone too ill to go skiing. In fact, she had never looked healthier or more beautiful. Her pink lounging robe clung flatteringly to her figure. The subtle fragrance of exotic perfume followed her as she fluttered from kitchen area to bench, making sure Duane's plate remained full.

Finally, when he declared he could eat nothing more, Gina settled down beside him and rested her head on his shoulder. In silence they watched the fire for several minutes.

"You don't know how I've looked forward to your visit. I've admired you a long time," she sighed at last.

"Thank you for inviting me. You have an attractive place here."

"There's something I haven't shown you. Please come upstairs."

She took his hand and led him upstairs to the room the women had occupied the night before. At the door he hesitated, but Gina tightened her grip on his hand. Sitting on the edge of the bed, she pulled him gently down beside her. From under the pillow she drew out an envelope containing a letter that she unfolded and handed to him.

"Dearest Gina,
  "Sorry I cannot accept your invitation for the weekend at your cabin this time. If the young man is as fine a pianist as you say, I should like to meet him. Bring him to see me sometime.

>   *"With fondest memories,*
>   *"Phil"*

Duane finished reading, but continued staring at the letter, one elbow resting on his knee. Gina stroked his back. "Phil and I are the best of friends. I can help you if you will let me."

Turning toward her, Duane found himself looking into her searching eyes. He could not think of anything but her touch.

Abruptly he stood up.

"Where are you going?" she asked in a startled whimper.

"Skiing," was the determined reply.

Laurel was despondent. Duane had not told her of his weekend plans, but she had overheard in the lunchroom Friday that Gina had invited him to her cabin. To make matters worse, tales of Gina's earlier escapades had begun filtering back to school. While Laurel did not doubt the stories, she could not see how Gina's type could interest Duane.

That evening she told her parents nothing of her problems but went to her room immediately after supper. She lay on her bed sobbing as she imagined what was happening at Mount Snow. After awhile she glanced in the mirror. Her swollen, red eyes and disheveled hair made her no match at all for the other girl. No wonder Duane found Gina more attractive. The night dragged on, and she barely slept.

The next day she played the organ for church but paid little attention to the sermon. Afterward her friends noticed that she went through the formalities of being pleasant but that her mind was elsewhere. Driving home with her parents, she was not her usual cheerful self.

While helping her mother prepare dinner, Laurel said, "Don't set a place for me. I'm not hungry."

"Dad and I have noticed something seems to be bothering you. Do you care to talk about it?"

The girl stood silently for a long time. Finally, "Do you remember Duane, who brought me home after the concert?"

"Yes. A nice boy."

"Well, I liked him, too. And I thought he liked me. At least he's been spending a lot of time with me. But this weekend he's with Gina, who's a . . . a . . . a real . . ."

Mrs. Lambert looked startled. "I'm sorry to hear that. It seems out of character for him. Perhaps you should give him a chance to explain."

"I don't want to see him again. That girl has—has no principles."

Mrs. Lambert replaced the lid on the pot of soup she had been stirring and studied her daughter a moment. "It would be unfair to him for you to jump to conclusions. Of course, you have to consider your own reputation, but if he still wants to be friends, I suggest you let him explain about Gina. But please try not to become too fond of him or of anyone else who does not share your religious convictions."

Laurel frowned. "That's hard advice to follow."

"I know. But if you don't want a home full of constant

heartache, don't attach yourself to someone who doesn't share your faith. I know you want a home and family. God will help you find a good husband.''

"Maybe a happy marriage is not in God's plan for my life," Laurel murmured.

"Don't be silly. God wants all His children to be happy.''

The girl wiped a tear with her apron. "Happiness is not my only goal in life," she said, trying to convince herself.

Monday morning Laurel sat in a practice room, improvising at the piano and vainly struggling to gain inspiration for a composition assignment due the following period. Suddenly the door opened, and a leg in a cast made its appearance, followed by a crutch, then Duane.

"Whatever happened?" Laurel gasped, jumping to her feet.

"I went skiing."

"I didn't know you ski."

"I don't. It's a long story. Let's just say I consider myself lucky."

"Lucky?"

"It could have been worse—a lot worse. Broken bones can heal.''

"I don't think I understand you."

"Never mind. I'll explain some other time. I'm late now for a lesson I'm accompanying for Madame Wolfinger." He tried to laugh. "Hope I can pedal with my left foot. See you at lunch.''

As Duane went hobbling off, Laurel felt better—much better.

Chapter 8

"THE CONSUL"

The opera department began casting for *The Consul* by Menotti, which they would stage in late May. Gina wanted desperately to sing the lead role of Magda, and had let it be known she felt quite sure she would be chosen. So Laurel was completely unprepared when Madame announced at her voice lesson, "Vee look for a zinger to be Magda, und vee pick you. You do a good chob, ja?"

Laurel blushed. "I'm afraid I couldn't."

The older woman put her hands on her ample hips. "Vat you mean? Iss a great honor vee gif you."

"Yes, yes, I know." The girl was flustered. "I really appreciate it. But I think Gina would do much better."

Madame cocked her head to one side. "You let us decide dat. You zang so gut der Schumann's *Frauenliebe und -leben* vee all tink you make a great Mutter in *The Consul*."

"Really, I have no operatic aspirations."

Madame stared at Laurel. "Vat iss wrong mit you, girl? Vy you vaste time studying voice if you not vant to zing opera?"

"There are other ways to use one's voice."

"Sure, sure. You can zing for churches. You can zing Lieder. But you starf, I tell you. Unless you teach or zing opera, you starf." Her voice, always loud, increased in volume.

41

The girl's face now burned. "An operatic career just isn't for me. I don't mind singing in churches and teaching," Laurel replied softly.

"I tell you vat I tink." Madame shook her fist for emphasis. "You vill get married and vaste dat beautiful voice. For lullabies you don't need training. Bah!" She grabbed her large handbag and slammed the door behind her.

Duane had been quietly sitting at the piano, listening in amusement. He had witnessed several of Madame's outbursts before. Laurel had blushed at her reference to marriage and lullabies. Now she appeared to be on the verge of tears.

"Don't mind her. In a few minutes she'll be back and probably won't mention the opera again. Anyway, you have a right to sing the role or not as you choose. I'm not too enthralled with opera myself, but it's Madame's whole world. Not to be an opera star is, in her eyes, to be a failure." He arose from the piano bench and limped to her side.

"I'm sure she thinks I'm crazy," the girl said, trying to control herself. "*The Consul* is not as ridiculous as most operas. But I promised myself long ago that I wouldn't become stagestruck."

He appeared surprised. "That's rather unusual for a singer. Just wait till Gina learns that you turned down the role."

"I wouldn't tell her if I were you. She has never liked me."

"Huh? What makes you think that?"

Just then Madame opened the door and stood surveying the pair as she cleared her throat and adjusted her ample proportions to create proper resonance for what threatened to be a major proclamation. "Laurel, I giff you two days to reconzider. Meet me in der opera director's office at eleffen Zaturday morning. Vee can vait no longer dan dat for your dezision. You go now."

The girl wanted to say that her mind was already made up, that Saturday morning she could not be at the school. But the finality of Madame's dismissal left no opportunity for discussion. Picking up her music, Laurel fled.

Hurrying down the hall without glancing at anyone, she rushed out the front entrance and across the drive to the clump of yews that hid the bench where she sometimes came for a breath of fresh air. Her cardigan sweater offered little protection from the March wind. About three inches of fresh wet snow covered the ground. She buried her head in her hands and sobbed aloud, "O God, I don't know how I got into this mess. Help me get out of it without making my church look ridiculous. Help me to make them understand. Help me to be Christlike."

Duane had gotten permission from Madame to try to "talk some sense" into Laurel. He asked the students in the hall which way she had gone. When told that she went racing out without even a coat, he stopped by the locker room and got his. Still unaccustomed to his crutches, he had to hobble slowly after her.

When he reached the front entrance he marveled how she could disappear so fast. Then he noticed tracks in the snow leading around the clump of yews that flanked the Thornton School of Music sign. Remembering the bench, he started toward it as quietly as his crutches would carry him. As he neared the yews he heard sobs.

Laurel still had her head buried in her hands when she felt something warm descend upon her shoulders. With a startled cry she sprang up. When she saw Duane she collapsed on the bench again.

"Sorry I frightened you. I thought you might be a bit chilly." Sitting beside her, Duane placed his arm around her shoulders, which were shaking from a combination of cold, fright, and sobs.

"Thank you for coming," she whispered. "Thank you so much."

It didn't take long for news of Laurel's refusal to spread around Thornton. Gina was furious. True, she had the role she wanted, but the fact that it had first been offered to Laurel humiliated her. Madame had made no effort to hide the fact that Laurel was a fool to reject it.

Many students who couldn't believe that she would voluntarily pass up such a chance to further her career questioned her about her decision. Some admired her stand, but more found it incomprehensible. The letter she had written the opera director explaining her reasons for rejecting the offer and why she could not meet him Saturday morning also created considerable discussion. That a seemingly intelligent and talented girl would let matters of conscience interfere with her success and that she considered the Ten Commandments—even the fourth—still binding upon Christians, made many regard her as a relic from a bygone era. But while most disagreed with her opinions, her fellow students still respected her integrity. And though she had cultivated few close friendships at the school, everyone generally liked her—everyone except Gina, whose outward civility masked her intense hatred.

As the weeks passed, the students forgot the stir Laurel's refusal had caused. Laurel herself was so busy studying and practicing that she did not realize the long awaited day of the opera had arrived till Duane asked her to accompany him to the performance. That night the theater was packed, and people lined the walls. She and Duane chose inconspicuous seats in the balcony.

Gina's superb acting compensated for her small voice that the orchestra at times drowned. A wildly applauding audience rose as the cast filed on stage after the final curtain.

It recalled Gina again and again, whistling and stomping approval. She glowed as she bowed and received the floral sprays.

After the crowd had dispersed, most of the voice students went backstage to congratulate the cast. Gina radiantly accepted praises from friends standing in line to shake her hand or to hug or kiss her.

Duane and Laurel took their place near the end of the line. When they offered their congratulations, Gina's jaw suddenly hardened and her eyes narrowed.

"No doubt you would have sung the role better," she sneered at Laurel.

"Oh, no, indeed! You were superb. I don't have your ability for acting."

"I prefer to be acclaimed for my singing, thank you," Gina snapped as she turned her back on Laurel and greeted her next admirer.

"Duane, you can see how intensely she dislikes me, can't you?" Laurel commented as they slipped out into the hall.

"Yes. I hear she vows to get even with you someday."

"I wonder how she plans to do that."

He shrugged. "Who knows? I wouldn't worry about it."

Chapter 9

THE STUDIO

It was early June, and in a few days Duane would have his master's degree in piano. He expected to continue his studies eventually, but he felt that he would like to teach and perform for a few years first. Though he had never been to see Phil Sumpsion about his concert career because he felt that he needed Gina's friendship for success there, a concert manager from Boston, Aaron Jude, had arranged a few recitals of a local nature. A small college in Maine had offered him a position teaching piano, but because he felt that such a remote location might hamper his concert career, he decided to teach privately and continue to live in the Worcester area.

He wanted to move from his studio apartment in a decrepit section of town to a neighborhood more likely to attract professional people. Also, he was tired of wasting time going to students' homes. Therefore he decided to look for a furnished three-room apartment that would have a living room large enough for the grand piano he hoped to buy.

After three frustrating weeks of searching he found a suitable place on the first floor of a four-apartment dwelling, where the landlord did not object to his profession. The apartment would be available the middle of July, but the rent was triple what he had been paying. He would have to find many new students, and unfortunately, summertime was slack season for music teachers.

What to do about a piano was another problem. Should he move the old clunker he had used on weekends and holidays when the school pianos were not available for practice? Should he buy a rebuilt grand that might develop pin block trouble and thus be impossible to keep in tune? Or should he obligate himself to years of debt to buy a new one? He decided to consult his tuner friend, David Holden, whose judgment in such matters he valued.

David obligingly agreed to check for mechanical soundness any pianos that appealed to Duane. In the days that followed, David checked several, but in each case advised against the purchase because the so-called rebuilding had not been sufficiently thorough. When Duane had about decided that only a new instrument would meet David's exacting requirements, his friend excitedly took him to see a three-year-old grand that the owner was selling for half the original price.

It was an exceptionally fine seven-foot grand. The owner had purchased it for his ten-year-old daughter before she had demonstrated that her declared interest in learning to play the piano was strong enough to survive the practice her teacher demanded. Chagrined, the parents now wanted to get rid of it. Duane made a small deposit to hold the piano till he could arrange a bank loan. Two days after he moved into the apartment the piano arrived.

It was one of the happiest days of his life. Not even the new bicycle he had bought at the age of ten with savings from his paper route had brought him so much satisfaction. As soon as the movers departed, he started to play, and continued until he felt the neighbors might be retiring for the night. Then he sat and gazed at it for a long time before going to bed.

For the next few days he was too engrossed with his new piano to worry about soaring food prices and bills, but then a

trip to the grocery convinced him he had better strictly limit
his purchases to staples and bargains. Also, he remembered
that his rent would soon be due again as well as the first
payment on his piano loan. Although he had sold his car to
save garage rent, what he had received for it wouldn't be
enough to see him through the slack season.

Deciding to run an ad in the *Telegram*, he used his name,
thinking it might have some value in attracting advanced
pupils, though at that point he would have welcomed even
beginners. He had had a phone installed when he moved,
considering it a necessary business expense. Now he used it
to call in the ad, hoping that by the time the bill arrived, his
financial status would have improved.

The next day the *Telegram* carried his ad:

> **DUANE MANNING**
> Concert pianist; teacher
> Now accepting pupils
> MM from Thornton School of Music
> 3816 Thoreau Drive   853-1712

Of the two dozen responses, three resulted in new pupils
starting immediately and three sounded like good prospects
for the fall. One of those beginning right away was Spencer
Schwab, now nine years of age but still not sharing his
mother's conviction that he was destined for the concert
stage.

Mrs. Schwab felt that her son should have an hour lesson.
Duane readily agreed, especially as the fee for an hour was
almost as much as for two half-hour lessons. Unfortunately
he hadn't taught many children and so overestimated the
attention span of a nine-year-old.

The first lesson was somewhat of an ordeal. Mrs.
Schwab, who insisted on being present, dominated it. She

discussed in her son's hearing his special gifts and his weaknesses. The boy was good at playing publicly from memory, she said, but could hardly read notes, so had to learn chiefly by rote. But she was willing to spend an hour a day teaching the music to him. When Duane suggested beginning him on easier pieces than those he had been playing so that he could figure them out himself, Mrs. Schwab argued that psychologically it would be bad for him to feel he was retrogressing. To his offer to give Spencer a slow piece so that he could work on tone and expression, she replied that since the boy's interpretation would naturally improve as he gained maturity, she preferred he continue to specialize in sparkling showpieces.

During the discussions Spencer sat at the piano, vigorously swinging his feet so that they bumped the pedal braces from time to time or experimenting with the tone produced by laying paper, pencils, clips, and other objects on the strings. By the time the lesson ended, Duane wondered whether he had made a mistake in not accepting the offer from the small college in Maine.

For the next several weeks he dreaded his encounters with the Schwabs, though he tactfully managed to conceal the fact. He followed Mrs. Schwab's suggestions at first, but gradually helped her to see that his ideas of what her son needed most were sound. She became quite vocal in extolling the merits of her son's new teacher. Since she was an influential citizen of nearby Hudson, her recommendations resulted in Duane's acquiring several students from that area.

He finally succeeded in balancing the budget again, thanks to Mrs. Schwab. But he disliked being obligated to anyone with such a dominating personality and hoped he could soon become independent of her. While he felt fortunate to have her good will, he shuddered to think what would happen if he dared to cross her.

Chapter 10

LARRY

The summer was nearly over. Duane had seen little of Laurel since his graduation. Though he had thought of her often and had called her on the phone several times, his impoverished state and lack of a car had curtailed any visits to her home.

Toward the end of August she invited him to spend a weekend at Three Elms. He arrived on the five-thirty train Friday afternoon. Mrs. Lambert and Laurel met him and drove the mile to the house. Mr. Lambert was still milking the cow.

When they entered through the back door the house smelled delightfully of baking bread and freshly waxed floors. The dining-room table was set for five. "Do you have another guest?" Duane asked.

"No," Laurel replied. "I guess I forgot to tell you that my brother, Larry, is home for vacation from med school. I'm sure you'll like him."

Just then the back door opened, and Mr. Lambert's bushy gray head appeared. He carefully cleaned his feet on the doormat to avoid spoiling Laurel's waxed floor.

"Hi, there, Duane," he exclaimed in his rich bass voice. "Good to see you." He strode over to clasp Duane's hand. Of medium height, Turner Lambert was inclined to be somewhat stocky.

Behind him stood a young man whose athletic build and handsome face made his shy smile seem a bit incongruous. He appeared to be about Duane's age. His eyes told Duane that he would like to be friends but needed an introduction. Fortunately, Mrs. Lambert took care of that.

"Duane, I would like you to meet our son, Larry. Larry, this is Laurel's favorite pianist. Go get acquainted while I put supper on the table."

Supper was a happy occasion. All joined hands while Mr. Lambert asked God's blessing on the food, thanked Him that Larry and Duane were there to share it, and asked for His continued guidance. The simple meal consisted mainly of what the garden, chickens, and cow had produced. But it was a real treat to Duane, who was thoroughly tired of his own cooking.

As they cleared the supper dishes away, Mr. Lambert looked at his watch. "The sun will be setting in ten minutes. It's about time we have worship."

The two men followed him into the living room, while Laurel and her mother finished putting the dishes into the washer. Duane wondered what worship would be like.

"We begin by singing hymns," Mr. Lambert answered his unexpressed question. "Would you play the piano for us?"

"I'm afraid my experience playing hymns has been nonexistent. I'd probably make a fool of myself. Why not let Laurel do it when she gets here?"

"As you wish. Here she comes now. Let's begin by singing 'Abide With Me.' Laurel, it seems you won't get a vacation from playing after all."

Duane and Larry looked off the hymnal Laurel played from while Mr. and Mrs. Lambert shared the other one. When Duane's thoughts turned to his mother, he was unable to finish the last stanza:

"Where is death's sting? where, grave, thy victory?
    I triumph still if Thou abide with me!"

Laurel had rarely discussed her religion, though Duane
knew she kept the seventh-day Sabbath from sundown Friday
evening till sundown Saturday. She had refused to attend
concerts or perform in recitals that fell on Friday nights.
Madame Wolfinger had accepted the girl's stand as another
evidence of a fanaticism that would prevent her success as a
singer.

Duane's knowledge of the Bible was limited. As a child
he had gone fairly regularly to Sunday School, but as an adult
he had found himself attending church rather infrequently. In
fact, he recalled that the last time he had attended a service
was at his mother's funeral. It seemed that most sermons
were variations on the theme "Love thy neighbor as thy-
self." Granted, he hadn't achieved that goal as yet and
probably never would. Yet he didn't seem any closer to it
after some of the sermons he had heard.

After several more songs, Larry took a chair, and Duane
and Laurel sat on the piano bench facing the others. Mr.
Lambert picked up a well-worn Bible and handed it to
Duane. "We'll each read a favorite passage tonight. We'll
let Duane begin. Join in from memory if you can."

Duane remembered that the Book of Psalms was about in
the middle of the Bible, so without too much trouble he
located and read the twenty-third psalm. All repeated it with
him.

Laurel chose John 14:1-3 and let Duane read along while
the others recited: "Let not your heart be troubled: ye believe
in God, believe also in me. In my Father's house are many
mansions: if it were not so, I would have told you. I go to
prepare a place for you. And if I go and prepare a place for

you, I will come again, and receive you unto myself; that where I am, there ye may be also.''

Her brother chose the Beatitudes as recorded in Matthew 5. Only Duane could not recite them.

As her favorite Mrs. Lambert quoted the next to the last verse of the Bible: ''He which testifieth these things saith, Surely I come quickly. Amen. Even so, come, Lord Jesus.''

Mr. Lambert chose Revelation 14:5-12, which he referred to as ''the three angels' messages.'' Surprisingly to Duane, who had always heard that the Book of Revelation was a mystery, all of the family quoted along from memory.

After the preceding texts, Mr. Lambert's choice came somewhat as a shock. Duane cringed at phrases like, ''the hour of his judgment is come, . . . drink of the wine of the wrath of God, . . . smoke of their torment.'' And what was this beast whose mark in the forehead or hand determined who was to be a victim of God's wrath?

He asked no questions, and no one offered any explanation. It seemed to him that Mr. Lambert was too relaxed a person to be concerned with hellfire. The fact that his family could quote the passage indicated that it must have some special meaning for them. Duane determined to find out what.

Following worship Laurel and her mother hurried off to finish straightening up the kitchen. Mr. Lambert spread out his Bible, his Sabbath School lesson quarterly, and volume 6 of *The Seventh-day Adventist Bible Commentary* on the dining-room table. Donning his reading glasses, he prepared to teach a Sabbath School class study on Romans 3 the next day.

Larry asked Duane whether he would like to brave the mosquitoes and sit outside where it was cooler. Duane welcomed the opportunity to get better acquainted with Larry. They sat in lawn chairs near the petunia bed. Darkness hid the flowers, but their fragrance permeated the air. The stars appeared one by one, while tree frogs and crickets tuned up for their evening symphony.

Duane had almost forgotten the scents, sights, and sounds of dusk in the country in August. He felt reluctant to break the spell by speaking. Laurel's brother became uneasy as the silence continued.

"Played any concerts recently?" he asked at last.

His reverie broken, Duane answered, "No. But I have one in a couple of weeks. Nothing impressive. Just a ladies' club."

"Do you get enough out of it to make all that practice pay off?"

"Not in money. Mainly I get experience. One never knows when a performance for a small group will lead to something more important. Fortunately, I have enough pupils to keep soul and body together, and hopefully I'll have more when I get established."

Larry shook his head in the darkness. "Getting established can be rough. Even in my field."

"Do you plan to set up practice near here?" Duane shifted in his chair.

"Well, that's a long way off, so I really don't have any specific plans yet. Mainly I'm just concerned with keeping my grades up."

"Are your studies that bad?"

Laurel's brother leaned toward him. "Let's put it this way. My knowing the answer at the right time can be a matter of life or death for somebody. Loma Linda University wants to make sure it doesn't turn out physicians who make wrong guesses."

"Yes, I see your point. How many more years do you have?"

Larry sighed. "Forever, it seems. Actually one before I

graduate. Then a year in internship. More if I decide to specialize. I'll be close to thirty before I'll be a practicing physician.''

"Oh, you'll still probably have forty years to practice." Duane chuckled. "You'll get back your investment in time and money many times.''

Laurel's brother stood and began to pace back and forth. "In all honesty I must say I don't expect to practice anywhere near forty years. I may not even get to practice at all.''

He sounded extremely serious, and Duane wondered whether Larry might perhaps be suffering from some incurable disease and debated whether he should drop the subject. Then he blurted, "Why do you say that?''

"Conditions in the world tell me clearly that Jesus is coming very soon.''

Duane had once learned to recite the Nicene Creed, which declared that "Jesus Christ . . . ascended into heaven, and sitteth on the right hand of the Father; and he shall come again, with glory, to judge both the quick and the dead.'' But that it might happen in his day was an idea that had never occurred to him. He didn't even know for sure whether he believed in a literal return of Jesus.

Finally he asked, "What makes you think this may happen soon?''

The young medical student turned to face him. "Prophecies—especially those found in the books of Daniel and Revelation. Those concerning the time of the end are either fulfilled or just about so. The recent passage of a national Sunday law is a sign that Adventists have long predicted. We expect the enforcement to become harsher until violation becomes punishable by death.''

Duane tried to laugh. "You surely don't believe that could happen in America!''

"I'm sure of it.''

"Well, I suppose you could refrain from violating Sunday laws and still worship on Saturday."

"I'm afraid that won't satisfy those who are intent upon enforcing uniformity of worship. I'd like to study Revelation 13 with you some day." In the dim light that spilled from the house Duane thought he could see a grim smile on Larry's face.

Duane shook his head. "I'm a firm believer in law and order myself."

"Well, so am I. But only insofar as it respects human dignity and the right to hold divergent opinions."

"But don't you believe it is legitimate for the government to invade the privacy of criminals?"

Larry resumed his pacing. "How do you define who is a criminal? Here in Massachusetts there were, and I believe still are, laws on the books from the time of the Indian raids saying it is illegal to attend church without carrying a gun." The darkness obscured the twinkle in Larry's eye as he added, "Of course, the more recent law making it illegal for anyone to carry a gun perhaps solves the problem, though the Indians now have the advantage with their bows and arrows."

At that point Laurel and her mother came out to join them, and the conversation turned to other subjects.

Two hours later as Duane passed through the living room on his way to the bedroom Larry had graciously vacated he stopped by the bookcase and took out volume 7 of *The Seventh-day Adventist Bible Commentary*. He wasn't used to retiring so early, and his curiosity about Revelation 13 and 14 had been whetted. He thought reading in bed for half an hour or so would make him sleepy.

Chapter 11

SABBATH AT THREE ELMS

The next morning he awoke at 6:30. Whether it was the bright sun streaming through the window or the rattling of Turner Lambert's milk bucket, he wasn't sure. He knew only that after reading till 4:00 AM he was extremely tired. Although Duane tried to go back to sleep, the cackling in the hen yard and realization that breakfast was scheduled for 8:00 prevented him from relaxing.

When he did at last lapse into a semiconscious state he seemed to be standing on a seashore. A leopardlike creature with seven heads and ten horns rose out of the sea. One of the heads hung almost severed from the body, and though dripping blood into the seawater, it talked. What it was saying he couldn't understand. The beast swam toward him. As its paws touched the sandy shore a few feet from where he watched, the dangling head swung back into place, and the flow of blood ceased. Duane struggled to flee, but his feet seemed to stick in the sand.

A knock on his bedroom door and the announcement that breakfast was almost ready shattered the nightmare, though it didn't stop the pounding in Duane's chest. Quickly he dressed, shaved, and hurried to the kitchen where breakfast waited.

Laurel stood at the sink, slicing a cantaloupe. She had drawn her hair back in a bun, giving her a maturity that he

57

found rather attractive. Walking over to the sink, he encircled her waist with his arm. "I've never seen you with your hair back. It is very becoming," he whispered. "Do you always wear it this way on Sabbath?"

Laurel blushed. "No. Only on special occasions. I'm glad you like it."

After breakfast Mr. Lambert and Larry donned their neckties while the women went after their purses and Bibles. During the drive to church, Laurel commented, "When we first moved to the farm we attended the Worcester Church. But not being able to drive in the city was such a nuisance that we joined the little group still meeting in New Braintree, even though our academy there has closed."

"Why did it close?" Duane asked.

"Financial reasons. Parents couldn't afford the high tuition, which climbed every year as the state imposed more and more requirements on secondary schools. Most of the secondary schools the Adventists used to operate in the United States met a similar fate."

"That's too bad."

"Five or ten years ago it would have been a disaster. Now, since the passage of the national Sunday law, most of our church members—young and old—are more serious about their religion than ever before, so the schools are not so essential."

"Has the law inconvenienced any of your members?"

"Yes, definitely. Like Mr. Smith, who used to operate a grocery till he went bankrupt because he could operate only five days a week. Sunday used to be his busiest day, with people coming for miles when the supermarkets were closed."

"Maybe he could go into some other business."

"I don't think he has enough money to begin again."

"Don't forget Mrs. Frazer, who just got out of jail," Larry added.

"Oh, yes. That was ridiculous. You tell about it, Larry."

"Well, the problem was that the Frazers don't have a clothes dryer. The two youngest children are still in diapers, and Mrs. Frazer didn't have enough to last the weekend. Usually on Friday she washes them up so she can make it till Monday, but last week she had been to a funeral and didn't get it done. So when she hung them outdoors to dry Sunday morning, her neighbor, who has always resented having five noisy children next door, called the police."

"They jailed her for that?" Duane asked in surprise.

"The judge fined her for violating the law prohibiting work on Sunday, but since she was unable to pay the heavy fine, she had to spend two nights in jail."

"Who took care of the children?"

"One of the women from the church stayed with them during the day while Mr. Frazer was away at work. He drives a truck for a construction company."

"He should make good money at that. Perhaps he had better buy his wife a dryer or a good supply of disposable diapers."

Laurel laughed. "I'm sure he will as soon as he can. They have had heavy medical expenses, and he has just recently returned to work after weeks of illness."

"How could a neighbor be so unfeeling for Mrs. Frazer's predicament, even if the children are noisy?" Duane wondered aloud.

"She's elderly and has never had children of her own. Instead, she has beautiful flowers that she cares for daily, Sunday included. A few times the children had accidentally batted a ball into her yard. Once it broke off her prize dahlia. She probably figures that by reporting their Sunday violations to the police she can persuade them to move away."

The car turned off the road onto the drive circling the

brick academy buildings and stopped in front of the church.
"This is it, Duane," said Mr. Lambert. "We have a large
church building. What we need is a congregation to match
it."

"You have a splendid view from here. What are the other
buildings used for now?"

He replied that they were for sale, and although they had
received various offers, none as yet had come near their true
value.

As they entered the church Turner Lambert introduced
Duane to Peter Thayer, a young ministerial intern about
Duane's age, who had been assigned to the New Braintree
congregation. "Everybody here just calls me Pete. I'd like
you to meet my new bride, Peggy," he said, drawing up
beside him an attractive redhead. "Peggy, this is Duane
Manning, Laurel's friend."

"Welcome, Duane. I've been looking forward to meeting you. We hope you will worship with us often. Would you
sign our guest book?"

She led him to a small stand holding a guest register.
Duane noticed that it had been three weeks since the last
guest had signed. He had hoped to be inconspicuous in a
throng of worshipers, but he realized that in such a small
group a visitor could not escape notice.

During the Sabbath School class he was glad to learn that
these Adventists looked for salvation through Jesus rather
than through keeping the Ten Commandments. Just before
the time allotted for discussion ran out, Mr. Lambert directed
attention to the last verse of the chapter in which the apostle
Paul points out that faith does not make void the law, but
rather establishes it.

After church he met other members of the congregation.
When introduced to Mrs. Frazer he remembered the diaper
episode. "I heard about your misfortune. I'm truly ashamed

that anything like that can happen in America."

The woman smiled. "Paul says we must 'glory in tribulation' because 'tribulation worketh patience.' I'm sure God felt my patience needed some developing."

A different way of looking at things, Duane thought to himself.

On the way home Mr. Lambert asked him, "Do you think Pete will make a preacher some day?"

"He's an effective one already, and he seems sincere. You know, I would like to get better acquainted with him."

"I think we can arrange that," Mrs. Lambert commented. "We'll call him after dinner and see if he can come over for a while."

After dinner Larry went to telephone Pete, and Laurel suggested that her parents both rest while she and Duane straighten the kitchen. Afterward she asked him how he would like to spend the afternoon.

"I'm not in the habit of napping in the daytime, but I read most of the night, and I can hardly stay awake. I'll be much better company if I can rest an hour or so."

"Go right ahead. I'll be outside reading when you get through."

She picked up some church magazines and left through the back door. Soon Larry joined his sister, who had curled up in the shade of the largest elm. Laurel looked up and laid the *Adventist Review* aside.

"What do you think of him?"

"Seems like a fine fellow. But don't get too emotionally involved yet."

Smiling, she replied wistfully, "I'll try not to." Then she resumed her halfhearted reading.

Duane's hour of rest lengthened into three, but eventually he emerged, feeling more alert, and joined them on the lawn.

Early that evening Sheba's barking announced the arrival

of Pete and Peggy. Laurel and her parents greeted them at the car. Pete said he was sorry he couldn't come sooner, but he had had to visit two of his ill members and go to the jail, where he was having Bible studies with Bob, an inmate.

Mrs. Lambert suggested sitting on the lawn to enjoy the evening air and watch the sunset. Because they had only four lawn chairs, the three young men sat on the grass. Sheba lay, tail wagging and ears pricked, at Larry's feet.

"When do you go back to California, Larry?" Pete asked.

"In two weeks, I'm afraid."

"So soon? Will you get home again next summer?"

"I hope so, but it's an expensive trip. 'Fraid I don't have a wife supporting me like so many of my classmates."

"Are you doing anything to correct that condition?" Pete asked, a smile lurking at the corners of his mouth.

"I've been dating a girl rather steadily, but I'm not sure I love her enough to ask her to marry me. Anyway, I prefer to finish my education before marriage."

"Good boy! I wish more people were willing to postpone marriage. Much of my marriage counseling has involved young married couples, with the husband still in school."

Turning to Duane, Pete said, "I hear you're a fine pianist. I had seven years of piano lessons and at one time thought of majoring in music. When and where are you giving your next recital?"

"Two weeks from tomorrow in Bolton for a ladies' club."

"I wanted to hear you, but probably I'd be a bit out of place at a ladies' club meeting. Maybe Laurel can let me know when I might have another opportunity."

"Well, I'm playing a premiere of Engel's new piano concerto with the Worcester Symphony Orchestra in October."

"Who is Engel?"

"A member of the composition faculty at Thornton School of Music."

"And the date of your performance?"

Duane frowned. "It's on a Friday night, so I don't suppose you would be able to attend."

Pete sighed. "That's true. Too bad."

Turner Lambert called attention to the red arc of the sun peeping over the horizon. Pink and gold lined the few clouds in the western sky. "Let's sing a stanza of 'Day Is Dying in the West,' " he suggested, and all joined him.

> "Day is dying in the west;
> Heav'n is touching earth with rest;
> Wait and worship while the night
> Sets her evening lamps alight
> Through all the sky."

"What New Testament promises involving clouds can we remember?" Pete asked.

Mrs. Lambert responded first. "John tells us in the Book of Revelation, 'Behold, he cometh with clouds; and every eye shall see him.' "

Her husband quoted Paul: " 'For the Lord himself shall descend from heaven with a shout, with the voice of the archangel, and with the trump of God: and the dead in Christ shall rise first: then we which are alive and remain shall be caught up together with them in the clouds, to meet the Lord in the air.' "

"In His predictions about the end of the world recorded in Matthew, Jesus tells us, 'They shall see the Son of man coming in the clouds of heaven with power and great glory,' " Peggy said.

Laurel remembered that when Jesus ascended, "a cloud received him out of their sight" and that two angels told the amazed spectators, "This same Jesus, which is taken up from you into heaven, shall so come in like manner as ye have seen him go into heaven."

Neither Duane nor Larry had any further additions, so Pete concluded by saying that since the New Testament often associated clouds with the return of Jesus, he always longed for that happy event when looking at the golden clouds of a sunset.

After Turner offered a short prayer of thanksgiving for the past week, he and Larry left to gather eggs and close the hen house before it got too dark. The three women went to prepare some supper, leaving Duane and Pete alone.

"I really was interested in your sermon this morning," Duane ventured somewhat timidly. "I never thought Jesus might come in my day."

"I'm afraid most people, if they believe in a literal return at all, place His coming in the remote future. Jesus was right when He predicted that the last generation would be no more ready for His second coming than were the antediluvians for the Flood, in spite of Noah's warnings."

"I don't know much about the Bible myself, I'm afraid."

"Would you care to study it?"

Duane paused a moment. "Yes, I guess I really would. But I know you're busy, and I would hate to impose on your time."

"Don't think a thing about it. I'd be happy to help you. But I suggest that you take a book of studies I have in the car and go through them yourself, using your Bible as your text. Then perhaps we could get together once a week, and I could help you find answers to any questions you may have."

When Pete returned with the book they decided that Duane would begin studying it, and that Pete would come to his apartment on Monday nights. Just then they were summoned for supper.

As they walked to the house Duane suggested, "I'd rather you would say nothing to Laurel or her family about this."

"I understand. I'll have to tell my wife where I'm going, but she knows how to keep a secret, I assure you."

Chapter 12

THANKSGIVING

The rehearsal was tedious. It took two hours to go through the twenty-minute composition twice. Every few measures either the conductor, Julian, would call a halt to admonish or insult a player, or Engel would tap Julian on the shoulder to direct his attention to something that wasn't coming off as intended. Julian's patience began to wear thin, and Duane expected to be the next victim of his wrath. On the fifth time through an intricate passage he fumbled, and everything fell into confusion.

"What! You call yourself a pianist!" Julian stormed. "Did you just start practicing this past week?"

Flushing, Duane wanted to say that much of the orchestra's problem was Julian's poor conducting, especially his failure to indicate entrances and announce starting places clearly, but he controlled himself. "I'm sorry," he said quietly.

"Sorry, sorry. You'll be sorry enough if you pull that stunt tomorrow night," the older man muttered.

But surprisingly, the performance the following night went at least as well as Duane had expected. They had no breakdowns, and what flaws there were escaped the notice of the audience. Engel, who had been apprehensive, elatedly acknowledged the applause. Duane also received warm applause. He wished Pete and the Lamberts could have heard him.

The review in Saturday's newspaper was flattering to Duane as a pianist, though less enthusiastic about the composition and quite critical of the conductor. It was good for Duane's self-esteem, as he had begun to wonder whether a concert career was an attainable goal.

Sunday his manager, Aaron Jude, called to congratulate him on his performance. He said that someone who had attended the concert had called to see whether Duane would be available for a recital of contemporary music at Lowell State College in December. Duane quickly accepted.

Practicing and giving lessons filled his days. His class of students had grown to forty, and he felt he had about as many as he could adequately manage. He spent the mornings practicing and the afternoons teaching. Although he tried to keep the evenings free, he still found himself practicing quite a bit at night when preparing for a performance. The studies with Pete continued every Monday evening, but though he enjoyed them and considered Pete's theology Biblically sound, music occupied his mind more than religion.

At the close of the tenth session Pete suggested that probably it would be well that Duane have a few months to ponder what he had learned before his next visit. He presented Duane with some books and asked him to read them. He left with the understanding that Duane would get in touch with him when he was ready for further study.

The books lay unread beside his bed. Several weeks passed, and he looked at one only enough to know that it was an outline of the struggle between Christ and Satan from the beginning of the Christian era to the final destruction of the world and its restoration as a home for the redeemed. The book looked interesting enough, but Duane was generally too tired by bedtime to do any heavy reading.

He saw Laurel once a week. Since he had agreed to play for her senior recital, they usually practiced together about one hour on Fridays, then ate lunch together in the Thornton School cafeteria.

The Friday before Thanksgiving she asked him whether he planned to go home for the holiday.

"No," he sighed. "Since Mother died, home is not the same. Also, Dad has found a lady who interests him, and she will no doubt invite him to her house for the day."

"I'm glad he won't have to spend the day alone. You already know we are vegetarians, but if you could imagine a Thanksgiving dinner without turkey, you would be most welcome to come share it."

He laughed. "I would love to. What time?"

"We'll probably eat around one o'clock, but you're welcome to come anytime in the morning. Call us when you get off the train. We'll be glad to pick you up."

Thursday morning the first snow of the season fell. About two inches covered the ground when he left the train. The flakes felt good hitting his face. Since the day was not very cold he decided to walk the mile to Three Elms. The large, wet flakes clung to every twig, frosted every fence post, and turned telephone lines into ropes of white.

By the time he arrived at Three Elms his brown hair had turned white. "I didn't know I was inviting an octogenarian to dinner," Laurel laughed as she brushed him off at the back door.

The aroma issuing from the oven as he entered the kitchen reminded him of his hunger. "I don't believe I've had a good meal since my last visit here in August," he told Mrs. Lambert and her daughter, who were busy rolling out crust and preparing filling for the pumpkin pie.

Mrs. Lambert laughed. "You look as though you could stand a nourishing meal or two. I hope you don't mind warm pie. If we can get this in the oven soon, it should have about an hour to cool before we're ready to eat it. I'll cover it and set it outside where it's cold. Laurel, remind me to bring Sheba in when we set the pie out." Her hands were white with flour.

Duane looked at his watch: 11:30. He wished he hadn't skipped breakfast.

After they had the pie in the oven, the women turned to other tasks. He sat at the round table in the corner and noted Laurel's efficiency in the kitchen. His own meager efforts at cooking kept him alive—but that was about all. Now that he was fairly well established, he had begun considering marriage. His income was not large, but Laurel could retain her Sunday church job as organist and choir director, and could probably give some voice lessons as well. The only obstacle that occurred to him was that since religion seemed such an important factor in her life, she might not consider marrying outside her church.

Realizing he hadn't seen Mr. Lambert around, he inquired and learned he was in the barn caring for a new calf. Duane excused himself, saying he wanted to talk with him.

When he found her father he made small talk as best he could about calves, the weather, and the meal they would soon enjoy. After a pause he resumed nervously, "Mr. Lambert, I need to talk to you."

"That's what I thought you were doing, my boy. What's on your mind?"

"It's Laurel." A long silence followed.

Turner glanced at him. "What about her?"

"She will make someone a wonderful wife." He swallowed hard. "I hope it can be me."

Mr. Lambert, who had been bending over the calf, stood up and looked intently at Duane. "Have you talked to her about this?"

"No. I know it's terribly old-fashioned to ask the parents' permission first, but I felt there might be a problem of religion. I wanted to find out whether I stand a chance before I ask her.''

The girl's father paused before answering. "I know that Laurel loves you. I'm quite sure that were you of our faith, she would say yes. Whether she will choose to unite her life with a non-Adventist—only she can decide. We have always told our children that to marry outside the church is to ask for a home with an extra burden of problems. Unfortunately, she doesn't have contact with many young men of our faith, now that Atlantic Union College has closed. We all like you a lot and hope you will join our church. But—to be perfectly honest—we wouldn't want her to marry someone who joined it because of love for a woman rather than out of a strong conviction.''

Duane also hesitated before replying, then said, "Do you object if I ask her to marry me?''

"No, I don't object.''

After dinner Duane declared he had never eaten a better Thanksgiving meal in his life and that he didn't at all miss the turkey. Laurel was almost in tears because Sheba had made away with the pie, but the others comforted her by saying they were too full for pie anyway, and they felt Sheba was entitled to a Thanksgiving dinner too.

Laurel's parents retired to take a nap. She and Duane went to the living room and sat down together on the sofa in front of the fireplace. He was more quiet than usual.

After moments of silence Laurel asked, "Is something troubling you?''

"No, why?'' Duane glanced away.

"You have so little to say.''

"It's just that I don't know how to say what I want to.'' He fidgeted nervously.

"Are you afraid I won't understand?''

"No. But your answer is so important that I hesitate to ask the question.''

Laurel, too, lapsed into silence. Duane slid closer and put his arm around her. "Laurel," he said finally, "my happiest hours are those I've spent with you. If you will consent to marry me, I will do my best to be a good husband."

She did not respond immediately. Her face was flushed, and her eyes wet. Then in a quivering voice she said, "Duane, I do love you. Really. But I could not marry someone not of my faith. If I have made the mistake of encouraging you to this point, it was because I have never been as fond of anyone as of you." She bit her lip. "Please, please study the teachings of our church and come to some conclusion. Then we can discuss marriage."

"But I won't oppose your religious views or interfere with your church activities," he pleaded.

Laurel shook her head. "You don't understand. My religion is and must be the center of my life. You have higher principles than many Adventists. But you haven't fully given your life to God."

Desperation filled his eyes. "I—I was baptized as a baby and consider myself a Christian. Isn't anyone outside your church a Christian?"

"No, no—I mean—it's more than that. Do you believe that Jesus is coming soon and we must get ready?"

"I don't know. People have believed that He was coming soon ever since He ascended to heaven. Why should now be any different?"

She started to say something.

"I know," he interrupted, "you're going to say world conditions and all that. Haven't people of every age thought the world was in a mess?"

The girl bit her lip again, and tears streaked her face. She struggled for words. Then she tried another approach. "If you felt that God was using the Sabbath as a symbol of His loyal people, would you observe it?"

He shrugged. "Probably. But I don't expect a special revelation of His feelings in the matter. I don't see how your people could be right and all other Christians wrong."

"Oh, Duane!" Laurel burst into tears, and sobs threatened to shake her body. He pulled her closer. She tried to dry her tears, to compose herself. "Duane, would—would you read *The Great Controversy*? I can lend you my copy. Please?"

"OK," he slowly answered. "You know I'll read it for you. And you won't need to lend me your copy. Pete gave me one. I asked him not to tell you or your folks, but I went through a series of studies with him."

Hope flooded back into her eyes. "Really? You've studied our teachings? What do you think?"

Duane glanced away. "I am not enough of a theologian to find fault with your doctrines. It is just that Adventists are out of step with the rest of the world, and joining your church would jeopardize my career. I mean, how would Aaron Jude react if I were to ask him not to book any concerts Friday night or Saturday, or any that would involve travel on the Sabbath?"

She folded her hands in her lap. "It would be hard, but God would see that you were successful in spite of that handicap."

"Laurel, Laurel." Duane shook his head. "Laurel, maybe your religion has made you as wonderful as you are. If so, it must be genuine. But that I will ever join your church is unlikely. All that I ask is that you will accept me as I am. Please, don't give me your final answer now. Take as much time as you need."

The girl buried her face in her hands, and he felt her shoulders again shake with repressed sobs. He held her tightly, burying his face in her hair. The fire in the fireplace died down to embers. Duane added a new log, and Laurel curled up into a ball of misery.

When the fire roared again, they heard stirrings upstairs, followed by footsteps on the stairs. Laurel struggled to regain her composure. Mrs. Lambert joined them in the living room, pausing at the window. "I see it has started snowing again," she observed. "Must be five inches of new snow on the ground now."

"Wet snow piles up pretty fast," Duane replied, standing. "It's beginning to get dark, and I had better be heading for home."

"Needn't rush off," Mrs. Lambert responded.

He tried to smile. "I've been here nearly six hours and enjoyed a wonderful meal. I don't want to wear out my welcome."

"You'll always be welcome here."

"Always?"

The older woman's eyes revealed that she understood. "Yes, always."

Chapter 13

ALEXANDER

Laurel did not see Duane again till the following Friday. They practiced for her recital, but neither alluded to what had happened Thanksgiving Day. As usual, they ate lunch together following the rehearsal.

As Duane started to leave, she said softly, "It is kind of you to sacrifice your Friday morning practice to help me with my recital. I know the accompaniments for my songs provide no challenge to you, and now that I have sung with them several times, I have them pretty well in mind. I was wondering whether it might be best if I take no more of your time till a couple of weeks before my February recital."

Surprised and hurt, he studied her face for signs of indecision. Detecting none, he replied hesitantly, "I have never—uh—begrudged the time I have spent practicing with you. In fact, I have looked forward to Friday mornings. Aren't you really trying to tell me it would be best if we didn't see each other for a while?"

She glanced down at her lap and tugged nervously at the material of the skirt. "I think that would help us make our decisions more intelligently."

Both sat in silence for a long time.

"When in February is your recital?" he questioned.

"The last Thursday evening." Her voice was barely audible. Duane gathered their dishes onto a tray and carried them to the conveyer. Then he returned to the table where Laurel still sat and touched her shoulder.

"If you ever need me . . . call."

He turned and walked slowly away, his leaden feet matching the heaviness in his heart. As she watched him go, tears welled in her eyes. She longed to call him back but did not dare.

A week before Christmas he mailed her a recording he had recently made. On the label he wrote: "To the most wonderful girl I know. Love, Duane."

He had hoped he might get a call from Laurel inviting him to have Christmas dinner at Three Elms. But none had come by December 23, so, rather than spend the holiday by himself, he decided to leave the next morning for New Hampshire to surprise his father, whom he hadn't seen for a year. Because most of his pupils preferred to take a vacation from their piano lessons, he expected to spend a week there. Since he knew the time would drag, he shoved into his suitcase the copy of *The Great Controversy* that he had not yet found time to read.

The inhabitants of Three Elms spent the afternoon of the twenty-fourth wrapping packages, replacing burned-out Christmas tree lights, and compiling a long grocery list. Mrs. Lambert noticed that, in spite of the apparent festivity, Laurel was sad. The girl had seemed depressed ever since Thanksgiving. Her mother realized the intense struggle she was experiencing and sympathized with her daughter. She herself felt a certain emptiness because her son, Larry, was not home. True, he had been gone the two previous Christmases, but she still missed having the family together on Christmas.

Finally she commented, "An empty chair won't seem right at the table for Christmas dinner. Laurel, could you think of anyone who might be lonely and would like to come for the day?"

For the first time in weeks Laurel looked happy. "I'll call Duane and see if he can come."

She let the phone ring a long time before she decided he must be out on an errand. An hour later she tried again. When her third attempt in the evening failed to reach him, she decided he must be away for the holidays. Saddened, but feeling that perhaps it was all for the best, she resigned herself to her loneliness.

His recording had not yet arrived in the mail. Having wondered whether they should exchange gifts, she had bought him an electric metronome and wrapped it in case he brought her a present. Not wishing to appear forward, however, she had not mailed it. She knew she could use it if they did not exchange presents. Her own windup metronome was old, and it no longer kept a steady beat. Yet she didn't really want the new one. The brightly wrapped box sat under the tree with the other gifts. The sight of it brought a lump to her throat.

After supper the family gathered in the living room, trying to decide whether to open their presents on Christmas Eve or wait till morning. They recalled how Larry and Laurel, as children, would shake and squeeze the gifts, trying to figure out their contents. They had generally been so eager to learn if their guesses were correct that Christmas Eve had become the time for opening them. But the excitement of Christmas had diminished somewhat over the years, so it was decided that the packages could wait till morning.

Mr. Lambert proposed that they sing some carols. Laurel went to the piano, and her parents joined her. They sang the last song so lustily that no one noticed Sheba's barking or the sound of a car in the driveway.

Suddenly the front door opened, and there stood Larry and a handsome young man with auburn hair and brown eyes. The singing stopped in midstanza as Laurel and her parents rushed to embrace Larry.

"What a wonderful Christmas present!" Mrs. Lambert exclaimed, brushing away tears of joy. "Who's your friend?"

"My roommate, Alexander Robertson. Alex has spent all of his life in southern California, and he wanted to experience a New England Christmas. He furnished the transportation in exchange for a place to stay. I was sure you wouldn't mind."

"Of course we don't mind! And we're delighted to have you, Alexander. We were feeling pretty lonely, but now Christmas is going to be as wonderful as it used to be." Turning to Larry, she asked, "Did you get our Christmas package before you left?"

"No, but I was sure one was on the way."

"Well, you can enjoy a second celebration when you get back to school."

"Want to tell me what was in it?"

"No, we'll let you be surprised."

Since the boys had driven nonstop for three days, taking turns at the wheel and sleeping, they were exhausted. Their meals had mostly consisted of snacks picked up at grocery stores along the way; so they were hungry as well. Mrs. Lambert and Laurel quickly warmed up some leftovers, which the young men consumed eagerly.

During the meal Alexander answered questions about himself. He held a Bachelor of Arts degree with a major in biology and was in his second year of medical school. His father was a surgeon, and he expected to follow his example. Eventually he would probably settle in California and inherit his father's practice, but first he would like to gain experience elsewhere. He might consider a term in some mission field that desperately needed surgeons. Money held no allurement for him because he had never experienced any lack of it.

As soon as the two finished supper, Larry suggested they

get a good night of rest. Alexander could use the single bed in Larry's room while Larry would sleep on the sofa in the living room. Though it was still early, the others decided to retire also.

In bed Mr. Lambert asked his wife, "Madeleine, does Larry know that Duane has proposed to Laurel?"

"Yes. I wrote him about it right after Thanksgiving. Why do you ask?"

"I wonder whether that had anything to do with his bringing Alex here."

"I'm sure a young man as attractive and eligible as Alex needn't go far to find a girl friend. He probably has a fiancée back home."

Turner Lambert smiled. "You know, I like him. I hope he's unattached."

"You just like him because he's also a biologist, Turner. One of those in the family is enough! How about going to sleep?"

Mr. Lambert and Alexander got along well from the start. Alexander, whose background made him more at home with a yacht than a tractor, found helping Mr. Lambert with the farm chores a form of education. On the third day of his visit, while they sorted apples to separate the marketable ones from the ones suitable only for home use, the conversation turned to women.

"Some women are sound, others are rotten like this apple." Alexander laughed. "But the dangerous ones are those whose rottenness doesn't show on the outside."

"You talk as if you've had some experience with the rotten ones."

"I was going steady with one—a real beauty. I asked her to marry me. When we went to the preacher to arrange the ceremony he asked her whether she had told me her background. She just shook her head and started to cry. The preacher suggested postponing the wedding. It took me three days to find out what she had been concealing—she had a two-year-old illegitimate daughter that her parents were keeping. She had told me the child was her baby sister."

"I'm sorry. No doubt that was a real disappointment. Do you still love her?"

"I should say not!" He dropped several apples and had to retrieve them from under the sorting table. "I walked out and haven't seen her since."

Turner Lambert sadly shook his head. "Though one can't excuse her dishonesty with you, she's to be pitied more than anything else. Probably she thought your love for her was great enough to overlook her previous lack of judgment. How recently did this happen?"

"About six months ago. We had planned a June wedding. It didn't take her long to forget me. In September she married some poor sucker who probably fell for her face and smooth tongue."

"Have you found someone else?"

Alexander shrugged. "I've dated several girls, but I'm not serious with any. I'm in no rush to get married."

Mr. Lambert nodded his approval, and the conversation turned to other matters.

Larry and Alexander had a two-week vacation, but half of that time they had to allot for travel. The afternoon before they started back, Alexander suggested they find some way to celebrate New Year's Eve. The little town of West Brookfield had few attractions, and the New Braintree Church did not have enough young people to organize a party. Alexander hadn't visited Boston yet, so he searched a newspaper to see what might be happening there.

He found that the Boston Symphony Orchestra was playing and offered to take all four Lamberts as his guests. All accepted but Mr. Lambert, who felt that his farm duties did not permit him to stay up so late.

At the concert Alexander revealed considerable musical sophistication. He said that though he often attended concerts in Los Angeles, he considered it a treat to hear the venerable Boston Symphony. Afterward he offered to treat the four of them at the Amalfi Restaurant near Symphony Hall. While none were used to eating so late at night, all agreed that something like ice cream might be in order. The Lamberts, accustomed to pinching pennies, planned to order a small dish of ice cream each, but Alexander insisted on four deluxe supreme banana splits. It was more ice cream than any of them could finish.

Alexander left a handsome tip, and the four went out to Prudential Center, where a shivering crowd awaited the New Year. The ice cream had done nothing to warm them, and Laurel complained her teeth were chattering. He quickly shed his overcoat and put it around her shoulders in spite of her objections that he would catch pneumonia. Fortunately the midnight strokes soon tolled, and the four hurried to catch a bus to return to the parking lot, where they had left the car.

The bus was crowded. Mrs. Lambert found a seat, but the others stood for several blocks. When someone vacated another seat, Alexander motioned for Laurel to take it. At the next stop Laurel's seatmate got off, and Alexander sat down beside her. "Still cold?" he asked.

"No, I'm fine. Here, you may have your coat back. And thanks." He helped her remove it, then folded it across his lap.

"I think Larry is fortunate to have such an attractive sister." Laurel blushed. "He has told me a lot about you. I wish we could have gotten better acquainted."

"Never believe what a brother says." She laughed. "He

might be prejudiced in my favor. It was quite the reverse ten years ago, I assure you.''

''Ah, but I have eyes and ears of my own and can form my own opinions.'' He hesitated a moment. ''How would you like to visit California sometime?''

''I'm afraid we haven't much money for travel.''

''If I sent you a round-trip plane ticket, would you come?''

''Well . . . er,'' she stammered. ''I really don't know. It—it's very kind of you to offer.''

He laid his hand on hers. ''It would make you a good graduation present.''

As Duane had expected, his week in New Hampshire was rather dull. He and his father spent Christmas Day with the widow Jenkins, who was pleasant enough but who had few interests that Duane shared. He felt she was inferior in every way to his mother and hoped his father wasn't considering marrying her. His father seemed to sense his feeling, so neither discussed the subject of marriage.

The days following Christmas afforded plenty of time for reading. Duane found *The Great Controversy* most interesting. It intrigued him that a book written in the late 1800s could have so graphically foretold current trends. He thought it quite probable that the predictions still unfulfilled were also correct. But it seemed that he still had time to build a successful career before he made some kind of decision about Laurel's church.

He wondered how much his love for Laurel colored his conviction that the Adventists were right. If he were to join her church and marry her, would his conviction be strong enough to withstand the scorn of his associates and the diminished opportunity for professional growth?

On the way home he decided to drop by Three Elms and

tell Laurel of his quandary. So on the evening of December 31 he knocked at the kitchen door. Turner Lambert went to the door.

"Well, Duane! So good to see you. Come on in." He took his coat and hung it in the closet as he added, "Sorry to say, I'm alone. The others are in Boston."

"I thought I saw the car in the driveway."

"They went in Alexander's car."

Duane looked surprised. "Alexander? Who's he?"

"A medical student Larry brought home for the holidays. Fine fellow. Took the family to a concert by the Boston Symphony Orchestra."

"I'm sure Laurel is enjoying it," Duane said gravely. Mr. Lambert motioned for him to be seated at the kitchen table. Without enthusiasm Duane resumed, "It must be good to have Larry home. Will he stay long?"

"I'm afraid not. They have to start back tomorrow. How are things with you?"

The younger man gestured in frustration. "Confused. I don't feel I'm ready to make a decision yet."

"Take your time. Your decision is extremely important."

Duane moved the salt shakers to conform more symmetrically to the design of the tablecloth. Then he shifted them again. Keeping his gaze on them, he said hesitatingly, "I just wanted Laurel to know I'm still hoping."

"You had better talk to her about that. I'm not very good at conveying that kind of message," Mr. Lambert chuckled.

"Did she get my recording?"

"Yes, it came two days after Christmas. She has played it many times. We all enjoy it. And she has something for you and was wondering how to present it."

"I didn't expect anything in return."

"She had it all along but was afraid to send it. You know

how women are. Excuse me while I go get it.''

A surge of happiness swept over Duane. In a moment Mr. Lambert returned with a medium-sized, brightly wrapped package.

''I'll save it and open it tomorrow. That will be my New Year's celebration.'' The huge red-and-white bow hid a little card. It said, ''To Duane. All my love. Laurel.''

Larry and Alexander slept late the next morning, but Laurel was too excited to sleep. She reviewed Alexander's offer and wondered whether the trip to California was just some fleeting whim. It seemed strange coming from a man she hardly knew, but she figured a round-trip ticket was as small a gift for him to give as a bottle of perfume or a dozen roses had been for other boys she had dated. Still, as much as she wished to see California, she didn't want to obligate herself.

Throwing back the covers, she went to the window where she looked down on his immaculately clean red sports car. He had spent the previous afternoon polishing it, and it gleamed in the pale morning sun. It would be fun to escape the rigors of New England for a while and roam the highways of fabled California with him, she mused. Then she chided herself for thinking such things.

She dressed in her most becoming skirt and sweater and styled her hair carefully. Her reflection in the mirror rather pleased her. Before she left her room she sprayed her wrist with a little cologne from the dispenser that contained nearly as much as when she had received it as a gift two years before.

Her mother was already in the kitchen, setting the table and scrambling eggs, when Laurel joined her. ''I guess it's too early to start making toast,'' the girl said.

Mrs. Lambert shut the doors from the kitchen, then said

quietly, "Your father has already eaten, but let's not awaken the boys. They have a long trip ahead and need their sleep."

Laurel wondered whether she dared tell her mother about her invitation to come to California. "What do you think of Alex?" she asked instead.

"He seems like a boy of high ideals and considerable ambition. What do *you* think of him?"

"I really haven't thought much about him," she answered, trying to appear nonchalant.

"I've noticed that he watches you a lot. He raved over that apple pie you made more than it warranted."

"I didn't notice." Laurel straightened the already neatly arranged silverware.

"He asked me last night at the restaurant when we were alone whether you had decided to marry Duane."

The girl drew in her breath slightly. "What did you tell him?"

"I told him it was a hard decision since Duane was not of our faith."

Laurel walked to the kitchen counter and began to carefully stack slices of bread for toast. "Would it be proper for me to accept a plane ticket to California as a graduation gift?" She did not turn around to face her mother.

Her mother hesitated only a moment before answering. "I would think so. That is, if his parents agree. After all, it would actually be a gift from them."

There was a gentle knock on the kitchen door. "Mind if I come in?"

Quickly Laurel opened the door for Alexander. "We didn't want to disturb your sleep. Is Larry awake yet?" she asked.

"Yes, he's shaving now. Should be ready for breakfast soon."

"Good. I'll start making the toast."

With breakfast out of the way, Laurel and her mother prepared a lunch for the boys as they packed their suitcases. By eleven o'clock, lunches, suitcases, and the two young men were settled in the sports car, ready to start the long journey.

Mrs. Lambert admonished them to drive carefully on the icy roads and stop when they were sleepy. Her husband wished them success in their studies and God's blessings. Laurel had little to say, but when Alexander asked whether she would be willing to write him occasionally, she consented. He shook hands with all three, but it seemed to her he held her hand an embarrassingly long time.

Turner suggested that a short prayer for protection would be appropriate. Alexander switched off the ignition. "Dear Father in heaven," Laurel's father prayed, "we thank Thee for letting us have Larry back home these few days. We thank Thee that we have made a new friend in Alex. Protect them as they travel and guide them in their future plans. May they use the skill they are acquiring in Thy service. Above all, help us all to be ready to meet Jesus. Amen."

As the car backed out of the drive and started down the hill Laurel and her parents waved until it disappeared. Mrs. Lambert wiped away a tear and continued to gaze down the road. Turner Lambert put an arm around Laurel's shoulders as they turned toward the house.

"That was quite a surprise Larry arranged. Wasn't your Christmas vacation far better than you expected?"

"Yes. It was wonderful to have him home."

"That wasn't exactly what I meant."

"Wasn't it?" Her blush told her father that no further explanation was necessary.

Chapter 14

SENIOR RECITAL

The evening of February 22, despite a blizzard, Laurel's parents, Madame Wolfinger, two other members of the Thornton School vocal department, several voice majors, Pete Thayer, and a number of friends had assembled in the recital hall of Thornton School for her senior recital.

She vocalized softly backstage as Peggy Thayer pinned the bow between the shoulders in the back of Laurel's long fuchsia gown. Duane watched as Peggy adjusted the way the dress hung. "There. That should keep the bow looking pert all evening. Doesn't she look stunning?" the young minister's wife asked him.

"If she sounds half as good as she looks, the recital will be a success."

Laurel looked like a Greek goddess, with her hair drawn back and her floor-length, high-waisted gown unadorned except for the velvet bow with its long streamers in the back.

"I'd better go join my husband," Peggy said. "Best of success, Laurel. I know it will be great." She squeezed her and left.

"Thank you. Say a prayer for me."

"I'm scared," Laurel confided to Duane when they were alone.

He smiled. "I know you are, and I don't blame you. Just try not to let it show so much."

"Are you ever nervous before you play?"

"Always."

Her eyes widened. "You never appear to be."

"I try to fool the audience, hoping to fool myself at the same time."

She sighed. "I'm afraid of only two people out there—Madame Wolfinger and Gina."

"Well, I know Madame thinks highly of your ability and respects you. As for Gina, she's so wrapped up in herself that anyone would suffer by comparison in her eyes. Ignore her."

"I wish I could."

Duane glanced at his watch. "It's five minutes after eight. Time to muster your courage and go on out." Holding the music for the first group of selections in his hand, he slipped his free arm around Laurel's waist and kissed her cheek. "I'll be right behind you."

The recital gave evidence of careful preparation. Laurel's voice gained in certainty after the first group. By the time she came to the Schumann cycle she put herself into the music wholeheartedly, and even Gina had to acknowledge to herself that Laurel was a fine interpreter.

In her last group Laurel included a song entitled "Dedication" that Duane had written especially for her. She had not known he had any interest in composition till he presented her with it. It was her favorite of the pieces programmed and she sang it tenderly.

Before Laurel could realize it, the recital was over. That seventy minutes of music could slip by so fast seemed incomprehensible to her. Backstage she asked whether she had omitted something, but Duane assured her that she had not. The audience was still applauding, and he told her to acknowledge the ovation. As she walked to the center of the stage and bowed, someone placed a spray of red roses in her arms. She wondered who could have sent them.

Backstage, she hurriedly opened the envelope as Duane peered over her shoulder. The little card read: "Congratulations. Alex." Duane studied her face but could not tell whether she was elated, annoyed, or merely surprised. Without comment she carefully replaced the card in the envelope and laid the flowers beside her coat.

By then most of the audience had found their way backstage to offer congratulations. To Laurel's relief she saw that Gina was among the few who didn't come. Madame Wolfinger told her she spoke for the three voice teachers in pronouncing the recital a success and a worthy fulfillment of the senior requirement. "I vas proud off you," she said as she hugged Laurel.

A number congratulated Duane for his playing. As he stood by Laurel in the receiving line she graciously gave him credit for the success of the evening. Several people commented upon the unity of their interpretation.

When they had a few minutes alone he whispered, "I hope that I won't be seeing less of you now that the recital is over."

"I hope not too. Thank you for the many hours you spent helping me get ready, and for the wonderful song you wrote for me."

He took her hands. "You can't imagine how much I enjoyed it. I hope it isn't the last time we perform together," he said, looking searchingly into her eyes. Her lips trembled and tears began to form.

Just then Mr. Lambert brought her coat and held it for her. "We must be going, Laurel. We don't want to keep Pete and Peggy waiting."

After Laurel slipped the coat on, Mother Lambert handed her the roses. "Here are your flowers. They're lovely." Then turning to Duane, she said, "Thank you for your wonderful playing. We all appreciate your help so much.'' The older woman smiled, but he sensed a hint of reserve in her manner.

As Laurel walked off with her parents, red roses cradled on her arm, he watched her disappear. He felt lonelier than he had in a long time. The janitor came to turn off the lights, and donning his topcoat, Duane started for home.

Chapter 15

VENTURA

Laurel thoroughly enjoyed her first flight. She had departed Boston only three hours before, yet now was almost ready to land at the Los Angeles International Airport. She was eager to see Larry, but felt somewhat apprehensive about greeting Alexander and meeting Dr. and Mrs. Robertson. Although she had been reluctant to accept this graduation gift of a trip, Larry assured her it was proper and that Alexander and his parents would be disappointed if she refused to come.

She took a mirror from her purse. Deciding her nose looked shiny and her hair needed attention, she squeezed past her seatmates and started down the narrow aisle. There were others standing in line waiting for the restroom. The ride that had been so smooth suddenly became jerky. The jet lunged a few times, alarming her, but the more seasoned travelers didn't even look up from their magazines. By the time she was seated before the mirror, she wished she hadn't nibbled at the meal served on the plane. Her skin was clammy, and her usually pink cheeks were ashen. Combing her hair and powdering her nose, she hurried back to her seat.

When the plane came out of the clouds she anxiously peered out the window and prayed for a safe landing as the ground loomed closer and closer. Finally, with a slight bump, the wheels made contact, and the jet slowed to a screaming stop. Greatly relieved, she settled back in her seat, reluctant to join the passengers scrambling for their belongings. When almost all had disembarked, she took her coat, which a seatmate had gotten down from the rack, and went to the end of the line of passengers.

Once inside the terminal, she was greeted with a hug from Larry. Beside him stood Alexander, looking rather nervous. She wondered whether he felt as apprehensive as she did. His greeting was more formal. "Welcome to California. How was the flight?" His casual clothing suggested affluence and good taste.

While Larry went after the suitcases, Alexander asked whether she would prefer to see some of the sights of Los Angeles now or go directly to his home. She replied she would leave that up to him. He thought it best to take her home and return when they were unencumbered with luggage.

The airport bus carried them to the parking lot. Laurel recognized the red sports car. Soon the three young people headed toward Ventura. The highway, which followed the coastline, afforded a magnificent view of the ocean. Laurel asked how far the Robertson home was from the water.

"About four miles," Alexander replied. "There's a good beach near the yacht club if you like saltwater swimming. Of course, you can always swim in our pool at home. That's where Mother spends most of her time—more reading and sunning than actual swimming, though."

"Oh, good. We'll have something in common."

A frown shadowed the corners of his mouth a moment. "Well, I trust you'll have something in common, but I doubt that reading will be it. She subscribes to about twenty magazines, which she reads from cover to cover. Probably doesn't read more than a couple books a year."

Laurel had imagined Mrs. Robertson as a gray-haired, motherly matron in her late fifties, fond of entertaining,

active in cultural events, and a leader in church activities.
How she had arrived at that image she didn't know. She
suddenly realized that the Mrs. Robertson she had created
was quite similar to her own mother and that she actually
knew nothing about the real one. Somehow she couldn't fit
the long hours of sunbathing and the magazine reading into
her previous conception.

Soon the car slowed and turned off the highway. Laurel
was becoming more uneasy. After several turns the car
pulled into the driveway of an expansive contemporary ranch
home with neatly manicured lawn and shrubbery. The house
was of white stucco, forming a perfect background for the
profusion of color in the oval rose garden in front of it. A low
hedge trimmed to formal perfection framed the garden. The
yard, which extended only a few feet beyond the house on
each side, had a six-foot redwood fence enclosing it.

"What an attractive home!" Laurel exclaimed. "How
can you keep the lawn and shrubbery so perfect?"

"Jim comes over twice a week to care for the grounds.
He has been our gardener for years. With not much frontage,
the lawn is small. But the lot is deep enough for a pool,
barbecue pit, and picnic area out back."

"You must entertain quite a bit."

He grimaced. "We used to. Seems most of Mother's
friends have moved away. Last time we had a group from the
church over, some of the children picked the roses, and
Mother vowed she would never invite them back. Dad has
some professional friends who come over occasionally."

Larry climbed out and held the door for Laurel while
Alexander got her bags out of the trunk. As they neared the
entrance a white toy poodle bounced against the glass door,
yapping excitedly.

"Quiet, Bijou," Alexander commanded as he opened
the door. The high-strung little animal danced around on two

ridiculously tiny feet, his pom-pom tail wagging frantically, while he pawed Laurel's stockings.

Laurel stooped down to pat the little head, but the puff of fuzz on top insulated the pat. When she decided Bijou wouldn't hold still, she stood up, and her eyes met those of a woman of no particular age, with well-groomed blond hair, a dark tan, and a youthful figure wearing a brightly flowered shell over yellow shorts.

"Laurel, I'd like you to meet my mother." He drew the woman forward. She seemed somewhat reticent.

"I've been looking forward to meeting you." Laurel smiled warmly. "You have a beautiful home."

"Thank you. We're glad you could come. Let me show you where you can put your things."

She led Laurel to a large bedroom with gold wall-to-wall carpeting. Black-and-gold-flocked wallpaper covered the walls. Tufted red crushed velvet covered the headboard of the king-sized bed, matching the bedspread and elaborately swagged draperies. Tall "antiqued" gold figurines used as lamps and a bouquet of flowers made of dyed feathers on the long French provincial dresser, all implied more money than taste and left Laurel feeling uncomfortable. Alexander set her suitcases down beside the bed.

Mrs. Robertson suggested she might like to unpack and freshen up a bit before lunch. When Laurel had shut the bedroom door she flopped down on the bed. It was as soft as it looked. She realized she was tired from nervous exhaustion, but reluctantly made herself get up and unpack her clothes. Then, deciding to change into something more casual than the suit she had traveled in, she laid out the three disposable paper sundresses she had purchased for the trip. Finally she selected the pink one with a random design of lavender and yellow. It was the most frivolous thing she owned.

They ate lunch in the picnic area of the backyard. The

entrée, individual frozen beef-style vegetarian dinners
warmed in the microwave oven, was served with an exotic
fruit salad. The dessert was an elaborately decorated cake
with "Welcome, Laurel" in yellow letters on top surrounded
by red roses. Mrs. Robertson did not sample the cake—too
many calories, she said—but hoped it came up to her baker's
usual standard of excellence. It did.

While Alexander and Larry cleared away the dishes and
leftovers, Mrs. Robertson suggested to Laurel that they sun
themselves in the hammocks by the pool. Laurel settled back
and gazed through the wispy mimosa tree at a hummingbird
darting from flower to flower and to the blue sky overhead.

"This is so comfortable I hope I can stay awake," she said.

"You must be tired from the trip. It's three hours later by
Boston time, so you've had a full day. Take a nap while I read
some." Mrs. Robertson reached for a magazine from the
rack by her hammock. In a couple of minutes Laurel fell
asleep.

Two hours later she awoke when a drop of water hit her
nose. She opened her eyes and saw the mimosa tree with a
hummingbird still flitting from flower to flower rather than
the ceiling of her room. When she heard splashing and the
sound of masculine voices, she realized where she was.
Larry and Alexander were diving and swimming under water
the length of the pool. When Alexander dived the water
seemed to part without splashing a drop. Laurel's brother
was a less skillful diver, and from time to time would create a
geyser, some drops reaching all the way to her hammock.

The boys hadn't noticed that she had awakened, so she
watched them. Laurel had always been proud of her handsome older brother. He stood poised on the springboard, his
golden brown hair falling over his forehead, his determined
chin indicating that he would practice diving till he mastered
it. She marveled how his muscles could still be so well

developed after months of grinding study. By comparison, Alexander looked weak, though his tan showed he had been out in the sun more. Both boys were about six feet tall, but Alexander looked taller because of his slimness.

Alexander's auburn hair glinted red in the direct sunlight. It was his most striking feature, well complemented by his freckleless complexion and brown eyes. He lacked Larry's look of determination, but he was handsome in a less rugged sort of way.

Seeming to sense he was being watched, he glanced in her direction. When he saw she was awake, his face broke into a smile, and he came over and squatted down beside her. "Had your beauty nap, I see. How about coming in for a swim?"

"I haven't met your father yet. Should I get my hair wet now or stay presentable till I've met him?"

"There is no telling when he'll get home. Sometimes six, sometimes midnight. We have loads of hair dryers. You have time to swim and dry your hair before dinner. If Dad gets home and sees you with wet hair, don't worry. A surgeon sees worse sights than that." He steadied the hammock and took her hand to help her out.

In a few minutes she approached the pool's edge in her bathing suit, and Alexander swam to meet her. "I'd say you have a glamorous sister, Larry," he called above the slosh of the water against the edges of the pool.

"Sure do. Come on in, Laurel. It's not cold."

Laurel tested the water with one toe, then the whole foot, followed by the other foot. Finally she slid off the edge into the water. Larry showered her with a huge splash as he attempted another unsuccessful dive. Alexander raced her across the pool and won easily.

By dinner time Laurel was feeling wonderful. The nap and the swim had erased the weariness she had felt earlier that day. She had set and dried her hair and donned one of her prettiest dresses. Now as she helped Mrs. Robertson in the kitchen Bijou started the special commotion that he reserved for the entrance of Dr. Robertson. His wife removed her apron and went to greet her husband with the routine kiss and questions about his day. His answers rarely told anything more than the score of living versus dead. It had been a good day—no dead.

Mrs. Robertson steered her husband to the kitchen. "Here is Alexander's friend Laurel, from Massachusetts."

"How are you, Laurel?" He looked kind, though careworn. "I hope your trip was pleasant."

"I'm fine, and the trip was wonderful. It was so kind of you to give me this opportunity to see California."

"Alexander very much wanted you to come. Seems none of the girls around here suit him. They chase him too vigorously, I suspect." She blushed, and Dr. Robertson changed the subject. "We understand you're a fine singer. I took the liberty to tell our church organist, who will probably be calling you about singing next Sabbath."

She was suddenly flustered. "I didn't bring any music with me."

"That's no problem. Mr. Patterson probably has stacks of pieces, and there's a well-stocked music store just a ten-minute drive from here."

The five sat down at the table. Mrs. Robertson lighted the candles, then Dr. Robertson asked God to bless the food. Before the meal was finished the phone rang. It was the hospital calling Dr. Robertson to come at once for surgery on an accident victim. Grabbing his bag and a sample of Laurel's Welcome cake, he headed out the door.

A few minutes later the phone rang again. This time it was Mr. Patterson, the church organist, wishing to speak to Laurel. A brief conversation revealed he had music for quite a few songs she knew. He suggested she come over to the church to practice with him. She let him talk to Alexander, and they agreed to be at the church in one hour. They asked Larry if he would like to go along, but he preferred to get a good night of rest before returning to Loma Linda and the dormitory the next day.

At the church Laurel and Mr. Patterson went through several numbers before selecting a contemporary setting of the Beatitudes by Murdoch. Mr. Patterson was a competent organist, and the church, though small, boasted a fine new pipe organ. Laurel enjoyed the evening and looked forward to performing with Mr. Patterson on Sabbath. She also accepted his invitation to sing the solo part in a choir anthem after he assured her that his wife, the usual soloist, would not be offended. Alexander, listening contentedly, sat on the front pew throughout the practice.

Back in the car, he asked her whether she would like to see whitecaps roll in by moonlight. She noted that it was nearly ten o'clock, and she didn't want to worry his parents. When he assured her that no one at his house ever went to bed before midnight, she agreed to go.

It was not far to the ocean. Parking the car, they strolled along the sand till they came to a large, dry rock. Silently they sat close together, listening to the roar and hiss of the waves. The tide was coming in, and as the foam crept closer and closer to their feet, Laurel felt two opposing forces compelling her to flee, yet gluing her to the spot. She knew the creeping water only symbolized something she was experiencing within.

Getting chilly, she wanted to suggest that they leave. Yet she said nothing. Alexander, noticing she was shivering, put his arm around her and drew her close. When the foam finally touched their shoes, they silently rose and walked hand in hand to the car.

Chapter 16

A DECISION

Next morning she awakened early. Laurel tried to ignore her feelings of apprehension as thoughts of Duane, Alexander, Bijou, and Mrs. Robertson in her yellow shorts whirled in her mind. She wanted to talk to Larry before she and Alexander drove him back to the Loma Linda campus. A couple of hours later as she helped Mrs. Robertson clear away the breakfast dishes she was still wondering how she could arrange a little time alone with her brother.

"Mom, did you say you needed a ride to the hairdresser?" Alexander inquired a few minutes later.

"Yes. My car is at the garage, and your dad left early with his. If you'll drop me off I'll get a cab home."

"Be glad to. Would you like to come along, Laurel?"

"How would it be if I stayed and prepared a lunch to take along to the university?" she responded quickly.

"Do we have anything Laurel can make sandwiches from?" Alexander asked his mother.

"I think so." She went to the refrigerator and began to set containers of various shapes and sizes on the counter. "Help yourself to whatever interests you. The bread is in here," she added, opening the bread drawer.

"I'll be back in a few minutes," Alexander said as he and his mother left.

As soon as they were out the door, Laurel called to her

brother, who was packing his suitcase in another room. "Larry, can you come to the kitchen?"

"I'm almost through packing. Be with you in a few minutes."

"This can't wait."

He came as bidden. "What's up, Sis?"

"Alex is gone for a few minutes, and I need to talk to you alone."

"Go ahead."

"Why did he invite me here?" She stared at him intently.

Her brother laughed. "He likes you."

"How much?"

"I don't know. I never asked him."

"What if he asks me to marry him?"

"Hold it! Hold it! I think he plans to finish medicine before he gets married. After all, he's just finished his second year."

"Do you think I could fit into his life-style?"

Larry smiled and put his arm around her. "It would be a change, but you're adaptable. He's basically a good fellow, and his father is a well-respected surgeon. I'm not too impressed with his mother, but I don't think Alex is looking for a wife anything like her."

She cocked her head toward the door to see if she could hear Alexander returning. "Has he talked to you about what he wants in a wife?"

"Several times."

"What kind of person is he looking for?"

"A lot like you."

Laurel blushed and studied the floor a moment. Finally she looked up and continued, "You know I still love Duane."

"Yes, I know. He's a fine fellow, but he's not of our faith."

She drew circles on the floor with her toe. "He is studying our beliefs."

Her brother frowned. "Even if he joins the church, you won't know whether it is out of conviction or to get you."

"Is Alex a good Christian?"

"So far as I can tell. He complies with church standards and talks of the possibility of a term of mission service before setting up his practice."

"Is his motive service or adventure?"

"I don't know. Probably both."

"Larry, I'm confused. I'm scared." Her wrinkled brow and trembling chin revealed her seriousness.

"Sis, I wish I knew how to advise you. But only God knows the future. It's a decision you alone must make."

Just then they heard Alexander's car in the driveway. "Promise me, Larry, you won't breathe a word of this to him."

"I promise."

When Alexander burst into the kitchen seconds later, Laurel was busy with her sandwiches and Larry was in the bedroom packing. They were soon on their way.

Laurel could hardly wait to see the university that had figured so prominently in Larry's letters. As they drove onto the campus, its beauty impressed her. She made mental note of various buildings, the classrooms and laboratories, the campus nooks Larry showed her. And she especially studied two young women who rushed up to be introduced. Larry's remark to Pete Thayer the preceding summer that he had a girl friend came back to her. But his matter-of-fact introductions gave no indication that either one was more than a passing acquaintance.

When it was time to say good-bye Larry hugged Laurel tight and whispered he would pray that God would guide her. He admonished Alexander to drive carefully and take good care of his baby sister.

During the trip back to Ventura the conversation turned to their future plans. "Have you accepted a teaching position for next year?" he asked.

She shook her head. "I always planned to teach in one of our Adventist academies, but now that most have had to close, I'll either have to teach privately or in a high school. My plans aren't definite yet."

He glanced at her. "Can you earn enough to stay alive teaching privately?"

"It isn't easy. It takes awhile to get established."

"There are still a few academies operating in California. I heard the one at Glendale is looking for a music teacher."

"Where is Glendale?"

"It's a suburb of Los Angeles."

"Surely they wouldn't wait until June to find a teacher."

"Seems the young woman who has been teaching there got involved with some fellow, and they asked her to resign just last week. If you would be interested, I'd be glad to introduce you to the principal."

"I'd be happy to talk to him," she said after a slight hesitation.

"I'll phone from the next filling station and make an appointment."

After the call, he reported that Mr. Nelson would be in church Sabbath to hear Laurel sing, and he would come to their place Saturday night to talk with her.

"I wish you hadn't told me he'll be in church." She frowned. "I'll be very nervous."

He laughed. "You'll do fine. I'm not worried."

Saturday night Mr. Nelson arrived at the Robertson home a few minutes after sundown. Laurel parted the drapes and watched as he walked confidently from the car to the front door. He appeared to be in his mid-thirties.

"You'll find him very pleasant," Alexander told her as he went to the door to admit the man. "Try not to look so nervous."

Laurel seated herself and attempted to appear poised but found her hands and knees were trembling. She silently sent up a quick prayer for calm and guidance.

Mr. Nelson was unassuming, and she found herself speaking easily about her qualifications and aspirations. He told her Glendale Academy had two music teachers, and the position then vacant was for a choral director who would also give voice lessons and teach a class in basic musicianship. The choir did considerable touring in the spring of the year and had an established reputation for excellence.

"I believe after hearing you sing today that you are certainly qualified to teach voice, and your degree would adequately prepare you to teach the theory class. Do you believe you could handle the choral part of our program?"

She thought a moment. "My only directing experience in the choral field has been with a small choir in the church where I am organist. But I have sung under some excellent directors at both Atlantic Union College and Thornton School of Music. I believe I know how to obtain a good choral sound."

"Most successful choral directors I have known are quite dynamic personalities. Do you think you can maintain discipline and get the cooperation of the young people?"

"I don't pretend to be a dynamic person. But I have known successful directors who gain respect and cooperation by their sincere interest in people and their dedication to the highest artistic ideals."

"Our academy board is meeting Monday," he told her. "There are two other applicants for this position. Would you like to have me submit your name also?"

"Yes. Yes, I would."

"Could you please give me two references who have known you for some time and who are members of the Seventh-day Adventist Church?"

She wrote down the names and addresses of Pete Thayer and a former Bible teacher from Atlantic Union College. As Mr. Nelson prepared to leave, he told her he would call Monday after the board meeting to report the decision. He added that he thought she could be a real asset to Glendale Academy.

It was 2 AM Tuesday, but Laurel hadn't yet fallen asleep. Finally she arose, turned on the light, and, taking a pen and stationery from her suitcase, started to write:

"Ventura, Calif
"Tuesday, 2 AM

"Dear Duane,
"It seems like such a long time since I talked to you last on the phone. I've been in California a week now and find that I'm eager to get back home. The family I'm staying with are doing all they can to show me a good time, but this life of idleness doesn't suit me too well. I've been swimming almost daily, and my skin and hair have approached each other in color till I'm one shade of tan.

"Today, rather yesterday now, I made an important decision. I'm telling you about it first of all, though I'll write my parents later today. I accepted the offer of a teaching position for next year in an Adventist academy here in California. I am somewhat apprehensive about the position, but as I have spent years preparing myself to teach, I'm really happy to have the opportunity.

"It has been a long time since you asked me to become your wife, and I am unfair to you if I postpone my decision

indefinitely. I do love you dearly, please believe me, and wish I could marry you. If we shared the same faith, I wouldn't hesitate to do so. But under the circumstances, I believe that to remain only friends is better for both of us.

"I'll never forget your kindness and understanding. I have not given my heart to someone else. I doubt that anyone will ever really take your place. I couldn't bear the thought of never seeing you again, so I hope you'll come visit occasionally after I return home next week to spend the rest of the summer.

"As ever,
"Laurel"

As she sealed the envelope the tears she had been blinking back trickled hotly down her cheeks. Licking the stamp, she was pressing it down firmly when a tear splattered on the return address, causing the ink to run. She blotted it with the hem of her nightgown and decided not to repair the illegible address. Duane would understand, she felt sure.

Chapter 17

HEARTBREAK

When Duane received her letter, her decision did not surprise him. Nevertheless he was deeply disappointed. He had hoped she would accept him as he was and that they could operate a joint studio that in time could grow into a music school.

Not knowing how to relate to Laurel, his one visit to Three Elms following her return had been friendly but short. Somewhat awkwardly and without much enthusiasm he wished her well in her teaching and promised to write.

Weeks lengthened into months, but neither had sent the first letter. Duane tried to convince himself that he would soon forget, but time didn't seem to ease the ache. In November he finally wrote and asked whether Laurel would be coming home for Christmas. He said he had missed her terribly and that he had reread *The Great Controversy* and decided that the author was truly a prophet.

Laurel replied that she would love to come home for the holidays, but she could not afford the expense of the trip. Her choir was giving a Christmas Eve concert in one of the churches, and she had an invitation to spend the vacation with the friends who had made her first visit to California possible. She added that she was glad he agreed with *The Great Controversy* and hoped he would not content himself with a mere intellectual assent.

The next few months Duane was despondent. His dream of a concert career seemed unattainable. True, he could continue playing occasional recitals in small halls to undistinguished audiences, but he realized that the glamor of the great concert hall would never be his. As he spent less time practicing, he spent more time composing, though more from the inner satisfaction it afforded than from any hope of attaining fame or fortune. His piano pupils were his livelihood, but he began to begrudge the time spent teaching.

Most of his pupils offered little musical challenge. Rather, the challenge came in exercising the necessary patience and trying to spark the pupils' enthusiasm for hard work. But he had a few pupils with considerable potential. One, strangely enough, was Spencer Schwab, who at age ten was his youngest pupil. His mother still entertained hopes of a concert career for her son. Spencer was preparing a recital to give at the time of his eleventh birthday in April. His love for music ranked considerably behind his love for baseball, but he was making steady progress nevertheless. His interpretation, though far from inspired, was rather good for his age.

A more interesting pupil was Sheila Cofield, a high-school junior who idolized Duane and practiced hours every day to please him. The girl planned to attend Thornton and major in piano. She was fairly advanced, considering that she had studied piano only four years. Duane was careful to treat her kindly, while not encouraging her infatuation.

His most advanced pupil was Mrs. Conrad Eaton, a piano teacher herself. About his age, she was married to an engineer whom Duane knew only through Mrs. Eaton's description. According to her, he was unsympathetic to the arts, unconcerned about his wife's happiness, and in no way bound by his marriage vows when away for weeks at a time on business. Duane suspected that she also viewed marriage as a socially acceptable custom not intended to limit one's sexuality. He tried to be as businesslike as possible at her lessons, but it was hard to keep her attention on music.

A major cause of Duane's unhappiness was his indecision about whether God's commandments were still binding. He knew few educated people who considered that any of God's law still applied in the twentieth century, if ever it had. The commandment forbidding adultery had just about joined the Sabbath commandment as a relic of a bygone era.

One Friday evening in March after his last student left, he turned to Exodus 20 and reread the commandments, dwelling long enough on each to think of ways in which the so-called Christian world had ignored them. It seemed he must make a decision either to accept all of them, including the fourth— with its concept of God as the Creator—as the will of God or live for the present and reject the idea of a future life. Duane felt it possible for those who had not studied the history of the change of the Sabbath to fulfill the requirement of the fourth commandment by observing Sunday. But for him to keep Sunday would be a rejection of—what could he call it?— truth. Determining before he went to bed that he would begin to shift his Saturday lessons to other days of the week, he slept peacefully for the first time in weeks.

His decision had not come lightly. The next day he began to reschedule lessons. Gradually, over a period of several weeks he managed to shift most of his Saturday lessons to other days. When he finally had Saturday morning cleared he looked up the address of the local Seventh-day Adventist church and took the bus to Airport Road to attend the worship service. He slipped in unnoticed and left during the closing hymn.

The fourth time he went, the visiting minister was Pete Thayer. Duane arrived late and didn't notice Thayer sitting on the platform at first. When he finished reading the bulletin and looked up he saw Pete smiling at him. He wanted to remain after the service to talk to him but had to leave early to meet his one o'clock student.

That afternoon his phone rang when he was in the midst of a lesson. Motioning to his pupil to play softly, he said, "This is Duane Manning."

"Hello, Duane. Pete Thayer."

"Oh, hello, Pete. Good of you to call."

"I was happy to see you in church today. Have you been attending regularly?"

"I've been a few times."

"The pastor there doesn't know you. Why not introduce yourself to him?"

"I always have to leave early. I wanted to hang around today to talk with you, but had to be home by one o'clock."

"Maybe Peggy and I could visit you later today."

"Sure. Anytime after four o'clock."

"I see by the phone book you're at the same address."

"Yes. Nothing has changed. I'll be looking for you."

At 4:15 Pete and Peggy arrived. After the usual pleasantries, Pete came to the point of his visit. "We have been praying for you ever since our Bible studies. Have you begun observing the Sabbath?"

"I'm convinced it is what I must do. In fact, I'm gradually shifting my Saturday lessons to other days of the week. It will be a few weeks before I can complete the changeover."

The Thayers smiled. Pete shook Duane's hand. "We are happy for your decision. We trust God will give you courage to carry out your convictions. I do think, however, a less gradual approach would be preferable."

"I'm afraid courage is not one of my virtues. I want to obey God, but I'm not eager to ally myself with a group as socially stigmatized as the Adventists seem to be."

"Do you disagree with any of our doctrines?"

"No." Duane glanced down at his hands, which he nervously clasped and unclasped.

"Do you think it will be easier to be an undeclared Sabbathkeeper?"

"No. It will probably be harder if I don't take a stand. I'm just not quite ready yet to make that kind of decision."

The young minister was silent for a while. "May we have prayer together?"

Duane nodded. He felt God's Spirit come near during the prayer. He was unable to talk when the prayer ended.

"God can use you and your talents, Duane," Peggy said. "Don't wait too long."

As Pete and Peggy started to leave, he asked them about the Lamberts. Pete said the parents were in good health, but he had not seen Laurel since August or Larry for over a year.

"How is Laurel enjoying her teaching?"

"I understand she loves it, but she misses Massachusetts," Pete answered.

"Will she teach there again next year?"

"Yes," Peggy replied. "She'll be there for one more year while her husband takes his internship at a Los Angeles hospital."

"Her husband?" Duane sounded shocked.

"You didn't know? She's to be married in June," Peggy explained. "Fine fellow. We met him a year ago Christmas when Larry brought him home for the holidays."

Duane turned pale. He didn't notice as Pete took Peggy's arm and waved good-bye. Finally he realized he was standing alone on the front walk, gazing vacantly into space. Slowly he turned and climbed with heavy feet the few steps to his door. Numbly he collapsed into an armchair.

When it became dusk Duane didn't turn on a light. Instead, he went to the bedroom, undressed, crawled into bed, and lay for hours gazing at the shadows on the ceiling created by the streetlight on the corner. Although he wanted to cry, no tears came. He felt the same emptiness he had experienced when he had learned of his mother's violent death three years before. Was this how God was rewarding his decision to keep the Sabbath? Or was he himself to blame because of his indecision?

He turned on the bedside radio, which he kept tuned to an FM station that interrupted its twenty-four hours of classical music only for newscasts. The music finally permitted him to get to sleep. Before he realized it, the sun was shining brightly and an announcer was giving the Sunday morning news:

"Evangelist Sunny Parker told an audience of 50,000 in Wallace Stadium last night that what the U.S. needs is a return to religion so God can again bless our nation. He regretted that dissenters have thwarted all attempts to bring unity to Christendom and bring reality to our claim to be a Christian nation. . . .

"The Supreme Court yesterday upheld a ruling by the Federal Court of Appeals that violation of the Sunday law can result in imprisonment regardless of whether the violator keeps the seventh-day Sabbath or not. A bill has been introduced into Congress making regular public church services on any day other than Sunday illegal. Similar bills have been thwarted in the past, but the recent Constitutional revisions have eliminated the arguments of those minorities who oppose the state and persistently refuse to yield to popular demand."

Duane turned off the radio and stared again at the ceiling. Finally he slid out of bed onto his knees. The words would not come. At last he gasped, "God, give me courage."

Then without rising from his knees, he buried his face in the covers and wept.

Chapter 18

BETTER THAT A FEW SUFFER

A few nights later Duane watched a special on TV in which a spirit medium invoked a shining being. CBS claimed there was no camera trickery involved and that what appeared on the screen was actually taking place. The being never spoke but placed his fingertips on a number of ill persons assembled in the studio, and all were instantly healed. In one close-up shot a cancerous growth shriveled and disappeared. In another the thick film that had blinded a man all his life disintegrated, and the bewildered man saw for the first time.

The being lit *yes* and *no* bulbs by touching them in response to questions from the audience.

"Are you an angel?"

"Yes."

"Did you once live on earth?"

"Yes."

"Are you happier now than when on earth?"

"Yes."

"Some people claim the dead are asleep and know nothing and that spiritualistic manifestations are the work of Satan and evil angels. Is this true?"

"No."

"Is God displeased with the United States?"

"Yes."

"Will God fight for us if we again become a Christian

nation with Christian laws and allegiance?''

''Yes.''

''Was the tidal wave which devastated Atlantic City a result of God's wrath?''

''Yes.''

''Will Los Angeles be destroyed by an earthquake?''

''Yes.''

''Will this happen within the next five years?''

''Yes.''

''Can Los Angeles repent and save itself?''

''Yes.''

''Is it necessary to keep the fourth commandment?''

''Yes.''

''Does this mean we should all keep Saturday?''

''No.''

''Is it wrong to persecute Sabbatarians?''

''No.''

''Will there be a millennium of peace?''

''Yes.''

Finally a teenager demanded, ''Are you a fake?'' Suddenly a blinding flash filled the studio, the being vanished, and the teenager lay dead, his scorched body toppled in a heap in front of his chair. The program director was as confused as the other participants, who fled the studio. The station abruptly switched to another program.

It took a year for the bill prohibiting regular services on any day other than Sunday to pass both houses of Congress. Duane hoped that President McGrath would veto it, but as she signed it, she stated, ''It is the duty of Christians to yield obedience to those civil authorities ordained by God. It is better for the few who stand in opposition to the laws of the land to suffer than for the whole nation to continue to suffer the wrath of God.''

The law would go into effect at the end of March so that those churches affected would have two weeks to notify their members of the change. On the last two Saturdays that the authorities permitted worship, police officers required those present to register their names, social security numbers, and addresses before leaving the building. Though attendance was less than usual the first Saturday, it was even lower the following week.

Word went out from General Conference headquarters in Washington that the churches would comply in changing their day of meeting to Sunday and that they should encourage as many non-Adventists as possible to attend. Members should meet in small groups on Friday nights and Saturdays in private homes for devotional services and Bible study, reserving Sunday for meetings of an evangelistic nature.

Though the government aimed the new law primarily at Seventh-day Adventists, it brought hardship to many orthodox Jews and other Sabbatarians. The Jewish people throughout their long history had learned to accept and adapt to persecution, thus the ones in the United States related to the new laws as a passing inconvenience to be endured. Some Jews who had strictly kept the Sabbath ceased doing so.

But because being a Jew involves an ethnic identity as well as beliefs, and since Judaism had never actively proselytized, the mainline Christian churches did not consider them a threat. So when the Orthodox Jews protested the law, the authorities granted a waiver for anyone who was a Jew by birth and who practiced the Jewish religion. The large number of Jews who had been recent converts to the Adventist faith lost their rights to special consideration.

The various Christian communions agreed that though Christendom must become unified, they should respect the rights of the Jews. Adventists and other dissenting Christians could be persuaded, they felt, to give up their heresies. The new law would not inconvenience atheists and non-Christian groups. It was felt that a giant step toward the unity of Christendom had been taken and that the blessing of God would return to the United States.

Chapter 19

LAID TO REST

Duane attended the first Sunday morning meeting in the Worcester church. To his surprise he found the sanctuary packed and a public address system carrying the service to the many seated in folding chairs outside. Not wishing to shiver throughout the service, he decided to try to slip inside. Since there were no seats available, he stood in the back, where the deacons cared for the offering plates and bulletins.

The sermon dealt with signs of Christ's coming and the need for individual preparation. At its close the speaker gave an opportunity for those who wished to obey all God's commandments to come forward in commitment. Duane joined the majority of the congregation pressing toward the front. But when the pastor invited those wishing baptism to remain after the service, he resisted the urge to stay.

On the way out of the church he picked up the mimeographed bulletin. It listed the topic of next week's sermon, hours the Community Service building would be open to assist the public, addresses of homes where Sabbath services would be held, and various other announcements. One at the bottom of the page shocked him.

"Funeral of Turner Lambert, former teacher at Atlantic Union College, will be held today at 2 PM in the New Braintree Church."

Without returning to his apartment, he started for New

Braintree. Sunday bus connections were poor, and he feared
he wouldn't arrive in time. He wondered whether Laurel had
been able to come for the funeral.

Duane arrived at the church a few minutes before two
o'clock. As he entered he saw one spray of white lilies upon
the closed casket at the front. The congregation was small,
and Duane sat a few pews behind the family. Mrs. Lambert
sat next to Larry. Laurel was there between her mother and a
handsome man whom he assumed was her husband. They
were remarkably composed, though he noticed Mrs. Lambert wipe away a tear as the organist played "Abide With
Me."

The one spray of flowers perplexed Duane till he noticed
the request printed at the bottom of the souvenir leaflet,
which read, "Memorials may take the form of gifts to 'The
Voice of Prophecy' or 'Faith for Today.' ''

After Pete Thayer read the obituary, Pastor Kline
preached a sermonette on the hope of the resurrection and the
nearness of Christ's return. He reminded those present that
God knows best and probably saw it was better for Turner
Lambert to sleep rather than endure the trials just ahead. He
confidently stated that some in attendance would be trans-
lated without experiencing death, while others would
perhaps be called to rest for a brief time during a period of
chaos unlike any in the world's history. All must trust God to
decide which group they would be in.

After a moving prayer by Pete the congregation filed out
of the church, followed by the pallbearers with the casket.
The family accompanied the casket to the waiting cars.
Though there were tears in their eyes, they smiled and nodded recognition to those who had joined them in the memorial
service. Larry supported his mother, and Laurel took her
husband's arm. Duane thought that she was beautiful in her
grief. Her eyes had an unusual softness, and when they met

Duane's she gave him an appreciative smile. He watched as Alexander helped her into the car, and the funeral procession slowly started on its way to the cemetery.

Duane turned to a man standing beside him and asked, "What was the cause of Mr. Lambert's death?"

"Heart attack, apparently. He seemed fine when he went to bed Wednesday night. Thursday morning he didn't arise at his usual time; so Madeleine tried to awaken him and discovered he was dead."

Shaking his head sadly, Duane started toward the bus stop. He wished he could have expressed his sympathy but was glad, at least, that Laurel had seen him.

That evening Mrs. Lambert, Larry, Laurel, and Alexander tried to reorient their future. Larry, still unmarried, was an intern at a hospital in San Diego. He offered to move to an apartment and let his mother live with him, but she said she didn't want to leave Three Elms.

Laurel was still teaching at Glendale Academy while Alexander was beginning his internship. He was willing to check into the possibility of taking his residency in Boston so that he and Laurel could live at Three Elms with Mrs. Lambert. Laurel suggested that her mother sell the cow and chickens and spend the next three months with them in California. The possibility that the young couple might return to Massachusetts delighted Mrs. Lambert, but she said she could manage alone temporarily. After all, she argued, the neighbors were kind. Hadn't they been dropping by to leave casseroles and other dishes and offer their condolences?

Just then the doorbell rang, and Larry admitted an awkward youth. "Hello, George. My, how you've grown!"

"Here is s-something my Mom s-sent," the youth stammered as he held a foil-wrapped pie plate out at arm's length.

"Thank you for bringing it. And tell your mom it was very kind of her."

George grinned and backed out the door. As he hurried off Mrs. Lambert commented, "He's a dear boy. Fine folks, too. I remember, Larry, how timid you were at his age."

Two days later Laurel was packing her suitcase to return to California. Mrs. Lambert sat beside her on the bed. "Do you have room to take back some strawberry preserves I put up last summer?" she asked.

"I'm sure I do. Alex will enjoy them. I'm not supposed to be eating sweets."

"What? You on a diet? You've never had a weight problem."

"Haven't you noticed that I'm larger around the waist?"

Her mother studied her. "Now that you mention it, I can see a slight change. You don't look fatter anywhere else, though."

"Here's a new dress I bought yesterday while Alexander went for his interview at the hospital. Do you like it?"

"The material is beautiful. The style is a bit unusual. Almost looks like a maternity dress."

"It is."

Mrs. Lambert's jaw dropped as she stared with amazement and joy at her daughter. In a moment she jumped up to embrace Laurel. "I'm so happy. When will it be?"

"Probably early September."

"Too bad Turner never knew. Won't he be surprised on the resurrection day?"

Chapter 20

FAMINE

During the months that followed Turner Lambert's death the United States experienced one calamity after another. The specter of imminent nuclear war terrorized the inhabitants of all the major cities. Epidemics raged at home. The labor unions and other power groups had a stranglehold on the legislatures. From time to time the unions flexed their muscles by cutting off services and supplies.

New York City experienced a reign of terror when a teamster strike rendered all bridges to Manhattan and Staten islands impassable for two weeks at the same time that police and firemen walked off their jobs. Business was suspended because employees could not get into the city. As food supplies dwindled, uncontrolled looting raged. To be seen carrying a bag of groceries was to invite assault. Thousands were homeless because fires raged uncontrolled.

In Chicago, hospital employees went on strike. With no one to check patients in and out, man the labs, keep operating rooms clean, prepare meals, run the switchboards, or perform other necessary functions, conditions were such that doctors advised all but the most critically ill to go home. Meanwhile morticians did a booming business.

Drinking water in most major cities had become unsafe. The wealthy bought bottled water, but the poor too often risked drinking unboiled tap water, which contributed further to the rapid spread of highly infectious disease.

Diseased animal products spread devastating infections. At first the government intensified its inspection, but before long it had to prohibit the sale of meat, butter, milk, and eggs. The authorities reimbursed ranchers and dairy farmers who destroyed their stock, but many sold great quantities of contraband animal products to anyone willing to pay the exorbitant prices.

Malnutrition appeared everywhere as millions who had no understanding of how to get adequate protein from vegetable sources had a vegetarian diet forced upon them. Protein food products rose astronomically in price, and the demand far surpassed the output of the factories. Fishing became such a profitable business that it attracted many fortune seekers.

The list of foods rationed increased as supplies dwindled. The government hoped that the summer and fall would alleviate the situation, as the country had put all available farmland into crops. But the fifth year of the drought forced additional farmers into bankruptcy. The authorities spent billions of dollars on a crash program to harvest the food resources of plankton, but the refining process was costly and most people did not find the product palatable.

By January the hungry were desperate. The number of coupons in the ration books had considerably decreased. People came from miles around to Three Elms to buy apples, which they could obtain without coupons since Mrs. Lambert was not a licensed food dealer.

Fortunately the garden she had tended that summer had not suffered much from the drought that had destroyed crops across much of the nation. Laurel had helped her mother with the canning, because soon after Chucky's birth Alexander had been able to arrange to take his residency in Boston. Rows of jars of canned beans, corn, tomatoes, pickles, pumpkin, sauerkraut, and strawberries lined the basement.

About two o'clock one morning Sheba's barking awakened Laurel. As she debated whether she should get up to investigate, she heard a crash of broken glass, which seemed to come from the basement. Alexander was working all night at the hospital; so she and her mother were alone with Chucky.

Slipping out of bed, Laurel threw a robe over her nightgown and tiptoed downstairs in the darkness. The door from the kitchen to the basement was closed but unbolted. She tried to bolt it but found the two parts of the barrel were no longer aligned. Sheba barked wildly at the small basement window near the chimney.

Soon there came another crash, followed by a third. Laurel recognized the sound as jars breaking. Thinking a basement window must have come open, permitting an animal to take refuge from the cold, she opened the basement door and switched on the light. Cautiously she descended the stairs, not knowing what to expect.

The basement was divided into a recreation room, a heater room, and a storage area. At the foot of the stairs she hesitated. Whether she turned left and went to the storage area through the recreation room or right and approached it through the heater room, the animal or thief could exit through the other door. Her heart pounded, and her throat was dry. She wondered if she was acting foolishly.

As she breathed a prayer for protection and courage, she heard someone begin in a coarse whisper, "There, there. Good dog. Good Sheba. You know me. Remember? How about cutting out the barking?" The dog didn't stop. Then the whisper became hoarse and threatening.

"Beat it, mutt."

Laurel swung open the door to the right. The heater room was dark, but the light from the stairs revealed a teenage figure cringing against the wall under the open window. At his feet were about a dozen jars of food. Laurel flipped on the light and recognized the fifteen-year-old boy. His eyes stared in terror as he backed against the wall.

"Are you hungry, George?" she asked as kindly as possible.

"Y-y-yes," stammered George. "All we've had for the past week is potatoes."

"Do your parents know you are here?"

"N-n-no. You won't tell them, will you?"

"I'm sure your parents would prefer a diet of potatoes to having their son a thief. How did you expect to explain these jars of food?"

"I was goin' to tell them someone gave them to me."

"Bring me that large empty box, George." Laurel pointed to a box they had used to ship Alexander's medical books in.

The boy obeyed, and she put the jars of food into the box. Then she added some apples to fill it up. "Are you strong enough to carry this?"

"Sure am."

"Well, take it home and tell your mom that Mrs. Robertson sent it."

"Thanks so much, Mrs. Robertson. You sure are kind." A broad smile replaced his expression of terror.

Chapter 21

THE SHAKING

President McGrath and her chief adviser, Rasmussen, claimed to have had communications from the spirit world indicating that Sabbatarians were the root of the nation's woes. Because their numbers were increasing so fast that no accurate figures were available, religious and government leaders tended to panic. When asked to report its U.S. membership, the General Conference of Seventh-day Adventists replied that baptisms represented only a small percentage of professing new members.

The majority in Congress felt that the Sabbath foolishness would have to stop and that it was time to close Adventist institutions and require Sabbatarians to work on Saturday. The labor unions promised to cooperate by making rotation of any four-day workweek mandatory.

On April 15 the government confiscated all Adventist-operated educational institutions and publishing houses, though it did permit Adventist hospitals to continue, since a critical need existed for medical facilities and personnel. The FCC banned Adventist radio and TV programs. The communications satellite companies terminated their contracts with the General Conference, and the selling or distribution of Adventist publications became a crime.

On May 2 McGrath signed a law requiring that anyone—other than Jews by birth—refraining from secular

activity on Saturday or holding worship services involving
more than his own family on that day should forfeit all right to
food-ration coupons. Anyone reporting violation of the law
would, if proved correct, receive the food-ration coupons
allotted to the violator. Surveillance could include tapping of
phone lines, forced entry by authorized officials into private
homes, remote listening devices, and censorship of the mail
of those on the lengthy lists of suspected Sabbatarians in the
police computer systems.

The latest laws touched off a series of investigations all
over the country into the origin of the Sunday-Sabbath controversy. Many Americans who had supported the government in requiring Sunday observance felt Congress had gone
too far in requiring Saturday labor and in closing Adventist
institutions.

Protestants who had never previously investigated the
matter became uneasy at the lack of Scriptural authority for
Sunday. The evidence seemed to indicate that the shift had
occurred well after the time of the apostolic church. But as
many Christian leaders valued unity above doctrinal consid-
erations, most felt that matters of conscience should be sub-
servient to a united Christendom. They stressed the prayer
of Jesus, ''Holy Father, keep through thine own name those
whom thou hast given me, that they may be one, as we are.''
The apostle Paul, they pointed out, enjoined the early church
to subdue differences, ''that there be no divisions among
you; but that ye be perfectly joined together in the same mind
and in the same judgment.''

That the Adventists admittedly kept a day in honor of the
creation of the world seemed ridiculous in a time when
almost all educated people ''knew'' that creation was only a
religious myth. True, a few scientists asserted that evolution
should be taught as a theory rather than as a fact. They
reminded others that Darwin himself questioned the validity

of some of his assumptions, that occasionally forms of life turn up unexpectedly after supposedly having been extinct for millions of years, and that certain necessary intermediate links between basic types had never been found. But the majority never questioned that evolution was a proved fact.

Adventists, though most acknowledged the demonstrable mutations within a species, maintained that God was the Creator of the universe and all life and that, whether the Genesis record was factual or poetic, God had commanded men to keep the Sabbath as a memorial to His creative power. Without doubt the present Saturday was the Sabbath of Sinai. Man had no right to substitute another day for the one God had commanded. To the taunts that the Sabbath applied only to the Jews, they referred to Genesis 2, where God sanctified the Sabbath long before a Jewish nation existed, and to the weekly miracle of the manna before the Hebrews received the law at Sinai. Such arguments carried weight with some. But as most educated people regarded the books of Moses a collection of religious myths, whether anyone observed Sabbath before Sinai did not interest them at all.

Unfortunately for the Adventists, two of their leading ministers in a well-publicized TV debate came off looking ridiculous when confronted with seemingly incontrovertible evidence from fossil deposits that shook their faith in seven literal days of Creation. Their theory that the Flood caused most fossilization seemed incompatible with the ages determined by various dating methods.

The two ministers belatedly researched various aspects of paleontology, eager to refute their opponents, but they never received the opportunity to undo the effect of the telecast. Thousands of new, ungrounded converts gave up their recent conviction that God required obedience to His law, and many, including some church leaders who had grown up in the Adventist Church, renounced their beliefs as being untenable in the light of scientific evidence.

The foes of the Sabbatarians eagerly publicized all defections from the church by any of its leaders. Since all Adventist periodicals were defunct, the various congregations had little communication with one another. Many isolated members had no way of knowing whether or not they were alone in adhering to their faith. But what few suspected was that for every member shaken out of the ranks of Sabbathkeepers, Adventists gained ten recruits.

Chapter 22

REVENGE

The inhabitants of Three Elms were grateful for the few remaining jars of the preceding year's crop. Within two weeks after the law cut off rations to Sabbath observers, they received a form letter stating that they were known to be Sabbatarians and therefore their names would be deleted from the list of those eligible to receive ration books, unless they made an appeal. The letter also stated that their child, being under twelve years of age, could continue to receive coupons if his parents would consent to let him leave home to become a ward of the state.

Laurel and Alexander resolved not to give up Chucky. They further decided that Alexander should appeal his case since his residency at the hospital often involved weekend duty. When he presented it the hospital director verified his statements, so the authorities reinstated his name on the ration rolls. Since he ate most of his meals at the hospital, where rationing was not in effect, Chucky, Laurel, and Mrs. Lambert managed to survive with his rations, the eggs of their few remaining hens, and their nearly exhausted apples and canned food supply.

Mrs. Lambert and her daughter planted a garden triple the size of the preceding year's plot. They paid a neighbor to clear an acre of aging apple trees and prepare the soil. Alexander helped as much as he could, but his time at home was limited and his knowledge of farming was nonexistent.

They planted the vegetable garden in stages throughout April and May. Last to go in were the tomato plants. The Lamberts had always put them in at the end of May, but because of the urgency, Laurel planted them three weeks early and listened each evening to the weather forecast, covering the plants whenever it predicted frost. By late May the garden produced peas and lettuce, which they eagerly gathered and shared with nongardening Adventists.

The Robertsons were fortunate compared to the city dwellers, who had to depend upon the generosity of others and who found that generosity diminishes when rations are meager. Many non-Adventists wanted the heretics to suffer, but the majority were not willing to see their friends starve.

Some opportunists made it their business to discover Sabbath observers not yet so identified, accuse them, and thus obtain their ration books. They would then purchase supplies and resell them clandestinely to the desperate at exorbitant prices. When the authorities finally noticed that some were collecting many ration books, they decided to limit the informant's ration book reward to one month's supply. The decision helped the Sabbathkeepers not yet accused because it lessened the reward to informers, but it created new problems for those who largely depended on black-market food to keep from starving.

Laurel and her mother worked long hours in the garden, hoeing, fertilizing, dusting with insecticides, and carrying water for the languishing plants. Alexander, rarely around to help, spent fewer and fewer nights at home. Though she never intimated that she suspected his hospital duties were less demanding than he claimed, Laurel was worried. When he did come home one or two nights a week he seemed preoccupied and eager to get back to Boston.

One Friday evening in August following worship he sat

staring at a book he held in his hand. His brow was wrinkled, and his lips pressed tightly together. Laurel noticed he kept his eyes on the book but never turned a page. When Mrs. Lambert announced she was retiring, he said good night without looking up. A few minutes later he rose and went to Chucky's room, where he leaned on the side of the crib, watching the sleeping child by the light entering the room through the hall door. After some time his wife joined him.

"Isn't he beautiful?" she whispered.

"He's perfect," he said after a moment.

"Too bad you aren't home more when he's awake. He's so cute now."

"Yes, it's too bad."

"All day he's been asking, 'Daddy tum home?' "

Alexander made no reply, but Laurel noticed him blinking rapidly.

Laurel tiptoed out and prepared to retire. She turned out the light and crawled into bed. After a few minutes she heard him leave Chucky's room, go downstairs, and out the kitchen door.

She slipped to the open window and drew the folds of the drapery around her, as her sheer gown offered no protection from the cool night air. A half moon bathed the yard in a soft light. As she watched he headed hesitantly toward a chair on the front lawn and sat down. He remained there a long time with his head in his hands, moving only to swat a bothersome mosquito or to wipe his eyes with his sleeve.

When at last he came to bed Laurel pretended to be asleep. She could tell by his breathing and an occasional sniffle that he couldn't sleep either. His back was toward her. Finally she put an arm around his waist.

"What's the matter, Alex?"

"Nothing," he told her. "Must be catching a cold."

"I know you're worried about something."

"Doctors always worry. Go to sleep."

The following week Laurel was baking when the phone rang. Mrs. Lambert answered, but the call was for her daughter, who had pie dough all over her hands. "Find out who it is and ask if I can call back in a few minutes," Laurel suggested.

Her mother wrote on a slip: "Attorney Caleb Schwartz, 756-9696."

As soon as she had the pie in the oven she called. While she listened, her face gradually lost its usual glow and turned ashen. She drew up a chair and sat down. "Yes, I see. . . . Yes, I can come. . . . Tomorrow at ten o'clock. . . . I'll be there. . . . Good-bye."

"Whatever is wrong?" queried her alarmed mother.

In an emotionless voice Laurel replied, "Alexander wants a divorce."

"No, it can't be!"

"I'm not surprised."

"Well, I certainly am. I've noticed he's home very little, but I thought it was his duties. Is there another woman?"

"Probably. I'll know tomorrow."

Laurel slept little that night. At ten o'clock the next morning she entered Attorney Schwartz's office. Alexander was already there. Both men rose when she entered, but her husband's eyes avoided hers.

When they were seated Mr. Schwartz explained matter-of-factly that Alexander wanted to remarry, so was suing for divorce. His intended wife was willing to accept Chucky so the child would not go without rations. The lawyer removed his reading glasses and fixed his gaze on Laurel. "Do you, Mrs. Robertson, care to contest the divorce, and do you consent to let Dr. Robertson have your child?"

Her face was pale, her eyes red-rimmed. "Mr. Schwartz,

I should like to talk to my husband alone.''

"Surely. I'll be in the next room when you are finished.'' He went out and closed the door.

Laurel stared at Alexander, who preferred to gaze out the window. Her lips trembled as she began. "Is this what you really want?''

"Yes.''

"Don't you realize what you are doing? You're not only turning your back on me, but on our church too.''

"Yes.''

Gasping for air, she struggled to control her emotions. "What do your parents think?''

"They don't know it yet.''

For a second she lost control of herself. Her pent-up emotions burst through the dam of her self-control and poured over her. Finally, biting her lip, she regained her composure. "Do you really think I would ever consent to give up Chucky?''

Briefly he faced her. "I don't think you will choose to let him starve. I will look after him much better than the state would.'' Neither said anything else for several minutes.

"Who—who are you marrying?''

"Gina Schiavina Sargent.''

A flood of memories came to Laurel's mind. In a way, despite her hurt, she felt sorry for him. Any man involved with Gina would be helpless and trapped. "I know her,'' she said at last.

"Yes, I know you do.''

"How long have you been interested in her?''

"About six months.''

She started to reach toward him, then let her hand drop slowly to her side. "Could you get away for a few weeks to think this through clearly? Without either Gina or me to influence you?''

"I've made my decision." He swallowed hard and unconsciously turned his back toward her.

"Did you make it, or did she?"

"We made it together."

Tears splashed down her cheeks. "You said her last name is Sargent. Does she have a husband now?"

"She divorced him a year ago. He's a lawyer."

"Why—why did she leave him?"

"Is it any of your business? Besides, we don't talk about him."

Another long pause. "Do you think she will make a good mother for your son?"

"I hope so. She will soon have a child of her own."

"How soon?"

"In about six months," he mumbled.

Her voice was dull, resigned. "Then you . . . you're the father?"

"Probably."

"Then you're marrying her out of a sense of responsibility . . ."

"No," he snapped. "I love her."

She sighed. "Do you still love me?"

"I respect you, Laurel, but I've got to be honest. I don't think I really ever loved you. You were the type of girl everyone expected me to marry." Her numbness grew; reality retreated further away. "There's an excitement with Gina—I don't know how to put it into words—she makes me feel alive. Besides, when I come home there's always a job to do. I didn't grow up working like a slave, and I can't take it!"

"But you never complained."

"The work was inescapable. But I'm still young. Gina and I have fun together. You're always serious. Anyone else would be screaming at me. But you always suppress your emotions. Look how calm you are now."

Laurel buried her face in her hands. "Do you think our marriage was a mistake?"

"Well, I'm divorcing you."

Suffocating silence filled the room. Several times she started to say something. Finally she said, "You'll be tired of her in a few months."

"So? You wouldn't want me back anyway." He sounded less sure of himself.

She looked at him pleadingly. "We all make mistakes. Is adultery more wicked than the more 'respectable' sins?"

Alexander suddenly opened the door to the room where Mr. Schwartz waited. "I've decided to wait a couple of weeks before proceeding further with the divorce," he told the lawyer. Then turning to Laurel, he said, "I'm going to try to arrange a short vacation to visit my parents. If I go, I'll stop by Three Elms for my things."

The next day Alexander came to pack his suitcase. He stayed only about an hour. No one said anything about the divorce. Chucky was playing with his blocks, trying unsuccessfully to build a tower. Alexander helped him. The boy laughed gleefully as he demolished it.

" 'Gain, Daddy."

His father rebuilt the tower and once more the child knocked it down.

" 'Gain."

"No, Son. Daddy has to be going now."

"Tum back soon?" His eager face brought a pained expression to Alexander's brow.

"I don't know," he replied as he hugged the child and waved good-bye.

A week passed, and Laurel had heard nothing from her husband. She wanted to call him, but restrained herself because it had been her idea that he go where neither she nor

Gina could influence him. Mrs. Lambert suggested that her daughter talk to Gina to see whether she could persuade her not to marry Alexander. Although reluctant to follow her mother's advice, Laurel finally agreed it could do no harm.

She got Gina's current address from the alumni office at Thornton. Laurel looked up the phone number and dialed, half hoping no one would be home. After three rings a woman's voice answered. "Is this Gina Sargent?" Laurel asked timidly.

"No, this is her mother. Gina's not here."

"When do you expect her?"

"She left for California this morning. Said she would be gone about a week. Can I take a message?"

"No—no, thank you."

Abruptly Laurel hung up the phone. Sinking onto a kitchen chair, she buried her head in her arms on the table. Her mother seated herself in another chair. "She's followed him," Laurel sobbed.

Alexander came home only once to get his things. Laurel was away buying their son clothes for fall. Mrs. Lambert expressed regret that they were gone, but he said it was better that way. He promised to send money and ration cards.

The money came regularly, though Laurel hoped to augment it by teaching voice lessons. The same church where she had been organist and choir director while in college offered her a job. It would have given her some publicity that would have brought her pupils, but she felt that with the case for Saturday versus Sunday so clearly before the public, she could no longer conscientiously ally herself with Sunday worshipers.

The family needed the ration cards even more urgently than money. But with the December cards came a note in Alexander's handwriting:

''After my marriage on the 25th I will no longer be able to supply ration cards. I hope this will not prove too great a hardship. I am still willing to take Chucky if you cannot feed him properly. In fact, the state will be checking from time to time to see whether he is adequately nourished.''

Chapter 23

A STRATEGY

Duane was lying in bed leafing through the Sunday morning paper on New Year's Day. As he started to lay the society section aside, his eye fell on a large picture of Gina. The caption read: "Mrs. Alexander Robertson."

In disbelief he read the announcement of the marriage. The statement that Dr. Robertson was currently a resident at Massachusetts General Hospital confirmed his assumption that she had married Laurel's husband. Though he had never met Alexander, the envy he had not even admitted to himself turned to contempt. He determined to visit Laurel and offer his condolences.

But he had a problem of his own. Spencer Schwab, now fourteen years old, had become advanced enough that his mother felt the city of Worcester should have the opportunity to hear her talented son. She had cultivated the friendship of Julian, director of the Worcester Symphony, and at the close of a dinner in her home for the director and his wife, had casually asked Spencer to "play something for kind Mr. Julian." The boy willingly agreed and played all three movements of Beethoven's Third Piano Concerto. While Spencer played, his mother had Julian's wine glass frequently replenished. By the end of the performance Julian jovially suggested that such a talent should be heard and asked whether Spencer would care to play the concerto with the orchestra. Mrs. Schwab and her son pretended great amazement, but with slight urging they agreed.

The performance was scheduled for the second Sunday in January, and the rehearsal with orchestra was to be the preceding afternoon. Mrs. Schwab had asked Duane to attend the rehearsal to coach her son. He replied that he didn't know whether it would be possible and that he would let her know later.

With the rehearsal only six days away, Duane knew he would have to make a decision. He was reluctant to endorse a debut that he believed was premature. But his main objection to attending the rehearsal was that he felt, even though he would receive no remuneration for going, it was part of his responsibility as Spencer's piano teacher and thus a secular activity. As such, he could not conscientiously do it on God's day.

How to avoid violating his conscience without having a showdown with Mrs. Schwab was his problem. She was a strong-willed, influential woman to whom he was indebted for many of his pupils. He dared not give his real reason for missing the rehearsal, but lying was as bad as breaking the Sabbath.

That afternoon he boarded the commuter train for Three Elms. During the mile walk to the house he remembered his last visit five years before when he had found only Mr. Lambert home because Alexander had taken Laurel, her mother, and Larry to hear the Boston Symphony Orchestra. He recalled the letter she had written the following summer explaining why she couldn't marry him. Had she ever regretted her decision?

As he approached the house he felt he should have phoned first. Nobody had shoveled the path to the front door since the last foot of snow had fallen; so he went to the kitchen door and knocked. A little boy opened it and stood staring in two-year-old fashion.

"Hello, Sonny. Is your mommy home?"

"Yes."

"Would you please call her?"

"Mom-m-meee," he yelled.

"Who is it?" Laurel asked from upstairs.

"Man."

"Tell him to come in and sit down."

The child opened the door, and Duane left his rubbers on the porch. He entered the warm kitchen and sat down at the table. The aroma of baking bread reminded him of the good meals he had eaten in that same room years before. He wondered how Laurel could buy flour and other staples. Chucky brought a shiny red truck for Duane to admire. "Was that a Christmas present from Santa Claus?"

"No, Grandma."

"Where is your grandma?"

"Bed."

"Is she sick?"

He nodded solemnly. "Real sick."

While the child sat on the floor, playing with his truck and making appropriate engine noises, Duane wondered how soon Laurel would come downstairs. His knees trembled slightly, and he had a hollow feeling in his stomach. After what seemed like a long time he heard her footsteps on the stairs.

In a moment she entered the kitchen. Her hair was in curlers, she wore a flour-dusty apron, and her collarbones were prominent above the drawstring neck opening of her checkered housedress.

Duane rose as she entered. Laurel was obviously flustered.

"Duane! What a surprise! Please excuse the dreadful way I look!" she gasped as she untied the apron and laid it on the back of a kitchen chair.

"You look good to me. You probably could use a few square meals, though."

She blushed. "We have enough. But we try to eat a minimum so we can share. What brings you here?"

"I came to offer my condolences. I saw the picture of the new Mrs. Robertson in today's paper."

"Oh! So you know. Was she a radiant bride?"

"Naturally." He grimaced. "Gina's always radiant. How did it happen?"

Laurel motioned for him to take a seat. "I don't know. Alex said I was too serious and Gina was more exciting. How their friendship started and developed I don't know."

He swallowed and cleared his throat. "What happens to an Adventist who deserts his wife and remarries?"

"He's disfellowshiped."

"Is—is his wife free to remarry?"

She nodded. There was a long pause.

"How are you getting food?"

"We had Alex's rations till he remarried. I don't know what will happen now. We're praying about it."

Duane looked puzzled. "How did he happen to have coupons?"

"He takes his turn working weekends at the hospital, so he is eligible. Because he eats most of his meals there, he doesn't need coupons."

"Why can't he continue to send them, then? Doesn't he love his son?"

She sighed. "I really believe he loves him. Probably he wants to force me to give Chucky to him."

"Will you?"

"I hope not. But I can't let him starve." Tears peeped out of the corners of her eyes.

Duane fumbled in his coat pocket. "Here's something

that may help," he said as he handed her a stack of cards for flour, sugar, shortening, and soybean milk.

"How can you spare these?" she asked in disbelief.

"I don't do any baking, and I've never learned to drink milk substitute. Can you use them?"

"Use them! I should say I can! Thanks so much. Before you leave, remind me to give you some canned food to take along."

"Thanks, but you keep it. I don't really need it, and I might be robbed on the way home anyway."

"You'll eat supper with us then, won't you?"

"I'd love to. I rarely get to eat a good home-cooked meal. Your little boy tells me your mother is ill. Is it anything serious?"

"It's a combination of undernourishment, flu, and loneliness. She misses Dad terribly. Alex's desertion was a hard blow, too. Would you like to go up and see her?"

He nodded.

The winter twilight was beginning to cast shadows throughout the house. The rounded edges of the carpeted stairs were faintly discernible as they went upstairs. Mrs. Lambert's room was lighted only by a small reading lamp on the head of her bed.

As Duane and Laurel entered the bedroom Mrs. Lambert laid down the Bible she was reading. Her hair had turned almost completely white around her thin face, and her frail hands protruded from the lace-trimmed sleeves of her blue bed jacket.

"Mother, I've brought you a visitor."

"Who is it, Laurel? I can't see too well."

"A real surprise. I'll turn on the light so you can get a good look." Laurel stepped to a floor lamp and flipped the three-way lamp till the room was flooded with light.

The older woman smiled. "Well, I do believe it's Duane.

How good you look! I won't offer to shake hands because I wouldn't want you to get my flu.''

"I'm sorry to find you ill," he said, not knowing what to say and feeling a little uncomfortable. "I've never known you to get sick before.''

"A lot has happened since you used to visit us. It hasn't been easy.''

"I'm sure it hasn't. When I see you and Laurel, I feel ashamed of myself.''

Her eyes widened. "Why?''

"You have each suffered physically for your faith, and it shows. I, too, have been keeping the Sabbath, but I've been too cowardly to accept responsibility for my decision.''

Laurel touched his arm. "How long have you been observing the Sabbath?''

"Almost four years.''

"That's wonderful! Did you ever join the Adventist Church?''

"No. To be honest, I've been too afraid of ostracism. Now I'm faced with a problem.''

Laurel and her mother listened while Duane told of the crisis he expected to face when he told Mrs. Schwab he could not coach her son on Sabbath. They discussed the problem a long time before the three agreed on a strategy they hoped would keep him out of trouble.

When he went home that evening he felt happier than he had been for a long time. It made him feel better that he had been able to leave Laurel some ration coupons, and he thought that he was gaining courage to follow his convictions. Perhaps, he hoped, in time Laurel might again love him.

When Spencer came for his piano lesson on Thursday his mother accompanied him. It had been at least two years since she had been present during his lesson. Duane did his best to pack six months' worth of instruction into one lesson without undermining Spencer's self-confidence.

When the lesson had stretched out to almost two hours and it was obvious that Spencer had absorbed all he could, Duane announced, "We'd better stop for today. If you remember all we've talked about, you should do very well Sunday. I'll be there cheering for you."

"You'll be there Saturday, too, won't you?" Mrs. Schwab asked in a tone that suggested he had no other choice.

"I'm afraid not. It will probably be better for Spencer's self-confidence if only Julian is there. I don't know of any further help I can give him, and anyway, I'll be out of town all day on Saturday."

The boy's mother looked rather unhappy. "We were really counting on your being there. This is an important occasion. We thought your interest in Spencer's career and what the performance can do for your professional reputation would take precedence over other plans. You didn't mention previously that you might be out of town."

Duane shrugged. "I didn't know it till a few days ago."

"But it was weeks ago that we asked you to attend the rehearsal."

"Really, Mrs. Schwab, it will be better for Spencer if I'm not there." He collected his music scores and put them in his case. "I've played with Julian, and I know how insulting and particular he can be." Then, turning to Spencer: "Just try to please him. When he tells you how to phrase a passage or what tempo to take it, do what he says, even though it may not be the way you or I like it. Don't argue with him. Remember, the conductor is the boss."

He noticed a sinister determination in Mrs. Schwab's eyes as she said upon leaving, "We're disappointed in you, Mr. Manning."

Friday afternoon, when he had finished teaching, Duane waited at the bus stop a block from his apartment. As the bus passed on the other side heading toward the suburbs he noticed it was crowded with housewives hurrying home to prepare dinner before their husbands arrived. A few minutes later when it stopped for Duane on its return, it was nearly empty. At the next stop a middle-aged man in a brown suit and tan topcoat boarded and took a seat behind him. Seeing his attaché case, Duane assumed he was a salesman.

Duane took the bus to the Greyhound station, where he purchased a ticket for Hartford, Connecticut. He boarded the bus destined for New York and, though he preferred to sit near the front, had to go nearly to the back to find a seat. Only two vacant seats remained—one beside a fat, forbidding-looking woman, the other across the aisle beside a man smoking a cigar. Duane chose to sit by the fat woman, though she glared at him and tried unsuccessfully to occupy only one seat. To his surprise the salesman in the brown suit took the other vacant seat.

Smiling at the salesman, he asked, ''Going to Hartford?''

''Yes, are you?''

Duane nodded. ''Do you live there?''

''No. And you?''

''I'm visiting a friend.''

''What part of Hartford?''

''I don't know. He's going to meet the bus.''

The man stretched, trying to find a more comfortable position in the cramped seat. ''Will you be in Hartford long?''

''I'll return Sunday.''

''I'm stuck there for the weekend. Know of anything special going on in the city?''

"Afraid not. What kind of entertainment do you like?"

"I'm not particular." The salesman closed his eyes. His expression indicated that his thoughts were no longer with Duane.

It was dark when the bus rolled into the terminal. Duane was one of the last ones off the bus. Pete Thayer grasped his hand and arm. "You're looking wonderful, Duane. I can't see that the past four years have changed you any."

Duane wished he could say the same of Pete, but he showed the effects of a meager diet. "It's been a long time. I've thought of you so often. How's Peggy?"

"Fine. She has supper ready for us. Here, let me take your bag."

"Pardon me," the salesman interrupted. "I see you're the friend who was to meet my busmate. Can you direct me to a clean hotel?"

"Certainly. The bus we'll be taking goes past several. I can show you where to get off."

"Much obliged. My name is Brooks Burnside." He held out his hand.

"I'm Peter Thayer."

"Do you live in the city?"

"No. In Blue Hills, just north of town."

While the bus lurched from block to block, Pete talked ecstatically about his two-year-old daughter, Julie. He was careful to say nothing about his responsibilities or the condition of the local Adventists. When they came to the hotel district he showed Mr. Burnside some hotels to investigate, and the salesman got off.

Once Duane tried to ask how they kept from starving, but Pete ignored the question and inquired if he knew where Larry Lambert was practicing medicine. Duane took the cue and turned the conversation to the Lambert family. "His sister told me that Larry's joined a clinic somewhere in

California. Also she said he recently married.''

"I'm glad. Hope he got a good girl. He deserves one.''

"I don't know any details, but Laurel and her mother seem happy with his choice.''

When they left the bus three blocks from Pete's home, Pete glanced around to make sure no one was near and then explained that it was dangerous to mention Adventists in public. Secrecy was necessary not only to protect the unexposed members from those trying to ferret them out to obtain their ration cards but also to keep open the sources of food from sympathizers and black marketeers.

"Haven't most of the Adventists left the cities?'' Duane asked.

"A great many have. But you would be amazed at the number of new converts we have here. We don't keep written records anymore.''

"Aren't you afraid to remain?''

"Yes and no. I'm an undershepherd. This is my flock. God will protect me and my family as long as He wants us here.''

"What did Laurel tell you about me when she called?''

"My phone is tapped, so our friends and members word their messages carefully. I write down the messages and try to decipher them later. Here's Laurel's.''

Pete pulled a slip of paper from his pocket. " 'Meet Worcester bus Friday evening around six. Duane will spend two nights. Fill the pool.' From her message I gathered that you wish to join the church, to be baptized. Is that correct?''

Duane nodded.

"What brought you to a decision?''

"I've been observing the Sabbath secretly for about four years. I've hated my lack of courage. And I'm still not very courageous. In fact, I'm running away from an awkward situation this weekend. But I trust God will give me strength to follow my conscience, whatever that requires of me."

"I'm sure He will."

The baptism was scheduled for seven o'clock the next morning. Pete and Duane entered the church by a side door at 6:30. A few minutes later Peggy arrived with a friend. A deacon and his wife came just before seven. The night before Pete had filled the baptistry and turned up the heat so the church would not be cold. They did not turn the lights on because, being the Sabbath, it was not legal to hold services.

In the dim light of early morning, Pete read the baptismal vows to Duane, who answered each question in the presence of Peggy Thayer and the three other witnesses. The little group voted to accept Duane into the church subject to his baptism. Then the two young men donned baptismal robes and entered the baptistry while the four witnesses sang softly. Pete raised his hand above Duane's head and said, "Duane Manning, in accordance with your faith in the Lord Jesus Christ as your personal Saviour from sin and your determination to lead a new life, I now baptize you in the name of the Father, and of the Son, and of the Holy Ghost."

At 7:30 old Mrs. Jacobs, whose home adjoined the church property, stretched, slipped out of bed, and looked out her bedroom window toward the church. She recognized Peter Thayer as he and a companion locked the side door to the building.

"I wonder why he is here so early in the morning," she mused. "Probably bringing church bulletins. Must admit he's obeying the law much better than I ever expected. When the police promised me a reward for each Saturday service I reported, I expected to get rich. Haven't made a dime thus far." Mrs. Jacobs turned away from the window and started to dress.

Chapter 24

LAWBREAKER

The next day Duane kept his promise to attend Spencer's concert. Duane took a taxi from the Greyhound terminal to the auditorium and found his seat just as the conductor raised his baton for the opening number. The concerto followed. As Spencer awkwardly walked to the piano and took a perfunctory bow, Duane suffered a severe case of empathic stage fright. His knees and hands trembled, and he felt mildly nauseated. As he wiped the perspiration from his forehead he realized that the man beside him was staring at him.

The assurance with which Spencer played surprised Duane. Things were progressing better than he had expected. By the end of the first movement he decided that perhaps he had underestimated the boy's ability. The gaiety of the rondo movement showed Spencer's clean technique off at its best. The boy's playing sparkled and appeared effortless. When the concerto ended, Duane rushed backstage to congratulate his pupil.

It was intermission time. Spencer nonchalantly accepted the praises of the conductor and various orchestra members. He had never doubted that the performance woud be a success, so he saw no reason for all the fuss. Mrs. Schwab, by contrast, glowed with ecstasy. Her moment of triumph had arrived. Vicariously she had achieved.

Duane stayed in the background till the orchestra members had extended their congratulations. As they returned to the stage to retune for the remainder of the program, he slapped Spencer on the back. "I was really proud of you, Spencer. It went even better than I had hoped."

"Wasn't he marvelous?" Mrs. Schwab chimed in.

"He did very well, indeed."

"Maybe next time you won't be so shy about letting folks know you are his teacher. I hope you had a good time in Hartford." Bitterness tinged her voice.

"It was an important trip. I would have stayed longer, but I didn't want to miss this concert."

"Thanks for your interest," she told him. He thought he detected a note of sarcasm. Back in his seat he heard little of the music. Instead he tried to remember whether he had said anything to Spencer or Mrs. Schwab about his proposed trip to Hartford. He recalled saying only he would be out of town.

When Spencer came for his lesson on Thursday he brought a note from his mother: "I am having a dinner party at our home Friday evening of next week and would like to have Spencer play the concerto. As the cost of hiring an orchestra would be prohibitive, and we haven't the space for a group anyway, will you please come and play the orchestral portions on a second piano? I'll rent a good instrument for you to play. We should be happy to have you play a solo selection or two, as well, if you are able on such short notice. The dinner will be served at 6:30, and the program will follow."

Duane replied: "If your party were any other evening next week, I would be happy to perform as suggested. Unfortunately I cannot attend Friday evening. I am sorry."

Saturday his mail contained a card from Mrs. Schwab: "Sorry I cannot change the date of the dinner party. The mayor is coming, and it is his only free night. Some important musicians will be present also. Please reconsider.''

"I'm sorry to have to disappoint you," he wrote back. "My former pupil, Sheila Cofield, is very talented and would do a good job. She has been studying that concerto at Thornton, where she is a freshman this year. You could reach her in the evening at 791-0003.''

Wednesday Duane received another card: "Sheila will play. Thank you. Spencer will not be in Thursday for his lesson. He thinks he needs a rest; so don't expect him anymore till further notice.''

Friday evening Duane welcomed the Sabbath by reading his Bible and having prayer. Then he resumed reading *The Desire of Ages*, which Peggy Thayer had given him at his baptism. After an hour Duane decided to take a short walk in the cold night air to counteract a touch of drowsiness. The sidewalks were empty, and only an occasional car passed. The snow crunched beneath his feet and sparkled under the streetlights. He wished he were at Three Elms, where street lights and buildings did not obscure the sky. He tried unsuccessfully to spot a few familiar constellations.

"Think I'll go to Three Elms tomorrow," he thought. "I'll take Laurel some January coupons. She'll be glad to get them. Hope her mother is well by now."

When Duane reached the corner he noticed a man standing by the bus stop. The man, wearing a hat and with his coat collar pulled up around his ears, turned his back as Duane walked past. Duane thought the man looked cold.

"Beg your pardon, sir," he ventured. "The bus left five minutes ago. They only run this way every half hour."

"Thank you. I'll wait," the man replied without facing him.

Retracing his steps half an hour later, Duane thought he saw the man or someone dressed like him by another bus stop a few blocks from the first. This time he got a glimpse of his face. It looked familiar, but as Duane couldn't place it, he quickly forgot about the stranger. Back at his apartment he called Laurel, who gave him an invitation to spend the Sabbath at Three Elms.

The young intern currently pastoring the congregation at New Braintree was also visiting Three Elms for the day with his wife. Alfred Kelly's most notable features were the broad smile illuminating his black face and his long legs that had brought him track-star fame during his student days in Boston. His wife, Helen, was a nurse.

The authorities had jailed Alfred for a month because he refused to furnish names of his parishioners. While in jail he had made converts of two fellow prisoners.

After sundown worship, before anyone left the living room, Alfred said he had some rather unpleasant news to share with all the church members.

"What is it?" Mrs. Lambert asked.

"You had better start saving up fuel oil or switch to some other method of heating."

"What's the reason?" Laurel wanted to know.

"The Public Affairs and Religious Liberty Department of the General Conference has discovered that before spring, oil will be rationed as well as gasoline, and Sabbathkeepers will be denied fuel as well as food."

"What will we do?" Mrs. Lambert gasped, consternation and unbelief etched on her face. "We depend on oil for heat nine months of the year. This old house isn't insulated well. Our one fireplace won't do much to heat the downstairs, let alone the bedrooms."

Laurel glanced from Alfred to Helen to Duane to her mother. No one offered any solution. While the others lamented the new development, she excused herself to prepare supper. As she peeled apples she started planning how to cut down on oil consumption while appearing to use it faster than normal. By the time supper was on the table she announced her plan.

She would get empty drums from the dump and siphon oil from the fuel tank into them. The oil company would keep the tank filled, and hopefully she and her mother could store quite a bit before the company cut the supply off. Mrs. Lambert would have to dress warmly and keep a fire in the fireplace so that Laurel could lower the house temperature ten degrees. They would buy electric heaters for the bedrooms, which they would close off and keep cool in the daytime. As for gasoline, they had a couple of fuel tanks from the time the farm had a tractor. They would save every extra drop they could get hold of.

The others agreed her plan had merit, and Duane offered to help her round up empty drums. He promised to start looking the next day.

After supper the Kellys drove him as far as the commuter train. As the train wheels clickety-clacked off the miles, they seemed to sing "oil drum, oil drum, oil drum, oil drum," till Duane in desperation began humming Beethoven to dispel the monotonous chant.

Two weeks had passed when he received a form letter notifying him that as a Sabbatarian he would no longer be eligible for ration coupons but that he could appeal his case if he chose to do so. Not wishing to deny that he was a Sabbatarian but curious as to how the officials had found out, he went to the specified agency. He waited for what seemed like a long time in the director's dingy waiting room before a secretary finally admitted him.

"Mr. Manning, you may take your case to court," the director stated in a tone that suggested Duane would be wasting his time if he pursued the matter.

"Will I be permitted to meet my accusers?"

"Yes."

Duane thought a second. "Can I find out in advance who they may be?"

"Just a moment." The director picked up the phone and dialed a number.

"Do you have a file on Duane Manning? (a long pause) . . . What are the charges? . . . I see. . . . Who reported this information? . . . Thank you." Then turning to Duane, he said, "It seems that a private detective hired by the mother of one of your pupils followed you to Hartford, Connecticut, on January 5. There you were baptized by an Adventist minister, Peter Thayer, the following day. Two weeks later you refused, without giving a satisfactory reason, to participate in a concert on a Friday evening. You remained in your apartment praying and reading the Bible and another book, then took a short walk before retiring. Frankly, Mr. Manning, it will do you no good to appeal your case if the charges are correct."

For a moment Duane felt numb. "Do you think a so-called Christian nation has any right to persecute a man for following his convictions?"

The director sighed, shrugged his shoulders, and slowly shook his head. "I don't make the laws. I just help enforce them. Discrimination against blacks or Jews is wrong because no one can choose his ancestors. But you Adventists needn't suffer. All you have to do is give up your silly ideas. That's all anybody wants. I have to leave for an appointment now. Good-bye, Mr. Manning."

When the director stood, Duane managed to thank him for his time, then hurried outside, where the temperature matched the chill in his heart.

Duane was glad the February coupons had already been

issued. What would become of him after he used them up he dared not try to imagine. At least the fuel shortage wouldn't affect him since he lived in an apartment and heat was his landlord's responsibility. He had been hoping to help Laurel feed herself, Chucky, and Mrs. Lambert with his unused coupons. Now, the thought that he might have to turn to them for help left him empty and weak.

That afternoon he had five piano lessons scheduled. Two called to say they were discontinuing their lessons but refused to give a reason. Later, other cancellations followed. He had been giving forty lessons a week. By the end of the week Duane was down to thirty-one, and he knew that if he lost any more, he would have to find cheaper living quarters.

He turned to his only source of courage—God. Instead of his usual two-minute prayer before retiring, Duane spent half an hour on his knees pleading for help. God seemed near. Duane felt impressed that what he needed was not so much physical help as courage to stand by his convictions. The words of Jesus flashed through his mind: ''Man shall not live by bread alone, but by every word that proceedeth out of the mouth of God.'' ''Take no thought for your life, what ye shall eat, or what ye shall drink; nor yet for your body, what ye shall put on. Is not the life more than meat, and the body than raiment? Behold the fowls of the air: for they sow not, neither do they reap, nor gather into barns; yet your heavenly Father feedeth them. Are ye not much better than they?''

For the first time he realized their significance. Crawling into bed, he slept soundly till the morning sun awakened him.

Two days later Mrs. Conrad Eaton came for her lesson. In the four years she had studied with him he had resisted her overtures and discouraged her attempts to discuss her personal problems with him. He had always made sure that her lesson was not the last of the day, but the high school girl who had followed Mrs. Eaton had now dropped him as a teacher.

When Mrs. Eaton's lesson ended she seemed in no hurry to leave. "I hear you've lost a good many pupils," she said, watching his reaction.

"Where did you hear that?"

"My husband heard it at work. You know, Mr. Schwab is an executive at Thornton Company, where Conrad works when he isn't traveling."

"Oh, yes, I had forgotten. Was Mr. Schwab campaigning to get you to stop too?"

She smiled and slid down the piano bench closer to him. "No. He just mentioned to Conrad that his son had switched to another teacher who would be a more worthy example for a young man."

"I see."

"I guess no one needs a worthy example more than I," she laughed. "But Conrad knows I'm hopeless and likes me this way. He says he wants me to enjoy myself when he has to be away for weeks at a time." She lowered her voice almost to a whisper. "How does it feel to be a lawbreaker?"

Duane hesitated a second. "It depends upon whether you mean man's laws or God's laws."

Her eyes widened. "Is there a difference?"

"Definitely."

"Well, if there is a God, I'm sure He wants us all to be happy. Starving to death surely can't please Him. Doesn't the command 'Thou shalt not kill' include suicide?"

He frowned. "I'm not nearly as concerned with the present life as with the future one."

"How noble!" She clapped her hands. "However, I prefer to enjoy the only life I expect to have. When you get too hungry to maintain your ideals or get thrown out of this apartment for nonpayment of rent, come stay at my house. I'm not too patriotic to harbor a criminal."

Chapter 25

THE VISIT

Duane would have liked to go to Three Elms every Sabbath, but he restrained himself as he didn't want to accept hospitality when he could give nothing in return. He made other Adventist friends and visited with them or invited them to his apartment. It was easier to keep the Sabbath now that he had officially joined the Adventist Church and no longer had reason to hide his convictions. Although he couldn't hold religious services with his friends, no one could send them to jail for studying the Bible together. On Sundays he regularly attended the evangelistic meetings at the church on Airport Road and even went along with more experienced church members who gave Bible studies to those requesting them.

Though his cupboard was never full, it seemed that he always had enough food on hand for another day or two. One day someone left a large bag of groceries on his doorstep. Another time he found a partially used book of food ration coupons lying by the curb at a busy intersection. Often students brought gifts of food. Somehow he managed to survive the months of March and April.

An equally serious problem was meeting the rent. When his lessons dropped to twenty-five a week by the end of March, it forced him to hunt for a cheaper apartment. He found one in an old section of town. It also had three rooms, but they were small, and he had to share the bath with two other apartments. It took him a week to scrub the apartment, poison the roaches, scrape and paint the peeling walls, and get moved in. His beautiful piano looked out of place beside the well-worn furnishings. He sincerely hoped his remaining students wouldn't desert him when they saw his new quarters.

Mrs. Eaton was aghast. "If I didn't have a very special place in my heart for you, I would never be found in a dump like this. Please, come live at my house. You could use the recreation room for your studio."

"If your husband weren't a traveling man, I'd accept your invitation," he told her.

"Let me know when you change your mind," she sneered.

Other students dropped their lessons rather than come to the crowded, older section where he now lived. But for every one who dropped, he got at least one replacement from the new neighborhood. They were mostly beginners, whom he charged less, but financially he managed to break even again by the end of April.

Since his move he had spoken to Laurel by phone several times, but he felt he had to talk to her in person. So the first Friday evening in May he called to see whether he could spend the next day at Three Elms.

He had not been to Three Elms since the increasing fuel shortage had caused the Adventists to be denied oil. The house was uncomfortably cool. Laurel lent him one of her sweaters to wear under his coat. The arms were considerably too short, and he didn't try to button it. Activity centered around the fireplace.

After dinner Mrs. Lambert and Chucky went upstairs to take a nap. When they were alone Laurel commented, "I see you have lost some weight. Are you managing to get enough to eat?"

"Yes, so far. I was wondering whether I could help you garden and share some of the produce. I've had a little experience."

"That sounds like an excellent idea." Sitting on the floor, she hugged her knees against her in an attempt to keep warm. "We'll talk about it this evening after sundown. How are you adjusting to your new neighborhood?"

He grimaced. "If I thought I would be there long, I couldn't stand it."

"Do you plan to move again soon?"

"I hope so." He drew his chair closer to her. "Laurel, I'm lonely. It has been over four months since your husband remarried. You must be lonely too." Pausing, he glanced at her.

She hesitated a long time before answering. A log cracked and popped sparks. "Yes, I am. Many a night I still cry myself to sleep."

"Chucky needs a father." The words stuck in his throat. "I—I have loved you since we first met over six years ago. I believe you once loved me, too. You know I can't offer you security, but I can offer love. You refused the first time because of our religious differences. Now we share the same faith." He paused and placed his hand on hers. "Will—will you marry me?"

Laurel did not answer immediately. He watched her intently. She blinked back some tears, then, after an eternity, she said with a tremor in her voice, "Duane, I'm honored. Yes, I think you know that I loved you. When I'm with you I feel the embers of our former love glow again. But I still pray that Alex will come home." She paused, choosing her words. "Duane, I feel sorry for him. He can't be happy for he knows he's disobeyed God and turned his back on the church. And he must miss Chucky terribly. If he still loves Gina a year from now, I'll marry you."

"You still love him then, don't you?"

"Yes, for real love doesn't cease when someone wrongs you."

He turned away from her in silence. Then, "Laurel, you're a remarkable woman. I doubt that I could be as forgiving. I won't mention marriage again till then. Will that make you happy?"

Her eyes filled with tears, and she nodded.

All summer Duane spent at least one morning a week cultivating Laurel's garden. She kept him supplied with produce. He watched the newspapers for ads about berry picking. Laurel canned or froze all the strawberries, blueberries, and raspberries he could pick. The early peaches were ready for harvest when she ran out of jars. In two days he brought her several dozen jars, which one of his students who was moving away was happy to give him.

So much fruit required large quantities of sugar. Duane bargained with his more overweight students to exchange ten-pound bags of sugar for piano lessons. He found the system worked quite well for other items such as flour and oil as well. Most of his students seemed willing to help.

One Sunday in September Duane was looking at the newspaper when he noticed that Gina would sing the leading role in a production of *Madame Butterfly*. Although he couldn't think of a person less like the Cio-Cio-San in character, he recognized that with her long black hair Gina could appear believably Oriental. Since he had been wanting to talk to Alexander Robertson, he thought this might be his opportunity.

Having seen Alexander only at Mr. Lambert's funeral, Duane could not pick him out in the audience. So at intermission time he slipped backstage, and as he had hoped, Alexander was there. Duane hadn't wished to have Gina see him, but she emerged from her dressing room just as he started over to speak to her husband.

"Why, Duane! It has been ages since I last saw you. I'd like you to meet my husband."

"How do you do, Dr. Robertson?" he said self-consciously. "I'm sure you're proud of Gina tonight."

Alexander gave his wife a squeeze, then said, "I didn't catch your name."

"Duane Manning."

"That name is familiar. Have we met before?"

"No. I went to Thornton School of Music with both Laurel and Gina. Maybe one of them mentioned me."

"Oh." Alexander looked shaken. "I remember now. Laurel often spoke of you."

Gina excused herself to retouch her makeup. When she had gone Duane continued, "I came tonight primarily to meet you. I would like to talk privately with you sometime."

Dr. Robertson hesitated. "Could you come to my office Wednesday PM? That's my afternoon off."

"What time?"

"How about four o'clock? Here's my card."

Alexander arrived an hour late for his appointment with Duane. "Sorry. We had an emergency at the hospital. Come into my office." He turned on the air conditioner. "Seems a bit stuffy in here. Care to remove your coat?" He motioned for Duane to be seated.

"It is quite warm for September, isn't it?"

Robertson seated himself at his desk and asked, "Well, what have you on your mind?"

Duane leaned forward. "I'll come right to the point after I've given you a bit of background, some of which you may know. I met Laurel six and a half years ago when she enrolled at Thornton School of Music. We became close friends, and I

asked her to marry me. She hesitated to marry someone not of
her faith and did what she could to convert me. I was cautious
about accepting the Adventist way of life, and she went to
teach in California. Just about the time I started to keep the
Sabbath, I learned she was planning to marry you; so I
dropped out of her life.

"When Gina's wedding picture appeared in the
paper—well, I was shocked. I visited Laurel to offer my
condolences. Since then we have seen a lot of each other, and
I have become a baptized Seventh-day Adventist. Again I
have asked her to marry me, but she still loves you. She hopes
you will return to her and Chucky. What I hope to learn is,
How likely is this to happen?"

Alexander had been resting his chin on his fingertips and
staring at the floor. He did not answer immediately. Finally
he stated matter-of-factly, "Not very likely."

"Are you happy with Gina?"

He shrugged. "Reasonably." A long pause, then he
strode over to the window, thrusting his hands into his trouser
pockets till only the thumbs protruded. "I'm not a complete
fool. Gina is a very selfish person. She'll no doubt desert me
if she finds someone more interesting."

Duane shook his head. "Don't you miss your son?"

"Yes, of course. I haven't seen him for about a year."
Robertson seemed to brighten a moment. "It's almost time
for his annual visit. I don't know whether Gina will take her
mind off our baby girl long enough to watch after him
though. Is he getting enough to eat?"

"Yes. He's doing well."

Alexander smiled. "I mailed him a toy yesterday for his
third birthday. Hope it arrives in time."

Duane cleared his throat. "What is your present relation-
ship to the Adventist Church?"

Turning his back, Dr. Robertson stared out the window.

"I was disfellowshiped when I remarried. Haven't had any contact with it since. I—I hope the members aren't . . . suffering too badly."

Slowly Duane stood. "Do you still believe it's the true church?"

"Yes." He grimaced. "But I suppose you would have to describe my present spiritual condition as—well, hopeless." He paled as he said the word.

"For my sake, I hope you remain as you are, but for yours, I hope you reconsider. Laurel wants you back. The church always accepts repentant sinners."

Robertson's brow wrinkled, and he pressed his lips tightly together. His reply was hesitant. "I can't give Gina up yet. I love her in spite of her—uh—self-centeredness. She is a very captivating woman. As for Laurel, perhaps we weren't meant for each other. And as for the church?" He shrugged. "May God have mercy on me." His voice began to tremble, and he stared out the window at the sky.

When Duane put on his jacket Alexander turned from the window and held out his hand. "Give Chucky a hug for me."

As the men shook hands Duane thought he noticed tears in the other man's eyes.

Chapter 26

COMMUNAL LIVING

President McGrath, in the midst of her second term in office, came under constant criticism for her inability to cope with national and world problems.

The economy increasingly lagged as the shortage of fuel curtailed industrial expansion. Years of an impoverished diet had brought multitudes to the point of revolution. Terror stalked the streets as strikes, riots, and crime became even more rampant. The growing opposition party responded with demands for stricter law enforcement and solutions to the food and fuel crises.

An increasing majority strongly felt that only God could help the nation. Evangelist Sunny Parker filled stadiums in every city as his voice cried out that only by a return to religion could the United States expect God's favor. He compared the nation's plight to that of ancient Israel's when it turned to other gods.

Sunday, October 1, was set aside for a national day of prayer and fasting. People who had not entered a church for years joined the faithful in participating in the prayer circles that began on the stroke of midnight and continued for twenty-four hours. Many who did not believe in God or prayer attended to avoid appearing unpatriotic. All that day the TV and radio stations were devoted to religious programs, urging Christian unity and stricter Sunday observance. A Spiritualist medium appeared on one popular TV show and told the viewers the spirits had repeatedly revealed that Sabbath observers were a cause of God's disfavor.

The following day the Senate ratified a House-approved law that would prohibit all business dealings with those Christians honoring Saturday as their worship day. President McGrath said as she signed it, "We regret that our previous measures against Sabbatarians seem to have aided rather than hindered their cause. We trust that by refusing them the right to buy or sell we shall force them to accept the will of the majority, which is also the will of God. We sincerely hope that they will not bring unnecessary suffering upon themselves and their children by foolish stubbornness. I would ask that those who may be sympathetic to their plight not postpone the achievement of unity by supplying them with the necessities of life." The announcement met with general approval throughout the nation.

The Adventists were perplexed but not surprised. When landlords evicted them or banks foreclosed mortgages and took over their homes, other Adventists who had their property paid for took them in. Those without friends able to house them camped in the forests or violated the Sunday laws in order to get put in jail. Soon Sabbath observers filled the jails. Their lusty singing on Saturday upset the guards and entertained the other prisoners.

When utility companies ceased to provide electricity, water, gas, and other services, Adventists quickly bought up camping equipment at stores where the sales people did not recognize them or where the merchants were so happy to dispose of merchandise during the off season that they were careful not to ask questions.

As Sabbathkeepers lost their jobs they banded together to supply services to one another. It was surprising how far a little money could stretch even during times of drastic infla-

tion. When children outgrew their clothes they passed them
on to younger friends or siblings, while accepting donations
from older children. They pooled their money as well as their
talents. Those with savings accounts withdrew the money to
help buy necessities for those in need.

Life at Three Elms radically changed as ten people
crowded into the modest house. Laurel, her mother, and
Chucky shared what had been Laurel's bedroom. Larry had
returned from California to claim his former tiny room. But
now he shared it with his bride, Joyce, who was three months
pregnant. The black Gordon family accepted the third and
largest bedroom. Zip and Dorothy Gordon were recent converts. They had a seven-year-old son, Rick, and a twelve-
year-old daughter, Jill. Duane, who had been evicted from
his apartment, slept on the couch in the living room beside his
piano that dominated the room.

Such a full house required some regimentation. A general
council convened and agreed upon a living schedule and
individual responsibilities. They set rising time at six
o'clock, retiring time at ten, and meals promptly at seven,
twelve thirty, and six. They would hold worship at breakfast
and after supper. Each person had a list of individual duties.

With so many people in close contact over a prolonged
period, some differences were bound to arise, and Mrs.
Lambert often found herself exercising her role as arbiter.
The problems centered around the schedule, personality
traits, and equalization of duties. They quickly agreed that
anyone wishing to sleep late need not expect to be served
breakfast upon arising. When Joyce complained that her
housework should not include picking up after everybody,
they established a system whereby someone confiscated the
offending garments or objects. The owner could redeem
them only by performing some distasteful task like washing

the windows of one room, scrubbing the kitchen floor, or cleaning the hen house.

Zip had been a service manager for a car dealer. An ingenious mechanic, he soon had a windmill operating a generator to produce electric current when the wind blew. It charged a set of batteries that ran the pump so that water once again flowed to the kitchen and bathroom. Everyone cheerfully abandoned the makeshift outhouse. All were thankful that the Lamberts had purchased a home with its own well rather than one depending on city water.

A camping stove kept the bathroom reasonably warm. But with only one bathroom for ten people, they had to set time limits for its use. Dorothy Gordon found she could no longer read in the tub. The men learned to do their shaving elsewhere. Chucky and Rick enjoyed taking baths together or skipping them when they could. Laurel preferred to rise before the six o'clock rush began. It also gave her a headstart on breakfast, which she tried to make as nourishing as possible with her limited supplies.

Cooking wasn't easy. At times Zip's generator supplied enough electricity for the stove, but the group couldn't depend upon it. The freezer was useless. Laurel was glad most of the garden produce had been canned. She was thankful, too, for apples to provide fresh fruit. As long as the money held out, Zip could bring home what groceries they needed by shopping where no one knew him. They had secured rationed items such as flour from neighbors in trade for apples. The permanence of that arrangement would depend upon the neighbor's reaction to President McGrath's request to refrain from assisting the Adventists.

Money threatened to become a problem. Larry had bought a beautiful home in California, which the bank took over a few months later when business dealings with Adventists became illegal. Fortunately the equity he lost was little more than the down payment. He had been enjoying a growing practice, but his cash on hand was slight because he had just bought furniture, draperies, carpets, and shrubbery for his home. Although he had tried to sell the furniture before leaving California, people were afraid to buy from him. Finally a physician friend took the furniture and promised to send him money for anything he could sell. Thus far, Larry had received nothing.

Three Elms was too isolated for him to open an office there. A fellow church member who lived on Route 9 offered to rent him office space for one fourth of what he took in. Larry hung out his shingle, hoping that tourists needing medical attention might see it and stop. Since Quabbin Reservoir, which appealed mainly to nature lovers, was the only nearby attraction, Route 9 was not heavily traveled. But the first day he had three patients. All paid cash. If they marveled at his lack of the usual equipment, they didn't complain. He figured that an average of three patients a day would make survival possible for the inhabitants of Three Elms.

Duane, however, felt useless. His water-carrying task had been short-lived, thanks to Zip's ingenuity. Since one teaches piano on a continuing basis, he was quite sure no one would have the courage to study with an Adventist, and he didn't care to run the risk of getting a student jailed. He did, however, place an ad for one month in the Worcester *Telegram*:

> Experienced concert pianist available
> to perform for private functions.
> Write W. Brookfield, P.O. Box 300.

During the month he had three responses. One function would be on a Saturday afternoon. The second came from Mrs. Schwab. Replying that circumstances beyond his control would make his appearance at her party impossible, he thought it prudent to sign her letter with a pseudonym. The third was for a small party on a Sunday afternoon two weeks hence. He quoted a reasonable fee and started practicing. Two days before the party a letter came saying that they had obtained a musician who would play for less.

While he had been practicing several hours a day, Duane had felt rejuvenated. Now he was despondent. Laurel tried to help him over his disappointment by saying that perhaps someone might have been at the party who would know him and cause either him or the hostess to be jailed. She suggested he make use of his time by giving piano lessons to the Gordon children. He replied that a mechanic and a telephone operator wouldn't be apt to have an interest in their children's musical education. But she promised to find out.

The next morning after breakfast Dorothy Gordon followed him as he left the table. "Laurel says you are willing to teach our children piano. I think that is wonderful!"

He tried not to reveal his lack of enthusiasm and asked, "Will you agree to see that they practice faithfully?"

"Of course. How much would you suggest?"

"Probably about half an hour a day for Rick. Jill should spend an hour. At twelve she ought to make excellent progress."

"You can't imagine how grateful I am, Duane. As a child I wanted piano lessons, but there was never any money. You see, my father was a drug addict. My mother tried to earn enough clerking in a dime store to feed the family. But as soon as I was old enough to stop school, I went to work to help support my younger sister and two brothers. I'm afraid I missed a great deal in life. I've always loved music. Your practicing these past two weeks has been a real joy to me."

Duane thought a moment. "We'll start lessons tomorrow. Maybe you would like to study too."

Her eyes widened in disbelief. "Do you mean it? at my age? I'd love to." Dorothy Gordon went running off to tell

Laurel the good news, leaving Duane feeling ashamed of underestimating the Gordons' interest in music.

In the following weeks Jill and her mother made excellent progress, while Rick was about as enthusiastic as the average seven-year-old. When Dorothy would lose patience with the boy's repeated errors and remark about his lack of intelligence, someone passing through the room might quote the portion of Revelation 14:12, which had become somewhat of a motto at Three Elms: "Here is the patience of the saints."

One day she stomped her foot and shouted, "Why can't you quote the whole verse for a change? If being a saint requires patience, I'll never make it!" That night she suggested to her husband that Rick discontinue his piano lessons.

"Then how would you know you haven't yet developed patience?" Zip replied.

So the lessons continued.

Joyce Lambert found her responsibility of keeping the house clean rather overwhelming. Longingly she remembered her spacious new California home with its decorator-coordinated carpets, furniture, and draperies. With only herself and Larry in it, she had been able to keep every room looking magazine-picture immaculate. Here at Three Elms there seemed to be constant clutter. She didn't know who belonged to the assorted books, toys, unread mail, towels, pencils, and pens that seemed to accumulate on every level surface. And she didn't see how Laurel could work in a kitchen where soiled glasses, a dish of apples, cereal boxes, a towel dispenser, dish and hand towels, a napkin holder, a useless electric mixer and blender, a grocery list, scouring pads, and assorted containers crowded the limited counter space. She found it almost impossible to remain tranquil and uncomplaining when the house was not orderly.

To complicate her problem she was nauseated for several hours each morning and feared the malady would afflict her all during her pregnancy. Also, she hated herself for bringing an innocent being into the world at such a time. She had hoped her child would be a few years old before the final period of persecution began. Now it seemed her timetable was faulty.

"O God," she prayed as she scrubbed the kitchen floor on her knees, "give me strength to care for this helpless child in the dreadful days ahead, or else take it before it's born."

Three Elms had no garage. The kitchen door opened onto a small uncovered porch with steps down to the driveway. It was January, and they could not leave boots on the porch to fill with snow. Someone had placed a large cardboard box under the table by the door to receive them, but not everyone was careful to remove his boots promptly upon entering. The children especially tended to rush upstairs to the bathroom with them on. Joyce mopped the kitchen daily, but rarely had the floor dried before boot tracks covered it. One day, feeling extremely frustrated, she looked at a fresh set of tracks and started to cry.

Duane had just come to the sink for a drink of water. "What's the matter, Joyce?"

"It's no use," she sobbed. "I can't keep this house clean. You people mess it up faster than I can clean it."

"You know we appreciate what you do. Think what a pigpen we'd have if it weren't for you."

"Look at my hands—rough from being in water all the time. Cold water in a cold house. Sometimes I wish I were in jail. At least I'd be warm and could keep my cell neat."

He patted her on the shoulder. "I'm sure you don't mean that. Let me think about this boot situation. Maybe I could build a roof for the porch and fix a shelf out there for boots."

"Ha—you a carpenter?" A touch of sarcasm lurked in

her voice, tinged with exhaustion.

"No, but I've used a hammer and saw a bit. With three men in the house, we ought to be able to come up with something."

The next day Zip and Duane took materials from the no-longer-needed outhouse and built a roof for the porch and a protected boot holder along the railing on two sides of the landing. They posted a sign on the door leading into the kitchen:

FINE
ENTERING WITH BOOTS ON—ONE MEAL.

It was amazing how much cleaner the house remained from then on.

It can be bitter cold in Massachusetts in late January. The fuel oil that Laurel had begun to hoard after Pastor Kelly's announcement the preceding January was almost gone. They had not received any more since April. Instead of the 60 degrees they had kept the house after Pastor Kelly's visit, they reduced the temperature to 50 degrees in hopes of stretching the waning oil supply. Sometimes the temperature in the house had dropped even below that.

Each day Duane spent about two hours roaming the forests looking for firewood. He found many birches snapped off by the wind and snow. Less often he found a recently toppled elm or maple. He especially prized the maple. While hard to saw up, it afforded heat for a much longer period than the quickly consumed birch. The apple trees which had been cleared to make room for an expanded garden when rationing began were cut into firewood. The logs, an excellent source of heat, produced colorful flames. But the long wall of carefully stacked firewood had diminished. Duane prayed fervently for an early spring. He marveled that, in spite of the cold and a meager diet, all at

Three Elms had remained in surprisingly good health.

One day in his wanderings in the forest he found a child's footprints in the freshly fallen snow. It appeared that the child could not be more than four or five years old. After following the aimless tracks for about an hour, he spotted a small form huddled under a bush. As he drew closer large blue eyes framed by matted blond hair stared in terror at him. The face was emaciated and dirt-streaked. The snow suit the child wore was ragged, and the holes in the once-red mittens revealed fingers blue with cold.

"Hello, there," he smiled. "Aren't you a long way from home?"

Seeming not to hear, the tyke watched him without blinking. Duane drew closer. The child attempted to run, but fell exhausted after a few feet. When he hurried to the little form and started to lift it up, the child struggled and attempted to bite his hand.

"I'm here to help you. If you come with me, I'll give you something to eat and a warm fire to sit by." The child's expression did not change. "I'll give you a place to sleep and some warmer clothes. I'll try to find your parents. Would you like that?"

Still no response. Duane sat down in the snow beside the frightened child and said nothing for a minute or two.

"My name is Duane," he almost whispered. "What's yours?"

"Kathy," a tiny voice answered.

"That's a nice name. I knew a Kathy once. We used to play house together when I was about your size. She had a one-armed doll named Coco. I was supposed to be the daddy and go to work and bring home groceries. Coco never ate the apples I brought, but Kathy and I enjoyed them. Do you like apples?" She nodded. "Well, I know where there are lots and lots of apples. I know a kind lady who likes to make apple

pie. Do you like apple pie?'' Again a nod. ''You could ride
high on my shoulders till we get out of the woods. Would you
like that?'' Another nod. ''Let's see if I can lift a big girl like
you.''

With a grunt and a pretense of great effort he wafted the
frail body over his head. He felt sure that Chucky weighed
more, though he was only three years old.

He kept up a one-sided conversation all the way home to
allay her fears. By the time they arrived at Three Elms he
knew nothing more about her except that she was five years
old and had eaten nothing for days.

Larry wisely suggested that she eat little at first. Duane
kept his promise by offering her a sliver of apple pie, which
she ate eagerly. Laurel heated some water and increased the
fire in the fireplace. When she had bathed the girl she gave
her a pair of Rick's pajamas and put her to bed. In minutes
she fell asleep.

Laurel took the car and drove to see Mrs. Morris, a friend
whose two daughters were five and seven years of age. She
told the woman about the child and asked whether she could
spare some warm clothes. When Laurel left she had a coat,
two dresses, a pair of corduroy play pants, a sweater, and
some underwear.

The next day, as Kathy played with Chucky, Rick, and
Jill, she talked about her parents. They were Sabbathkeepers
who had camped in the forest after being evicted from their
apartment. Then they found a small, rocky cave to protect
them when the snows began. Her father had gone in search of
food one day as usual, but he did not return. After two days
her mother went to look for food, but by evening she had not
come back to the cave. Kathy had been terrified all night,
especially when an unseen animal had entered the cave and
rested before moving on. At daybreak she started searching
for her parents. How many days had passed she didn't know.

Her father's name was Bill; her mother's, Beth. Their last name began with a T but Kathy's pronunciation of it was unintelligible.

In the days that followed, Kathy's gaunt face took on a childish roundness, and the terror in her eyes gave way to a merry sparkle. But there were times her thoughts seemed far away, and tragedy haunted her face.

Chapter 27

DEATH PENALTY

A narrow red arc peeking over the horizon promised temporary relief from the snow that had greeted February with a three-day blizzard. Alexander Robertson heard a thud signaling that the Sunday paper had arrived. As he unrolled it his eye caught the headline: "Los Angeles Destroyed by Earthquake."

"The quake, which came at 2:32 this morning, leveled most of the city and took thousands of lives. . . . It will be weeks before the number of dead is known. Flames are consuming what the quake did not demolish. The population is fleeing in panic, fearful that more tremors will follow. . . . A tidal wave following the quake lashed the California shore and swept away homes as far away as Ventura and San Clemente."

In a daze he dropped the paper. He had had no contact with his parents in the year and a half since his visit home when Gina had followed him to California. The announcement of his wedding had elicited no response. Now, out of concern for his parents' safety, he decided to call.

The operator informed him that no calls were being put through to southern California. She advised him to try again in about twelve hours. That evening he received the same message. Service did not resume until several days later.

Alexander tried to dial direct without success. The

operator secured the information that his parents' phone had been disconnected. So he tried to call Mr. Patterson, organist and choir director of the Ventura Seventh-day Adventist Church. His phone likewise had been disconnected. Then Alexander called the neighbor across the street, who was not an Adventist.

"Mr. Bunch? This is Alexander Robertson calling from Massachusetts. . . . I'm fine, thank you. Glad you survived the quake. . . . Any damage to your home? . . . What about my parents? . . . Really? . . . You don't know where they went? . . . Well, thanks anyway."

After he hung up, Gina asked, "What did you learn?"

"My parents moved away in November," he said without emotion. "Mr. Bunch didn't know where they went. They took the furniture in a rented truck and said they were going to look for a place in the country. He hasn't seen them since. Someone else is living in the house, which wasn't damaged."

"Oh?" Her tone indicated she wasn't particularly interested. She left the room, humming an aria from a new role she was studying.

Glad to be left alone, he sat in his easy chair with his eyes closed, trying to recall occasions when his parents and he still communicated. Somehow he couldn't recapture any feeling of closeness. There had been times up till his marriage with Gina that he nearly followed their advice to return to Laurel. Later when Duane visited him to see whether his marriage to Gina was permanent, he again had some stirrings of conscience. But now he felt nothing. His conscience was numb, and he accepted the inevitable. Even thoughts of Chucky failed to arouse him out of his spiritual stupor.

A call from the hospital interrupted his thoughts. It was Dr. Jewel asking his help in handling dozens of cases of an unidentified ailment characterized by painful sores.

When he arrived at the hospital he found the orderlies shifting patients around so that they could confine the strange disease to one floor. He examined a patient who had five large, inflamed sores scattered from her cheek to her thigh. They spewed an offensive, smelly discharge. As he cleaned them and applied dressings, he learned they had begun as pimples two days before. Their searing pain required an analgesic ointment. All night he cared for those admitted with the disease. When other physicians arrived in the morning, he wearily made his way to the cloakroom. As he put on his topcoat Dr. Jewel entered. "Quite a night, wasn't it, Alex?"

"I'll welcome some sleep." He rubbed his eyes.

"What do you suppose it is?"

"It's probably the first plague."

"Plague? What do you mean?"

"Never mind. I really don't know."

Alexander slipped on a glove. As he pulled on the second, he noticed a pimple on the back of his hand.

Fishing vessels had thronged the New England coast since the ban on meat products almost three years before. The entire Atlantic seaboard enjoyed a prosperous fishing industry as the demand for seafood exceeded the supply.

A few isolated spots of red tide had occurred during recent decades, but that March it affected the entire eastern seaboard at once. Dead fish washed ashore in such quantities that one could smell the stench of decomposing flesh for miles, and efforts to bulldoze them under proved futile.

Wealthy homeowners locked their coastal residences and moved to temporary lodgings inland. Poor transients living in flimsy houses built for the summer tourist trade settled for shoveling the putrifying carcasses from their doors. Airplanes sprayed the beaches daily with pesticides to discourage the maggots and flies that feasted on the carrion.

Gradually the red tide crept up the bays and rivers of the east coast. When the Potomac River began to reek with dead fish, President McGrath summoned Rasmussen to her office. "What's causing all this?" she demanded.

"I've told you before," he replied. "God is displeased."

"What more can I do? I've carried out every one of your suggestions."

Taking a seat, he leaned intently forward. "Listen carefully. On March 11 there will be a meteor shower over this city beginning at 9:57 PM. That will be your sign that the Adventists must die."

"But"—she spread her hands in frustration—"but I cannot condemn them. I'm not a dictator. Congress will never pass such a law."

"Ah, but they will. Leave it to me." He bowed and left the room.

The next day the Washington *Post* announced that "Rasmussen, influential leader of the Spiritualists in the U.S. has predicted that on March 11 a meteor shower over the city of Washington will be a sign that it is the will of God that Sabbathkeepers must die. The spectacle is supposed to begin at 9:57 PM and be visible for a radius of thirty miles from the center of Washington. One official, who asked not to be named, said, 'If this prediction is as accurate as those Rasmussen has made in recent months, we shall witness a most unusual instance of God's will revealed. We shall almost believe ourselves back in Old Testament times rubbing elbows with Moses, Gideon, and Hezekiah.' "

An editorial the next day continued to draw attention to Rasmussen's demand:

"Rasmussen has declared that the Adventists must die. Can liberty-loving Americans countenance the annihilation of nonviolent fellow citizens whose only crime is serving

God according to their concept of His demands?

"Is the commandment 'Thou shalt not kill' still in effect? If so, are we culpable when we take the lives of soldiers in opposing armies? What about the women and children our bombs destroy? Clearly, these foreigners have a different ideology from ours and are following another commander. Does this make them worthy of death? Perhaps the pragmatist's reminder that it is a choice of their lives or ours helps clarify our thinking.

"The Adventists, too, have a different ideology. It is clear they and we cannot both be led of God. If they continue to live among us, will God's wrath destroy us all? If they were on foreign soil, would we hesitate to annihilate them?

"Rasmussen claims to speak for God. That he represents supernatural power few would deny. As to the source of his power there are differing opinions. Will Heaven cooperate by providing the shower of stars he predicts? If so, the doubts of many will be removed."

The city of Washington extinguished its streetlights and neon signs at 9:45 on the eleventh. So many thousands of people jammed the streets that traffic ceased to move. Airplanes at Dulles and other local airports remained grounded. Planes scheduled to land were sent to Baltimore or ordered to hold at least thirty-five miles away. No one seemed to know how long the shower of meteorites would continue.

At exactly 9:57 the sky suddenly blazed. From a central spot myriads of meteorites streamed forth, leaving trails of light like a giant Fourth of July rocket. But unlike a rocket, the flow continued and became more abundant. No sound accompanied the spectacle. Viewers were for the most part too frightened to talk to one another, though many prayed fervently. Only the children expressed their delight. For two hours the impressive sight continued unabated.

Television beamed the spectacle to an expectant nation. A pilot in an airplane carrying a camera attempted to fly into the zone of meteorites but turned back when he noted that his instruments were useless in the vicinity of the display. NASA had positioned a research satellite to orbit through the area of the shower, but as soon as it started, the space vehicle's telemetry signals went dead. Newscasters found themselves without adequate words to describe the sight.

The shower of meteors subsided around midnight, and a bewildered commentator signed off with the comment: "When God speaks, man can only listen."

The next day anguished constituents plagued by sores, polluted beaches, hunger, or fear wrote to their congressmen, begging them to heed the voice of God. Rasmussen basked in glory as he accepted homage from those who had been skeptical of his claims as well as from his supporters. Even before the inundating mail peaked, Congress voted to give priority to the question of the death penalty for Sabbathkeepers.

Not all members of Congress were convinced that Rasmussen spoke for God. Some who knew him best could not reconcile his personal life with Christian principles. They found him shrewd, egomaniacal, and bloodthirsty. But they could not ignore the thunderous clamor of their constituents, and they feared to express their convictions.

So barely a month after the spectacle of March 11, Congress voted the death penalty for Sabbathkeeping Christians. President McGrath lost no time in signing the decree. It would go into effect on May 15.

Chapter 28

FAREWELL

The inhabitants of Three Elms did not learn of the death decree immediately because their wind-created electricity was hardly adequate for radio or TV, and the newspaper had ceased when business dealings with Adventists became illegal.

The afternoons were lengthening, and patches of green appeared here and there where a few days before only brown had been. The smell of spring was in the air.

Laurel, partly from habit and partly from a love of gardening, went to the closet and took down the jar of dried peas she had saved from last year's crop. Then, donning her oldest slacks and jacket, she headed for the shed where she had stored the hand plow and other gardening tools. As she pushed the plow on its wobbly wheel toward the garden plot, she passed her mother returning from the hen house.

"Don't tell me you plan to start the garden already!" Mrs. Lambert exclaimed.

"No, just a few peas for now," she said as she continued on her way.

"Why don't you let Duane or one of the other men push that plow, then?"

"I welcome the chance to be alone and to get away from the confusion inside. And I love the smell of freshly turned earth and the feel of the cool, damp soil."

Laurel soon had the ground broken in two straight furrows. She was on her knees, dropping peas with one hand while pulverizing the soil and covering them with the other when she noticed George, the boy who had once attempted to steal canned goods from her basement, leaning against the maple tree at the end of the furrow. Breaking off the song she had been humming, she stood. George eyed her narrowly and pressed his lips together tightly.

"Hello, George," she called.

The boy scowled and snapped, "You'll never live to eat it, you Saturday fool." Then he spat in her direction and shuffled off toward home.

Her eyes smarted with tears she tried to blink back. His remark did not surprise her. A satanic spirit seemed to have taken possession of her neighbors. As she recalled other insults and slights from former friends, her tears watered the soil.

Finished with the planting, she went inside and found everyone at Three Elms gathered in the kitchen, talking excitedly. It took only a few moments for Laurel to learn the tragic news Zip had brought back from the post office.

Congress had actually voted the death penalty for Adventists. The authorities were posting lists of known Sabbathkeepers in all public buildings, and persons capturing and turning over to town officials anyone on the list after May 15 would be rewarded.

There was no panic in the kitchen council—only sadness and uncertainty as they examined possible courses of action. Finally the inhabitants of Three Elms agreed that they would flee by families as inconspicuously as possible before the death decree was to become effective. The four Gordons would take Larry's car. Laurel, Chucky, Duane, Kathy, and Mrs. Lambert would travel together. Larry and Joyce would bring Zip's truck a few days after the baby, already several days overdue, was born.

The plan was for the Gordons to leave on the twenty-third and set up camp at a designated site in the Maine wilderness on a lakeshore, then somehow purchase food supplies at the nearest town. Laurel hoped to be able to stay till after the birth of Joyce's baby, but her car would leave no later than the twenty-fifth. Larry and Joyce would follow on the twenty-seventh regardless. They hoped that by going at different times they could avoid arousing the suspicion of their neighbors. With a thousand-dollar bounty on each of their heads, they wanted to avoid being followed.

On the morning of the twenty-third the Gordons wished Joyce God's blessing, told everyone good-bye, and drove off without a backward glance. All day Joyce prayed that her baby would delay no longer. That evening around the supper table Mrs. Lambert remarked how like old times it seemed having just the family, Duane, and Kathy. Suddenly Joyce gave a startled cry. All eyes turned toward her.

"Are you all right, Joyce?" Larry inquired anxiously.

"I . . . I'm not sure, but I think it's beginning."

He hurried her off to bed. Before long he returned to the table. "In a few hours I'll be a father." Although he tried to sound proud, he could not conceal his apprehension.

By midnight Joyce's pains were coming regularly, but they were still far apart. Larry insisted he could handle the delivery and that the others should go to bed, though he promised to call if he needed anything.

Awakening at six o'clock, Laurel rushed to Larry's side. Joyce struggled to stifle the screams that welled in her throat. Her husband told her to cry out, but she didn't want to disturb those still sleeping. Sweat glistened on her skin, and her hair stuck to her neck and face. The bed was wet where the waters had broken. Her breathing was fast and shallow.

Getting a cold washcloth, Laurel bathed Joyce's face and

arms. Larry then suggested his sister boil some water, so she hurried off to the kitchen. She remembered how grateful she had been for anesthesia during Chucky's birth. Her heart ached for Joyce. As she waited impatiently for the water to boil she heard a piercing scream, followed by another and another. Soon everybody in the house rushed to Joyce's bed.

Laurel arrived with her teakettle of boiling water, a large pan, a pair of scissors, and some clean towels. "Out, all of you," she said firmly as she steered Kathy and Chucky to the door. "Larry and I can manage this. Mother, you and Duane can fix some breakfast for everybody." She closed the door behind them.

In a few minutes a baby's cry punctuated Joyce's screams.

"Duane! Did you hear that? It's here!" Mrs. Lambert ran over and threw her arms around him.

"I surely did," he laughed. "Sounds healthy enough."

Larry shouted down the stairs, "It's a boy!"

That night, as Joyce and Larry admired little Paul nursing at his mother's breast, Mrs. Lambert lingered over an old photograph album. She brushed aside the tears as she looked for the last time at her wedding picture and at photos of her parents, Larry and Laurel as babies, Larry as an awkward twelve-year-old, Laurel as she graduated from academy, the family at Laurel's wedding, and Turner in his casket. When she reached the last page she closed the album, bowed her head, and prayed silently. "Dear God, please reunite us soon. How I long to see my parents and Turner. Protect us as we leave our home tomorrow. Thank You for little Paul, and give us strength to care for him." She placed the album back in the bookcase, patted it gently, then went upstairs to join Chucky and Kathy, who were already asleep.

Duane and Laurel were alone together for the first time

since he had come to live at Three Elms. It was unusually
warm for late April, and they decided to sit on the front steps.
Neither spoke for several minutes. Finally he said, "It must
be difficult to say good-bye to your home for the last time.
It's even hard for me after living here only six months."

"Yes, it is. There are so many memories connected with
this place . . . especially of Dad."

"And of Alexander?"

"Yes, of Alex, too."

Frogs croaked in the darkness. "I had hoped you would
be Mrs. Manning by now. Because of the confusion of these
past six months we have never had time to talk about marriage," he said without emotion.

She self-consciously glanced away from him. "You've
seen me as I really am. You should have no illusions. I'm
surprised you still want me."

"I've loved you for seven years." He took her hand.
"Wasn't that how long Jacob agreed to serve for Rachel?"

Her hand was stiff, as if she wanted to pull it away. "Yes,
but we can't get married now. We're leaving tomorrow."

"I suspect they perform weddings in Maine. Shall we
make that our first step in getting settled in our wilderness
home?"

Suddenly Laurel buried her head in her arms and started
to cry. Duane put one arm around her waist and lifted her face
with his free hand. His lips met hers. "I didn't mean to make
you cry," he whispered.

"I'm crying because—because I'm so happy. I was
afraid you didn't love me anymore. It has been a year since
you mentioned marriage."

"You asked me to give you a year to see whether Alexander would return, remember? Will you marry a poor
second choice like me?"

She straightened up. "Now, you're not a poor second,

and I'll gladly marry you. I would say rather that Alexander was the poor second. Please remember I loved you long before I met him.''

He laughed. "I'm flattered. But seriously, we must decide some things. Do you think with circumstances the way they are we should apply for a license and have a formal wedding?''

"What do you mean?''

"I mean that a church wedding is impossible, and I can't see that the formality of standing a few seconds before a justice of the peace has much meaning when all the laws of the land are against us. We could say our vows before our friends and relatives.''

She hesitated before replying. "You're probably right, but I'd feel more comfortable about our marriage if it were legal.''

Duane frowned. "Applying for a license may prove dangerous.''

"Here it might. But in Maine we won't be known." Excitement flashed across her face. "We could get it as soon as we enter the state—while we're still far from our destination.''

"All right." He hugged her. "If it will make you feel more truly married, we'll apply for the license tomorrow as soon as we reach Maine. I hope your mother won't object to the delay.''

"She'll be delighted." Laurel kissed him. "We can get camp set up for her and the children and then go off a few days by ourselves . . . Darling, won't the Gordons be surprised?''

"You know, I don't think they even knew we were interested in each other. I can imagine Zip's face now.''

They kissed and made plans till it was too cold to remain outside. Then they came in for their last night at Three Elms.

She tossed and turned for hours. Her mother snored softly beside her in bed. Laurel whispered his name and kissed her pillow, thrilled in anticipation of their honeymoon. At last she dozed just before the dawn began to gray the eastern sky.

With the departure of the Gordons and the birth of Paul, the schedule had relaxed at Three Elms. Only Duane awoke at six o'clock the following morning. He dressed, shaved, built a fire in the fireplace, and sat down cross-legged in front of the hearth to read his Bible.

When it sounded as though the others were getting up, he went over to his piano and carefully removed the dust that had settled during the night on the mirror-smooth walnut finish. The scratches on the nameboard that had so vexed him, put there by pupils whose long nails evidenced little interest in serious piano study, no longer mattered. Softly he played an intimate Brahms *Intermezzo,* followed by a Bach fugue. Next he turned to Mendelssohn's *Variations Sérieuses*. Its finale covered up the sound of Laurel's footsteps. When the last chord had died away, she placed her hands on his shoulders.

''Wonderful! Play as long as you like. I know it must be hard for you to leave your piano.''

He took her hand and kissed it. ''There have been many times these past five years when it seemed like my only real friend.''

Laurel made no reply. She hovered over him and pressed her cheek to his as her arms encircled his shoulders. Then she slipped away to prepare breakfast as he resumed playing.

Soon breakfast was over except for what remained in Chucky's bowl. Laurel helped him scrape up the last spoonfuls. Kathy wanted to run upstairs to watch little Paul finish his breakfast, but Mrs. Lambert restrained her. ''Just a minute, dear. We haven't had our morning worship yet.''

Duane picked up the Bible lying on the stand it shared

with the defunct phone book. "Larry, do you mind if I read this morning?"

"Not at all. Anything you like."

He opened to the second chapter of Genesis and began with verse 18: "And the Lord God said, It is not good that the man should be alone; I will make him an help meet for him."

As Duane read to the end of the chapter, Larry and his mother wondered why he had chosen the account of the creation of Eve and the first marriage. When he finished he returned the Bible to its place and cleared his throat. He seemed to be having trouble finding words. Laurel's cheeks were flushed, but only Duane noticed.

"God was certainly right when He said, 'It is not good that the man should be alone,' " he began. "Seven years ago I asked Laurel to marry me. We loved each other dearly, but because of our religious differences, she felt that marriage would be unwise. Probably she was right.

"Now again we find that we love each other. We know of no reason why we should not marry. Today when we get to Maine we'll apply for a license. Larry, as soon as you and Joyce arrive, both of you and Mother Lambert can be witnesses at a civil ceremony."

With tears running down her cheeks, Mrs. Lambert jumped up from her chair and threw her arms around Laurel. "I'm so very happy. Duane will be a wonderful husband." Then she turned to Duane and kissed him on both cheeks. "I've always been very fond of you. I know you'll take good care of Laurel. Welcome to the family."

By ten o'clock all was in readiness for the trip. Laurel took a last walk around the grounds. The chicken coop was silent as they had given the hens to a neighbor who had accepted them indifferently. She noticed Sheba's tombstone in the shade of an ancient elm and was thankful the dog had not lived to see this sad day. Pulling a weed from the row of peas beginning to break through the soil, she wondered whether anyone would harvest them. After plucking a giant daffodil from the joyously nodding yellow clump by the front steps, she pinned it in her hair. Then she thought how she would like to carry a cluster for her wedding bouquet. So she went inside and returned with a kitchen knife and a canning jar half filled with water to hold the flowers.

"What are we waiting for?" Duane said. "Let's go before we lose our courage."

"Chucky, Kathy," Laurel called. "Time to go."

"Yippee," the little girl shouted as she leaped out of the swing and came running. She stumbled over Chucky's dump truck and landed face-down in the sandpile, where he was playing. The little boy immediately began to wail. "Mommy, Mommy!"

"What is it, Chucky?"

"Kathy tore up my castle. She's mean!"

"No, Chucky. It was an accident. She was lucky she didn't get hurt. We have to go now. Put down your pail and shovel."

The boy's lip began to quiver. "Can't I take them along? Please, Mommy?"

Laurel was about to refuse when she considered that it was his only request. They would be camping by a lake that probably would have some sand along the shore. She took the pail, set her jar of daffodils in it, and secured it between two suitcases on the floor of the back seat.

Duane held the door as Mrs. Lambert and Kathy got in beside the suitcases. Then he helped Chucky and Laurel into the front seat. When he was ready to drive off, Larry shook his hand and suggested they have prayer. All heads bowed as Larry prayed.

"O God, the Help of Your children in ages past, guide us as we leave home and venture into the unknown. Give us courage to hold fast to our faith. Protect us from our enemies. Teach us to adapt to nature. But most of all, continue to prepare our hearts to meet Jesus. We thank You for the peace that comes only from Him, whose blood cleanses our sins. Amen.''

No one said anything else. As the car backed out of the driveway and Mrs. Lambert and her daughter looked for the last time on Three Elms, tears spilled down their cheeks. After the car had traveled about a mile Laurel began to sing softly. Her mother and Duane quickly joined in:

> "O God, our help in ages past,
>   Our hope for years to come,
> Our shelter from the stormy blast,
>   And our eternal home!

> "Under the shadow of Thy throne
>   Still may we dwell secure;
> Sufficient is Thine arm alone,
>   And our defense is sure."

Chapter 29

WILDERNESS HOME

The first few hours of travel on the interstate highway seemed more like the beginning of a vacation than a flight from persecution. The car sped past trailers and campers also headed north. The day was unusually warm for that time of year, though a few patches of snow dotted the hillsides. Kathy and Chucky took turns choosing what color car the other should locate. When a green car with a purple top failed to show up after many miles, Kathy fell asleep, leaning against Mrs. Lambert, who dozed in the back seat. Chucky soon succumbed as well, his head pillowed on his mother's lap.

"Somehow I never pictured the time of trouble to be like this," Laurel mused. "I expected to hide in rocks and mountains, but I never thought of being able to drive in comfort to the wilderness. What will we do when we need gas? The major companies no longer accept cash, and they won't honor our credit cards."

Duane shrugged. "We'll have to get off the interstate, look for independent stations, and hope they will sell to us without ration coupons. With so many campers flocking to Maine, I doubt that we'll arouse much suspicion. Everybody these days is trying to get extra gas. If folks begin to wonder, we can move on."

Soon they left the interstate and headed northwest. He

glanced at the lunch she had packed and placed on the pile of bedding at her feet. "It's been a long time since breakfast. When do we eat?"

"It's so peaceful with the children asleep I hate to wake them. Probably we should look for a roadside table soon, though."

"In about three miles we're coming to a town that should be large enough to issue marriage licenses. Or have you changed your mind?" He glanced quizzically at her.

"Do you think that I change my mind that easily? But I must admit I feel more like a harried housewife than a bride. Maybe Mother can help the children with lunch while we go for the license."

The town, though small, boasted a park with picnic tables and a courthouse. Duane suggested he was too weak to apply for a license till he had eaten, so he and Laurel quickly consumed their lunch.

"Take time to enjoy your sandwich," she laughed. "These are the last egg sandwiches you'll probably ever eat. I miss the hens already."

"Why didn't you bring one or two along?"

"Probably I should have. Don't know where they would have ridden, though. The car has every square inch of space crammed with something."

By the time they had obtained the license, Kathy, Chucky, and Mrs. Lambert had cleaned up the remains of the lunch, and Mrs. Lambert was eager to resume the trip. The children enjoyed the swings and slide.

"That was speedier than I expected," Mrs. Lambert commented when Duane and Laurel returned. "They used to make a couple wait days for blood tests. Do you have to come back to this county to be married?"

"No," Laurel replied. "This is good anywhere in the state after two days. The clerk who usually issues licenses was out, and his assistant asked us to wait till he returned. But when Duane mentioned our children were waiting for us in the park, he gave us an incredulous look and took care of it himself.''

They coaxed the children back into the car and resumed the journey. As the U.S. highway became a state road the towns gave way to villages clustered around white-steepled churches and separated by miles of forest broken only by frequent lakes.

Laurel studied the map and wondered whether they could reach their destination in time to pitch the tent before dark. They had to cover another thirty miles before getting to the dirt road that would take them to the lake where they were to meet the Gordons. Then they would have to leave the car and walk a mile or two to the campsite. Transporting the tent and other necessities would require several trips.

"Mommy."

"Yes, Chucky."

"Will we live like the Indians?"

"Very much like them. You had better practice walking as silently as an Indian through the forest."

His eyes grew big and round. "Will people scalp us?"

"Nobody scalps other people anymore."

"Will they shoot us?"

"I don't think so. God will take care of us."

The boy thought a moment. "Aren't you scared?"

"A little. Not so much of people as of how we'll keep warm, clean, and fed."

Chucky smiled to himself. "I'm going swimming every day."

She shook her head. "Not for several weeks yet."

"Why?"

"The lake water is like ice now. It will be at least six weeks before you can enjoy swimming."

"Shucks."

"I'm going to gather dandelions and birds' eggs so we'll have something to eat," Kathy chimed in.

"I'll appreciate all the help you can give me, dear," Laurel said. "I'm afraid we'll all spend most of our time looking for food."

The hum of the wheels on the pavement lulled the children into a sound sleep from which they did not awaken when the car began to jostle upon reaching the rutted logging trail. The sun sank behind the trees that fringed the lake as Duane parked the car at the end of the trail. "Jump out everybody. We're here," he called to the sleeping children.

They rubbed the sleep from their eyes and climbed out. "Mommy! It's cold. I wanna go home." Chucky's face began to pucker up.

"We have to be brave, dear. We can't go home. But we'll make a new home in this lovely forest. You'll get warm helping to carry our supplies to the campsite."

Laurel saw something emerge from behind a large tree about fifty yards away. The forest was dark with shadows, but she thought it was a man.

"Welcome!" he called. To her relief she recognized the voice of Zip Gordon. "I've made a sleigh of pine branches to make it easier to haul your equipment to the campsite." He led them to where he had hidden the sleigh a few feet from the road.

The four adults quickly loaded the tent, sleeping bags, and a few other necessities onto the sleigh while the children looked for footprints left by moose and bear in the soggy trail. Then while Duane and Zip pulled the sleigh toward the campsite, the others followed, carrying more provisions and replacing items that slid off the pine branches.

They soon reached the campsite, and the two men set up the tent while Dorothy Gordon served Laurel, Mrs. Lam-

bert, and the children some hot soup and skillet corn bread
she had prepared to welcome them.

When all had eaten, the campers sat around the bonfire
and told the news of the past two days. The Gordons were
delighted to learn that Paul had arrived and that Joyce was
recovering normally. They had a little news of their own in
that they had found another family of Adventists camping
about two miles away. The Gordons had gone for a walk
along the shore their first evening there and had heard strains
of "Lift Up the Trumpet." They had approached unnoticed
until they joined in on the chorus. The startled Ramsey
family was having evening worship and welcomed them
jubilantly. Although they had seen occasional boaters, they
had spoken to no other beings since fleeing to the wilderness
two weeks earlier.

When at last there came a lull in the conversation, Zip
suggested, "If no one has any more news, I'll let the fire die
down. It seems sensible to keep about the same hours as the
sun out here so as not to waste fuel."

Duane cleared his throat. "Well, there is another item
that might interest you. Here. Look at this." He handed the
marriage license to Zip, who tried to read it by the light of the
glowing coals.

"I can't make it out. What is it?" Duane handed him a
flashlight. "Well! . . . I can't believe it. . . . That's wonderful!"

"What is it, Zip?" Dorothy called.

He passed her the license and the flashlight. She read it
aloud as Jill gasped in amazement. "Congratulations! I'm so
happy for you," Dorothy exclaimed. "How long have you
loved each other?"

"About seven years," Duane answered.

"What?"

"Yes," Mrs. Lambert broke in. "Duane and Laurel

loved each other when she was still in college. But he was not an Adventist then, and Laurel didn't want to marry out of the church. I'm happy things have finally worked out for them."

"That calls for more wood on the fire," Zip said as he rolled on a large oak log. "When will the wedding be?"

"Probably Monday. We'll need some witnesses, and we told Larry and Joyce we'd wait for them," Laurel explained.

"Are you having a religious ceremony?" Dorothy asked.

"No, I'm afraid not. Not unless your new friend, Mr. Ramsey, is a preacher. We'll find a justice of the peace somewhere."

Zip shook his head. "Unfortunately, Virgil Ramsey isn't a preacher. He's a certified public accountant. Can we all come to witness the ceremony?"

"I really wish you could," Laurel reluctantly replied. "But we think it might create too much suspicion for so many to attend. We planned on only Mother, Larry, and Joyce."

"You're probably right," Dorothy sighed. "We'll look after Chucky and Kathy."

While the others enjoyed the heat from the newly added log and discussed the amenities of rustic living, Duane and Laurel took a stroll along the lakeshore. The stars in the moonless sky fragmented in the mirror of the inky water. As they paused to sit on a log, the glow of another campfire on the far shore and the gentle splash of wavelets laving the rocks a few feet away made them feel welcome in their new home.

Laurel's thoughts wandered back to an evening years ago and the ominous, creeping tide of the Pacific Ocean. She shuddered, and Duane, thinking she was cold, placed his arm around her shoulders.

Chapter 30

FUGITIVES

Friday morning Elmer Jenkins picked up the phone on his desk. "Hello. . . . Speaking. . . . Repeat those names, please. . . . Laurel Robertson and Duane Manning. . . . OK. . . . If they show up, I'll notify you."

He jotted down the names on a pad on his desk and went on reading his mail. What he didn't know was that every justice of the peace in the entire state of Maine had received a request to report the couple to the local police if they should come to be married.

Elmer Jenkins had forgotten about the call, when Monday afternoon Duane and Laurel arrived at his office with their three witnesses. He jovially commented that he had never seen a happier looking couple, while inwardly he wondered about the bride's bouquet of wilting daffodils. When Duane handed him the license he glanced at it perfunctorily, then scrutinized it more carefully. He said the names aloud as though trying to place them. Then he looked quizzically at them.

"I just remembered that I must make an important phone call." He sounded flustered. "I'll use another phone. Won't you sit down and wait?" Mr. Jenkins excused himself and closed the door behind him.

"His attitude certainly changed abruptly. I wonder what's up," Duane commented.

"Please be quiet," Larry said. "This phone is probably an extension." He lifted the receiver. His face went white as he listened. Quietly he replaced the receiver.

"Quick. Let's get out of here. The police are on the way. Both of our cars have Massachusetts plates and will be easily spotted. Don't go directly to the campsite."

Duane and Laurel fled in one car while Larry, Joyce, and Mrs. Lambert took the other. They went in opposite directions. The town was small, and soon Duane and Laurel were in the country. "They're sure to catch us"—Laurel sounded desperate—"that town was only a crossroad. Four police cars can cover all roads out of the town." Her face had lost the flush it had had when she entered the justice's office. Now it was ashen.

"You pray, and I'll drive," he said grimly. Suddenly he swung the car into a driveway.

"What are you doing?" she asked in alarm.

"Didn't you see that sign?"

"What sign?"

" 'White's Antiques.' It will get the car off the highway. I want you to examine everything in great detail and spend as much time looking as you can."

"OK. I'll try. I'm not experienced at putting on an act, though."

The driveway was long and curving as it climbed up to the house perched on a little hill. They parked the car by a clump of bushes that completely obscured it from the road. Duane stepped around the car to open Laurel's door, and he heard a police siren in the distance. "Wonder whom they could be after?" he said with a grin.

That he could smile at such a time gave her new confidence, and her knees felt a little steadier.

Once inside she tried to appear interested in antiques, but her acting ability was poor, and she didn't seem to know what kind of questions to ask.

Duane came to the rescue as he told the little shop owner, "We aren't experienced collectors. Our new home has kind of a rustic atmosphere, and we're just developing an interest in antiques. Why don't you describe each item for us and tell us what's unique about it?"

Mrs. White glowed and waxed enthusiastic over each of her treasures. After about an hour she said, "I see you have a Massachusetts tag. Are you on vacation?"

"No. We've recently moved to Maine," Laurel replied.

"Oh, do you live near here?"

"It's a few miles north."

"What town?"

"It's out in the country a ways."

"Some folks are putting up lovely homes out there in the wilderness. I'd be pretty scared, myself."

"Safest place I know," Laurel said. Then she added quickly, "It's not only large cities that are unsafe these days. Even small towns have plenty of crime."

"That's the truth. Guess God has about deserted us. Is there anything you folk have found here that you'd like?"

"There's a lot we would like," Duane answered. "But we'll have to purchase our antiques gradually. . . . Is there anything you want, Sue?"

Laurel looked startled at hearing her middle name, but recovered quickly. "I believe we could use that pair of iron candlesticks. What do you think, Jim?"

"How much are they?" he asked Mrs. White.

"I've had them a long time." She smiled. "I'll let you have them cheap—just fifteen dollars. Then maybe you'll come back again."

"OK. We'll take them," he decided. "You wouldn't happen to have any candles, would you?"

"Yes. I keep bayberry candles on hand—they're the ones

I get the most requests for. How many would you like?"

"We'll take four."

When they had paid and left, Laurel whispered, "We're going to have to be careful how we spend those few dollars we brought along for our honeymoon. What do you think we should do now?"

"I think we should get married."

She looked at him. "How?"

"Obviously all the justices of the peace throughout the state will be on the lookout for us. I didn't realize they were keeping Adventists under such tight surveillance. How about trying a preacher?"

"We can try. But let's get a little farther from where we made our first attempt."

At dusk they arrived at Bingham, a picturesque little town on the Kennebec River. From several churches she selected a small white one with truncated steeple that was floodlighted. A sign in front of the church identified it as Congregational and gave the name of the pastor. They hoped the spacious home beside the church was the parsonage. Duane parked the car. Carefully Laurel gathered up the daffodils scattered over the back seat, and together they approached the front door. After they rang the bell, a silver-haired man appeared.

"Good evening. Are you Pastor Kleppinger?"

"I am. Come in. What can I do for you?"

"We have just moved to this area and wish to be married," Duane explained.

"Congratulations. Do you plan a church wedding?"

Duane shook his head. "No. We cannot afford one. We thought maybe we could be married in your home."

"I see." The minister thought a moment. "You wish a small wedding. When would this take place?"

"How about tonight?"

"Tonight!" His face mirrored his surprise. "Have you given this sufficient thought?"

Laurel and Duane nodded.

"How long have you known each other?"

"Seven years."

"Hm-m. Well, I would think that would be long enough. Do you have a license?"

Duane produced the license, which Kleppinger studied.

"Don't you have a home church?"

"As I explained, we've just moved here and haven't gotten established yet." Duane swallowed nervously.

"It is customary for couples to come with witnesses. You must have some acquaintances you could bring."

"Unfortunately our friends and relatives couldn't come with us. Could your family perhaps be present?" He prayed the minister would not become suspicious.

"Well, my children are grown and married, but my wife might be willing. And I think our organist is practicing in the church. Maybe I could call on her."

A few minutes elapsed while Pastor Kleppinger rounded up his wife and the organist. He returned muttering about the irregularity, but as he had no grounds for refusal, he proceeded with the ceremony. Afterward Duane paid him, and they left just one hour after having entered his home.

With one hand Laurel held Duane's arm and clutched her daffodils in the other. As they went down the steps she mused, "Too bad there's no one here to catch the bouquet."

He placed his hand on hers and said, "Well, Mrs. Manning, how about getting a good meal at a restaurant and looking for a comfortable motel?"

His bride laughed. "After five nights in a sleeping bag on the tent floor, a bed would be most welcome. Great idea."

They drove around town and noted Riverside Lodge on the bank of the Kennebec. Duane discovered they had vacancies but no dining room. Next they came to Bingham Motor Inn. "Shall I try here?"

"We'd still need to find a place to eat. And since the tourist season hasn't begun, they don't appear to have many guests. I'd feel less conspicuous in a busier place," Laurel replied.

"We can go to Skowhegan. That should be large enough for us to lose ourselves."

At Skowhegan they entered Whittemore's Restaurant, which also doubled as the Greyhound bus station. The waitress ushered them to a booth in the front corner. The rush hour was over, but the room was nearly filled with diners.

As they waited to place their order, Laurel's eye caught a headline in the newspaper a man at an adjacent table was reading. Suddenly her appetite left her. "Duane, go buy a paper, please," she whispered.

"Can't we order first?"

"No. It's urgent."

Returning to the table with the Skowhegan paper, he, too, saw the headline. "Bride and Groom Sought in Local Manhunt." They laid the paper on the table and read silently:

"The statewide hunt for subversives Duane Manning and Laurel Robertson has narrowed on the area around Monson, where earlier today they presented themselves to Justice of the Peace Elmer Jenkins to be married. While he was notifying the police, they escaped. The groom is approximately thirty years old, the bride a little younger. The couple is not thought to be armed. A reward is offered for information leading to their arrest."

"Let's leave," she whispered.

"I think we're as safe here as anywhere. Anyway, I'm starved. I have no energy to flee."

Just then a waitress arrived to take their order. He ordered a full meal. Laurel ordered only a salad in spite of his insistence she should get more. "You'll be sorry," he said when the waitress had left. "We may have to go a long time on the strength of this meal."

"I know," she whispered. "I'm weak already. But I've completely lost my appetite. I guess I'm just a coward. I surely hope Mother and Larry and Joyce got home for the sake of the children, especially baby Paul."

"So do I. I don't believe the police were looking for them. It was probably our marriage license that tipped them off on us."

"What are we going to do with the car?"

He grimaced. "I don't know. We could take a chance on driving it out of here, or we could abandon it. I really think we should get out of town."

"So do I."

Duane thought a moment. "I noticed a Greyhound bus sign outside. Suppose you go to Waterville by bus while I try to drive down."

She clutched his hand. "Can't we go together?"

"You'll be safer on the bus, and I may not arouse suspicion if I'm alone. I'll try to think of someway to drive down without getting caught."

"Please don't take chances." She glanced over her shoulder. "If you see any police around, forget the car and come by bus."

"I will." He smiled and squeezed her hand. "I doubt that they have spotted the car yet. The parking lot is full."

Just then a bus rolled up and stopped in front of the restaurant. Duane noticed it was headed for Portland. "If you're through eating, you may as well take this bus. No telling when the next one will come."

Laurel's face showed her agony. "If you insist. I'll wait for you at the Waterville station. But please . . . please be careful." She blinked back hot tears she hoped no one noticed, fought the almost overwhelming desire to throw her arms around him and sob on his shoulder.

He hurried to the car for Laurel's suitcase. Noticing her daffodils on the dashboard, he picked them up, then handed the suitcase to the driver and the flowers to Laurel. Then he put his arm around her and started to kiss her.

"Please don't. Not here. We don't want to look like newlyweds."

"OK. Love you anyway. Take care."

He waved till the bus disappeared around the bend.

Chapter 31

WEDDING NIGHT

The bus slowed, and Laurel noticed a brightly illumi-
nated Holiday Inn on the left. Just ahead on the right was Elm
Plaza, which was nearly deserted, as all shops had closed for
the night. The bus turned in behind the plaza shops and
stopped at what appeared to be the back door of one of them.

"Waterville," the driver called.

Noticing the small, dimly lit sign identifying the terminal, she hoped her stay there would be brief. She picked up
her wilted daffodils and got off. Tenderly she laid the flowers
in the wire trash receptacle outside the station, waited for her
suitcase, and then entered the waiting room, where three
passengers glumly sat along the wall, awaiting the 11:30 bus
to Bangor. After it left, Laurel had the waiting room all to
herself for a short time. Even the ticket office was closed.
Resting her head against the wall, she hoped to get some
sleep, but just as she started to doze, a fat drunk staggered in.
He sat down beside her.

"Hi, beautiful. What's a nice chick like you doin' here?"

"I'm waiting for my husband," she said politely.

"Too bad. Hope ya won't think I'm rude if I go to
sleep."

She managed to shake her head, then ask him, "When is
your bus coming?"

"It ain't never comin'. My old woman's got me locked

out, so I'll hafta sleep here tonight. Don't let my snorin'
disturb ya none.''

In minutes his snoring and gaping jaw attested to the fact
that he was truly asleep. He leaned heavily against Laurel.
The combined scent of sweat and alcohol revolted her, and
she decided to abandon her seat and choose another at the end
of the row. As she attempted to ease out of her chair without
waking the drunk, his head lost the support of her shoulder
and flopped sideways in a jerk that awakened him momentarily. He looked around with bleary eyes, but seconds later the
lids drooped shut again.

Laurel sat down at the end of the short row of seats and
closed her eyes. She wanted to sleep, but she kept worrying
about Duane. Where was he? Had the police spotted the car?
What if they had caught him? ''Dear Father in heaven,'' she
prayed. ''Please look after Duane. Help him to escape with
the car and meet me soon if it can be Your will. Don't let him
get hurt. Give us both wisdom and keep us true to You,
and . . .''

The next thing she realized was that the back of her neck
was stiff and that she heard men talking. Opening her eyes,
she saw two policemen trying to awaken the drunk. She
straightened herself in her chair and looked at her watch. It
showed two o'clock.

''Come on, Bill,'' one of the men said. ''You can't spend
the night here. Shall we take you home or down to the
station?''

Bill didn't seem to hear; so they repeated the question
more loudly.

''Wot ya say?'' he mumbled. His eyes opened to slits.

''You can't stay here. Do you want to go home?''

''Naw. Lemme alone. Can't ya see I'm jus' sleepin'?''

''Come on down to the station. We'll give you a bed
down there.''

The two policemen helped him to his feet and ushered him out to the wagon. Then one returned and walked over to Laurel. "There are no more buses for three hours. I suggest you find a safer place to wait. Can we take you somewhere?"

She shook her head. "No, thank you. I'm supposed to meet my husband here, but I don't know just when."

"Which bus is he coming on?"

"I'm really not sure. He may be driving."

"Could we see your identification card?"

Laurel knew she had thrown her card into the trash can as she left Whittemore's Restaurant. Nevertheless, she went through the motions of looking. "I don't seem to be able to find it."

"You know, I'm sure, that it is a misdemeanor to be without your card. I should arrest you. However, this time I'll let it pass. What's your name?"

"Sue Lambert."

"Lucky your last name isn't Robertson or Manning."

Laurel felt her face flushing. "Why?" she questioned.

"I thought you might be the bride who's hiding somewhere around here. One of those Advent subversives. Hardly have time to worry about the real criminals anymore."

She heard the police wagon drive off. Too weary to worry, she soon fell fast asleep.

At five o'clock a bus arrived from Bangor. Two passengers got off and three boarded. In a few minutes the station was nearly deserted again.

The two policemen returned at six o'clock. "I see you're still here," said the one who had talked with her earlier. "We're going off duty now. Hope your husband comes soon."

An hour later the ticket agent arrived and opened the window. "You're mighty early," he said to Laurel. "Are you waiting to buy a ticket?''

"No. I'm waiting for my husband."

He glanced at his watch. "There's a bus due in at 7:30."
Grabbing a janitor broom, he began to rid the waiting room of
the previous day's accumulation of candy wrappers, cigarette
stubs, and chewed gum.

"Where does it come from?"

"Augusta."

"When does the bus arrive from Skowhegan?"

"Generally a few minutes after eight."

Laurel took her suitcase to the ladies' room, where she
washed her face, brushed her teeth, and combed her hair.
Feeling considerably refreshed, she realized that she was
hungry. Not wanting to be away when the bus from Skowhegan arrived, she investigated the station's vending machines
and decided upon a bag of peanuts. A few minutes later she
bought a second bag. Then she took her suitcase outside and
sat on it while watching for the bus.

At 8:15 it pulled in. Eagerly Laurel watched as six
passengers disembarked. Duane was not among them. Then
through the tinted windows she saw a man arise in the rear
and make his way down the aisle. He was about her husband's build and size, and her hope renewed. But when he
got to the door she was again disappointed. A lump formed in
her throat, and she blinked back tears.

She took a small photo from her purse and looked at it
tenderly. Then she went inside and handed it to the ticket
agent. "If this man asks for his wife, please tell him I've gone
out to eat. Have him wait for me. By the way, when is the
next bus from Skowhegan due?"

"11:30."

She went looking for someplace where she could get
breakfast. The plaza had a restaurant, but it opened for
business at 9:30. Then she remembered the Holiday Inn the

bus had passed when it turned off the interstate.

Before selecting a table Laurel took her suitcase to the ladies' room and changed from her wedding suit to a casual dress. She exchanged her high heels for comfortable walking shoes. After enjoying a warm meal she decided to see whether she could get a room where she could leave her suitcase and stretch out on a bed while waiting for Duane. She inquired at the desk.

"I believe we have one that somebody just left," the clerk replied. "One moment, please, while I check whether it is ready. . . . Yes, we have one available."

"Oh, good. I'll take it."

"May I see your identification card, please?"

"I don't have it with me."

The woman frowned. "Well, I'm sorry, but we have the strictest orders not to register anyone without an ID card. If you go to the police station, they can probably issue you a replacement."

"I see. Thank you anyway."

Laurel returned to the bus terminal, half expecting that her husband would be waiting when she entered. Eagerly she scanned the room. No Duane.

"Haven't seen anything of your man," the agent called. "Maybe he'll be on the next bus."

"Maybe so," she answered wearily.

The 11:30 bus came and went, as did the 2:10. Still no Duane. She was really worried. A passenger who boarded the 2:10 bus had left his copy of the Waterville *Sentinel* in the terminal. Laurel picked it up and went through the motions of reading, though few of the words penetrated her consciousness. As she turned to page four a name leaped out at her: "Manning Captured in Hinckley." With sinking heart she read:

"Duane Manning, the groom who was sought yesterday

in the Monson area, was found driving south on Highway 201 near Hinckley this morning about two o'clock. His bride was not with him, and he refused to give any information concerning her whereabouts. Rev. Kleppinger, of the First Congregational Church in Bingham, reports marrying them last evening. Manning is being held in the Somerset County jail. He and his bride, formerly Laurel Robertson, are both subversives.''

As Laurel read the statement her face turned pale. She folded the newspaper and laid it on the seat. Several minutes passed before her knees would support her, but then she went to the ticket window. ''I won't be waiting any longer. May I have the photo back, please?''

''Surely. What shall I tell him if he comes?''

''I don't think he'll be coming.''

Chapter 32

SOLITARY

"Dearest husband,

"I learned today from the newspaper about your capture. I cannot begin to describe the grief I feel. Seven years of waiting—for this! Will we ever meet again on this earth?

"Don't worry about me. I'll find my way back somehow. The others will join me in praying for your release. Remember Peter's experience when imprisoned by Herod!

"Whatever happens, don't compromise your faith. They will do all they can to get you to renounce your convictions. Remember that our few remaining days, weeks, or months on this earth are as nothing compared to eternity. Be brave! How I wish I could be with you!

"I can't write more now, as my bus is leaving in a few minutes, and I want to mail this in Skowhegan.

"Remember that I love you, and God loves you. I'll leave you in His hands.

"Good-bye, my dearest,
"Laurel"

The superintendent of the prison, Bruce Lawson, chuckled as he finished reading the letter aloud to Rocky, one of the prison guards. "Well, what do you think? Shall we cheer his stupid little heart with this letter?"

"Definitely not. Let him continue to worry about whether she got caught too."

A few seconds later the superintendent's face lit up with fiendish glee. "Say! I have a wonderful idea. Remember Funka, the handwriting expert?" Rocky nodded. "I saw him demonstrate his skill at forgery once. Let's turn the letter over to him and get him to create us one in her handwriting."

It was early Friday evening when Rocky came to Duane's cell. "Here's a letter for you," he said as he passed an envelope through the bars. Duane glanced at the handwriting, then eagerly tore it open.

"Dearest husband,

"I learned today about your capture. I cannot begin to describe the grief I feel. Seven years of waiting—for this!

"Don't worry about me. I'm living in a comfortable four-room apartment in Bingham. The car was returned to me by the police.

"You will marvel at what I'm going to say. Please try to understand. I was picked up by the police soon after we parted. I was taken to the judge who threatened to send me to jail and ultimately to the electric chair unless I chose to sign a simple statement to the effect that I would cooperate to the extent of honoring Sunday rather than Saturday. So I signed the statement they had prepared.

"God knows my signature meant nothing. I believe in the Sabbath as strongly as ever and plan to keep it in the privacy of my apartment. I'll go to church on Sunday to please them. I've always considered suicide a transgression of the commandment 'Thou shalt not kill.' My signature merely kept me from committing suicide.

"I would urge you to follow my example. You would then no doubt be released, and you could join me here in Bingham. I am so lonely for you. At night I toss and toss and

long to find you in my arms. Please come to me.
"All my love,
"Laurel"

"I can't believe it. It just can't be true," he told himself.
"After all Laurel has given up for her faith, she wouldn't let
the threat of death reverse her stand. It doesn't make sense.
Someone else must have written this. But yet . . ." He read
the letter again. "That's her handwriting all right."

Duane tore the letter into tiny pieces, dropped it into the
toilet in his cell, and flushed it away. "Good-bye, Laurel.
Let—let me remember you as I knew you."

He slept little that night. When his breakfast came in the
morning he didn't feel like eating it. He offered it to Max in
the next cell, who made a ritual of grumbling loudly over the
scant prison fare each time they brought his tray. Duane had
never seen Max, because a wall separated their cells, but he
pictured him as swarthy and obese. The slim arm covered
with blond hair that reached out for the food surprised Duane.

"Sure you can't eat this?" Max sounded less gruff than
usual.

"I'm sure."

He wondered what crime had brought Max to prison, and
how many prisoners there were in the Somerset County jail.
All he knew was that he was on the second floor.

His mind wandered to the campers. Remembering it was
Sabbath, he expected that Mrs. Lambert, Larry and Joyce,
and the Gordons were having Sabbath School by the lake.
Would the Ramseys join them? Mrs. Lambert would be
crushed if she knew of Laurel's defection. She would be
unable to understand her daughter's sudden change.

A baritone voice at the end of the corridor started singing,
"A Mighty Fortress Is Our God." After the first phrase a
second more cultivated voice joined it. The second voice

seemed to be only a cell removed from Duane, who timo-
rously joined in on the third stanza:

> "And though this world, with devils filled,
>   Should threaten to undo us,
>   We will not fear, for God hath willed
>   His truth to triumph through us."

At the end of the stanza the baritone boomed out, "Do we
have a visitor for Sabbath School or a new member?"

"A new member," Duane replied.

"Welcome. So glad you're on time. My name is Dwight.
What's yours?"

"Duane."

"How long have you been here?"

"Since Tuesday."

"Sorry you got caught, but we're happy for company.
Meet Keith, who arrived Sunday."

"Hi, Duane. Where are you from?" a new voice said.

"Until recently, Worcester, Massachusetts. Had less
than a week of camping in Maine."

"We'll let you choose the next song, Duane," Dwight
called.

"How about . . . 'Lift Up the Trumpet'?"

"Good selection."

The three sang fervently all four stanzas, happily noting
that a few of the other prisoners came in rather uncertainly on
the chorus. After a third song, Rocky entered the corridor.

"Knock it off, men," he shouted. "You're disturbing
the peace."

"So arrest them," somebody in a nearby cell quipped.

The fellowship of other Adventists did much for Duane's
spirits, though he couldn't get his wife's letter out of his
mind. He lay on his bunk staring at the gray ceiling and trying

to figure it all out. Somehow he couldn't imagine her relaxing with the children in a comfortable apartment. Instead, he could only picture her back in the kitchen at Three Elms, gathering firewood by the lake, or holding her daffodils as she boarded the bus in front of Whittemore's Restaurant less than a week before. When he remembered he hadn't been able to kiss her good-bye, a hot tear ran from the corner of his eye down into his ear.

Just then Rocky appeared in front of his cell. "Would you like something?" he asked pleasantly.

"For instance?"

"I have some magazines you might enjoy. Or perhaps you'd like to write a letter. Here's a pen and some stationery."

Duane glanced at the pornographic covers on the magazines. "I'd like to read the Bible I had in my suitcase. Could you get it for me?"

The guard scowled. "I'm not sure that's possible. I'll check, but it may take several days. Wouldn't you like to write a letter?"

"Possibly. You may leave the stationery."

When Rocky left, Duane picked up the pen and began, "Dear Laurel, . . ." Ten minutes later the page still had only those two words. He lay down again to stare at the ceiling. The close of her letter kept crying out to him: "I am so lonely for you. At night I toss and toss and long to find you in my arms. Please come to me."

Had she really sold out? he wondered. Or was the signature as meaningless as she suggested? At times Duane had wondered about the early Christians who fearlessly faced the stake or the lions rather than place a pinch of incense before an idol. Was God interested in the condition of the heart or in some outward symbol? "Maybe she's right," he told himself. "I hope she is. As for me, I can't afford to take the chance." Kneeling beside his bunk, he prayed to God for strength to follow his convictions.

The next morning a young minister, Pastor Raymond, came to hold a worship service. The guards escorted the prisoners one by one from their cells to the chapel. For the first time Duane saw his fellow inmates. The twelve men from the second floor were kept separate from the larger first-floor group. Duane wondered which were Dwight, Keith, and Max. He thought he recognized Max's arm as belonging to a bushy blond about thirty years of age.

It was Pastor Raymond's first visit. He opened the service by introducing himself and asking each inmate to give his first name. Duane had identified Max correctly. He was quite surprised to learn that Dwight's baritone belonged to a slightly built man of about sixty with thin gray hair. Keith appeared to be about thirty-five and had the build of a football player. Duane hadn't seen such a well-fed Adventist for a long time.

The short service consisted of read prayers, a scripture, and a brief sermon. Before the benediction the minister inquired whether anyone had a request. Duane asked if the prison furnished Bibles to those inmates desiring them. Pastor Raymond asked how many would like a Bible. Fourteen men, including the three Adventists, raised their hands. The minister agreed to try to procure them. Superintendent Lawson replied that they discouraged placing books in cells, because in the past, inmates had used them to clog the plumbing. The minister asked whether there was a library where prisoners could come to read. Lawson explained that the prison was too small for such a luxury.

The guards returned the second-floor prisoners to their cells one at a time, starting at the end of the corridor. Dwight was the first to go. Duane found that an empty cell was between him and Keith.

When they were back in the cells Duane called, "Keith, aren't you a recent convert?"

"Yes. What made you think so?"

"You look so well fed."

"So that's it!" Keith chuckled. "I weighed 260 pounds six months ago when I was baptized. Now I'm down to 215, and I could hold out quite a while longer. Of course, being in here you don't have to wonder where your next meal is coming from."

"How did you get caught?"

"My wife is not an Adventist. She felt disgraced when I joined the church. Then when I lost my job she sued for divorce on grounds of my religion. The judge granted the divorce and sent me here."

Both were silent for a moment. "What type of work did you do?"

"I was a brick mason."

"How long did you keep your job after you joined the church?"

"About a month. When I didn't show up for work four Saturdays in a row, the boss began to suspect it wasn't illness. He asked why I had been taking Saturdays off, and I told him the truth."

"How did you manage after that?"

Keith shrugged to himself. "I had always earned good wages and had never seen any need to save anything. So with no income and nothing in the bank, the wife and kids had to go on welfare. Of course I wasn't eligible, but for a while Martha had enough pity to share the groceries with me. Then one day while I was out on an errand she took the kids away with her and left a note saying not to look for any of them to return."

Duane did not know what to say for a moment. "I—I'm sorry. Have you seen them since?"

Emotion choked Keith's voice. "No, I haven't. Can't really say that I miss Martha too much, but—but Jimmy was just developing into a good ball fielder, and we used to enjoy practicing together on Sundays. And little Missy would come running to my arms each evening, squealing, 'Hi, Daddy.' " He lapsed into silence, then clearing his throat, continued, "Do you have a family?"

"In a way. I acquired a wife and two children a few hours before I was captured."

"You don't mean it! I assume your wife is an Adventist."

"I really don't know. I mean, she was. A most devout one. Seemingly. Then Friday night they gave me a letter from her saying she'd given it up. I just can't understand it."

Keith thought a moment. "Are you sure the letter was from her? You know the authorities will do anything to change your mind."

"I don't know. I've known her seven years and always thought her to be completely dedicated to her church. If she can't hold out, what hope is there for a recent convert like me?"

"Don't think things like that. The length of time we've spent in the church is not important. Our strength comes from God. We don't dare let our attachment to loved ones cut off our connection with Heaven."

"I suppose you're right," Duane soberly agreed.

"We all need encouragement at times. We're still too human."

Rocky appeared in the corridor in front of Duane's cell. "Superintendent Lawson wants to talk with you." He unlocked the cell and motioned for Duane to precede him down the hall.

Bruce Lawson loomed behind his huge walnut desk. As Duane and Rocky entered the room he tilted back in his swivel chair and interlaced his fingers behind his head.

"Well, Mr. Manning. I have had you brought here so I could deliver a message. Your wife keeps calling us, wondering whether you're persisting in your stubborn resistance, or whether you have considered her request and are ready to cooperate with the government."

Duane bit his lip, then answered, "You may tell her for me that I must obey God rather than man. I hope she will reconsider and ask God for courage."

Lawson frowned. "You seem to feel that you're on God's side and the rest of us are not. That seems rather unlikely. Doesn't the Bible command Christians to submit to the powers ordained of God?"

"Hitler's favorite Bible passage—and the one he liked to quote."

The superintendent rose angrily from his chair. "What—what are you talking about?"

"The Bible passage you're alluding to. Someone once told me that Hitler constantly repeated it during his struggles with the German churches. And anyway, those same Christians that Paul addressed his letter to did not hesitate to become martyrs when the claims of the emperor of Rome demanded an allegiance belonging only to God."

The official sneered. "Do you wish me to tell your wife that you're determined to become a martyr?"

Swallowing hard, Duane replied, "You—you may tell her I am determined to remain true to God's commandments."

Lawson turned away from him. "Very well. You have only a few days left to change your mind. Probably you could think more clearly if you didn't have the other prisoners to distract you. Rocky, take this man to solitary."

Twisting his arm, the guard led him down to a basement cell with one tiny window in the door, which admitted only a view of the boiler and oil tank. The cell was musty. The twenty-five-watt light bulb hanging from a short cord attached to the ceiling revealed evidence that rats were frequent visitors to the cell.

When Keith asked Rocky late that evening where Duane was, he answered that the prisoner had signed a statement renouncing his faith and had been released. Keith felt sick at heart. Why hadn't he tried to encourage the man more?

Chapter 33

LAKESIDE

After dropping her letter in the slot at the post office, Laurel hurried back to the bus station. The Rockwood bus was loading. She showed her ticket to the driver. "Monson," he read aloud and nodded her aboard.

Taking a seat in the rear of the bus, she placed the ticket in her almost empty change purse. She hoped Joyce would like the one-piece snowsuit with bunny ears she was bringing for Paul, bought on sale at Elm Plaza. He needed something like it for the chilly nights in the tent, but she felt foolish for having spent the money before buying her bus ticket.

Monson was a long way from her destination, but her funds had permitted her to go only that far. How she would cover the remaining fifty miles she didn't know. She was too tired to care. Her concern for Chucky and Kathy and her anxiety about whether her mother, Joyce, and Larry had been able to return to camp were incentive enough to impel her to walk if need be.

The sun was setting when the bus began to pull out of the station. Laurel caught a glimpse of one faded daffodil protruding from the wire trash receptacle by the station door. She felt too empty for tears.

Soon she dozed. The bus rumbled along, stopping frequently to take on or discharge passengers. After about an hour and a quarter the driver called out, "Monson." Laurel was sound asleep. Five passengers got off, and the bus went on its way again.

Eventually she awoke. She looked out of the window and saw moonlight reflecting on a large body of water. The road seemed to be following the shore. Not recalling any lake that size between Waterville and Monson, she became uneasy. Flipping on the reading light, she glanced at her watch. Almost 9:30. She knew she must have passed Monson during her nap.

Noticing a man reading across the aisle, she called timidly, "Pardon me, sir." He didn't look up, so she tried again, a little more loudly. When the man stared her way, she asked, "Can you tell me what our next stop will be?"

"Rockwood," he replied gruffly, then was again engrossed in his reading.

Silently she said another thank You to God for bringing her that much closer to her destination.

At Rockwood she got off at the service station that served as bus terminal. Placing her suitcase on the station floor, she sat on it and studied the wall map, trying to decide whether to follow the dirt paper-company road or the Brassua Lake shoreline. Finally she concluded that walking along the road carrying a suitcase would look too suspicious. Since following the shore would be hazardous at night, she decided to wait till morning.

"Lady, we're closing at ten o'clock," the elderly station attendant said. "Did you need to use the phone?"

"No, thank you."

He shuffled toward the door. "Is someone coming for you?"

"No."

"Which way are you heading?"

"North."

"Sorry." The old man began flipping off lights. "I'm

going west. There's a hotel just down the road off to your left." He motioned in the direction of Moosehead Motor Inn.

Laurel went out into the twenty-five-degree night. The attendant finished switching off the lights of the station and locked the door, got in his car, and drove off.

Laurel noticed two cars parked in front of the repair area. She tried the doors of the newer car and found them locked. The driver's door of the other one was unlocked, though. Letting herself in, she curled up on the back seat, using her coat for a blanket. Then she thanked God for a place to spend the night and asked for His protection.

The next thing Laurel knew, the first rays of the sun blushed the eastern sky. She looked at her watch and decided to start her journey immediately. Spotting a peanut vending machine, she used her last change on nourishment to sustain her for the ten-mile hike. Since she had eaten only breakfast the day before, she was feeling weak from hunger. The peanuts helped a bit.

Rockwood was on Moosehead Lake just below where the Moose River connected it with Brassua Lake. Laurel planned to stay by the road till it crossed the river. Her suitcase was small, and the occupants of the few cars she encountered didn't seem to pay any attention to her. Once across the river, she left the road and followed the river till it became Brassua Lake. Walking along the lakeshore wasn't always easy. Patches of snow still lingered in more shadowy places, and her bootless feet became wet and numb from cold. The shore was sometimes sandy, sometimes swampy. Tangled thickets that at times came to the water's edge made the detours around the swamps difficult. Had it been a couple months later, she would have welcomed the berries the thickets provided.

Although she saw animal tracks on the shore, moose

droppings, porcupine damage to the trees, and results of beaver activity, only squirrels, chipmunks, and birds welcomed her to their forest. By ten o'clock the temperature had risen sufficiently that her feet no longer ached from cold. She had been traveling about four hours and wondered how much farther she had to go. Her steps became slower and slower as her weakness and hunger increased. Occasionally she would find evidences of campers who had left empty cans and bottles or the charred remains of a fire. At one such campsite she found a bag containing a few soggy potato chips, which she eagerly devoured, and half a can of grape soda which had long ago lost its fizz.

The summer cottages she passed all appeared empty. Turning a bend, she saw a camping trailer and wondered whether it could belong to the Ramseys. Laurel had never asked the Gordons which direction the Ramseys' site was from theirs, so she sat down on her suitcase to watch. She remembered that the Ramseys had two children around the ages of Chucky and Kathy.

The trailer rested on a stump about three hundred feet away. It was small but could sleep four persons adequately. At least it was better protection from the weather than the tents at her site. Of course, the men had hoped to construct better shelters. She wondered whether they had started. If Zip was the only man there, it would take some time. What if Larry, Joyce, and her mother had not made it back safely? Who would take care of a week-old baby?

Laurel watched the trailer a long time before she saw the door open and a five- or six-year-old boy emerge. He ran to the water's edge and began trying to skip flat pebbles on the lake. Searching for more pebbles, he darted here and there, always approaching closer to where Laurel sat on her suitcase. When he was about fifty feet away, he spied her and froze with pebble in hand and mouth open.

"Don't be afraid," Laurel called. "Is your last name Ramsey?"

He nodded.

"I'm a friend. I live in the next campsite. Is your mother home?"

Another nod.

Laurel picked up her suitcase and started walking toward the trailer, followed by the boy. "I'd like to meet your mother."

"You said you were a friend," he replied suspiciously.

Mrs. Ramsey saw them and came to the door of the trailer, where she watched apprehensively.

"I'm Laurel Robertson . . . er, I mean Mrs. Manning. I believe you've met the Gordons. We share the same campsite."

The woman became all smiles. "Oh, of course. Do come in." An attractive woman about Laurel's age with black hair pulled back tightly in a bun, she created the impression of being most efficient. "Won't you sit down? I'm happy to have some company. My name is Karen."

Glad to rest, Laurel told briefly of her experiences of the past two days and asked whether the others had made it back safely.

"I really don't know. We keep so busy scrounging for food we don't have time to be neighborly. Jeff, do you know how our friends in the tents are doing?"

"Sure, Mom. Yesterday the old lady was sitting outside holding the baby. There were two men trying to build something."

Laurel's face lit up. Knowing they had returned safely made her willing to accept Karen's offer of a bowl of steaming rice and a salad of dandelion greens. In a few minutes she went on her way. The two miles was easy walking along a sandy shore. As she neared her campsite she heard Chucky and Kathy making Indianlike whoops. Then she saw them darting among the trees, blue-jay feathers attached to their hair.

When Chucky saw her he yelled to Kathy, "White woman," and each child attempted to hide behind the nearest tree. Laurel approached the tree where Chucky was partially concealed. She set down her suitcase.

"I wonder if I can find an Indian behind this tree," she said as her arms encircled it and the small boy on the other side.

Chapter 34

BACKPACKING

For three days Duane saw no one but Rocky, who brought him a few hard rolls and a jug of water once a day. Duane had to guard the food constantly from an aggressive rat. On the third day the superintendent again summoned Duane to his office. He was unshaven. The prison clothes he had been wearing night and day reeked of sweat and odors from the unemptied slop jar.

The guard ushered him into the presence of Superintendent Lawson and Pastor Raymond. Bruce Lawson pointed to a chair. "Sit down."

"Duane, we are grieved that you are having to suffer for your conscience' sake," the minister began quietly. "The United States is a Christian nation, and those in authority don't wish to persecute anyone. I brought you the Bible you requested. I would like to see you prove from the New Testament that Saturday is the Sabbath."

An hour later Pastor Raymond shook his head. "I see your mind is closed," he said sadly. "Do you realize the death decree for all Adventists takes effect one week from yesterday?"

Duane nodded.

"Well, you have until midnight of the fourteenth to reconsider. God have mercy on you."

Slowly the minister rose and turned his back on him.

Superintendent Lawson motioned for Rocky to take Duane back to solitary.

The Sabbath before the date of the death decree the Ramseys joined the Gordons, the Lamberts, and Laurel in a day of fasting and prayer. Though they prayed for Sabbathkeepers throughout the world, they pleaded primarily for Duane's deliverance. The children participated too. When Kathy's turn came, she said, "Dear God, take care of everybody who loves You, and don't let anything bad happen to my mommy and daddy. Help them to find me soon. Amen."

Laurel put her arm around the child, whose slight form shook with grief. The girl had never talked about her parents since the day after Duane had found her. The adults assumed that the intervening months had largely erased the tragic memory. Taking a cue from the child's request, each prayed for a speedy reunion of Kathy's family.

That night as Laurel lay in her sleeping bag on the floor of the tent she could not sleep for worrying about Duane. She recalled the story of Leonore's heroic rescue of her doomed husband in Beethoven's opera *Fidelio*. "If only I could work out some way just to see and encourage him," she told herself. But after hours of trying, she still had not thought of a workable plan. When eventually she accepted the fact she would have to leave him in God's hands, she fell asleep.

Monday morning Larry remarked that he was concerned about little Paul, whose cries were weak and who seemed listless. The baby did not appear to be regaining the weight lost the few days before Joyce's milk began to come, and his skin seemed more wrinkled than ever.

Joyce worried that her impoverished diet affected the supply and quality of her milk, so she begged Larry to take the car to the nearest town in hopes of securing some powdered formula and bottles for Paul. Her husband agreed to go, walking the mile and a half to the car that they had not driven for two weeks since the ill-fated marriage attempt.

When he got to the car it wouldn't start. Turning on the ignition produced no sound at all. Raising the hood, he discovered the battery missing. Then he walked around the car and observed that the back tires were slashed and the license plate was gone. When he checked the Gordon truck parked nearby he found it had met a similar fate. He felt trapped.

As he walked back to camp he wondered who might have done the damage. At first he could not think of any visitors, then remembered two men in a rowboat near the campsite on Sabbath. The campers were singing and had not noticed the boat till it was about five hundred feet away. Could the men have recognized the songs as Adventist hymns?

Larry preferred not to alarm the others, but he didn't know how to explain his return without the formula. The news of the misfortune spread quickly. While they debated whether to move to another location, Chucky ran in with news that a helicopter was hovering overhead. Of course, the noise it made amply announced the fact anyway.

Jill volunteered to notify the Ramseys that they were leaving as the others scrambled to pack up what supplies they could carry. They agreed to head north around the lake and westward toward Boundary Bald Mountain.

Within two hours they were on their way, backpacks loaded. Baby Paul rode papoose style on Larry's back. Larry carried the camping stove; Zip a lantern and extra fuel; the women, cooking utensils filled with food (except for Joyce, who had two bags for soiled and clean diapers); and the children, smaller necessities such as matches, a scout knife, a compass, and a flashlight.

Progress was slow, and it was nearly dark when they reached the northern tip of Brassua Lake. They decided to seek shelter and concealment in the thick forest that began a few feet from the shoreline. It was much darker in the forest than along the shore.

"Shall I light the lantern?" Zip asked.

"I don't think we should," Larry replied. "There's enough light to prepare our sleeping bags. Let's get our rest and leave at daybreak."

"But, Mommy, I don't want to go to bed." Chucky began to cry softly. "I'm hungry."

"Yes, dear. I know you're hungry. All of us are. Those horsetails and rock tripe we nibbled along the way weren't very filling. I'll see if I can locate the pot that has the dried apricots in it. We can chew on a few of those while we're falling asleep."

Jill Gordon brought a bag of shelled walnuts. "These were in the pot I carried. Can we eat them now?"

"I suppose we can eat a few. How about two halves each? No telling how long they'll need to last."

Laurel started shaking two nuts in Jill's open palm. "Hold it, Laurel," interrupted Larry. "We should thank God for the food and the safe journey thus far. Let's bow our heads. Mother, would you please offer our thanks?"

"Dear Lord, we thank Thee we have health and strength and can enjoy our apricots and walnuts," Mrs. Lambert began quietly. "Thou hast promised bread and water, but we are faring even better. May this food nourish our bodies.

"We thank Thee, too, for the good weather. Tonight seems unusually warm for mid-May, and we're grateful it isn't raining.

"Now protect us through the night, and be with those we love but who are not with us. Unite us soon in heaven with Thee, we pray in the name of Jesus. Amen."

Soon all was quiet except for the forest sounds, which grew louder by the minute. It seemed the woods had come alive with creatures large and small. The moon's rays did not penetrate the evergreen canopy, and one could only suspect that from all directions curious eyes peered at the strange new forest dwellers.

Chapter 35

DOOMSDAY

Tuesday promised to be an ideal spring day. As the birds greeted the first blush of dawn with their joyous chorus the campers rolled up their sleeping bags and headed toward Boundary Bald Mountain. It was May 15.

By noon they were well up the slope. Viewing the world from that point, it was hard to imagine that evil existed anywhere. Peace seemed to reign as far as the eye could see. A nearby mountain stream promised clear water for drinking and cooking. The campers felt fortunate to find a safe water supply.

Laurel began to gather sticks for the fire to cook some rice and whatever the children might bring back from their foraging expedition. She was getting tired of rice. Deciding to boil some birch roots for a tasty drink, she approached a clump of birches, found a sharp triangular stone, and started to dig. Soon she had a heap of tender roots. She gathered them up, then noticed an oval, white object at the base of one of the trees.

"No. It can't be!" she exclaimed, after hurrying over for a closer look. "What would a hen's egg be doing here?" Carefully she picked it up. "Wonder how old it is. I'll boil it and then find out." Then her eye caught sight of another egg and another. "Three eggs! May as well scramble them and let everyone have a taste. . . . No, Paul needs them most. I'll boil one for him. We'll see if he'll eat the yolk mashed up and mixed with water.''

The eggs proved to be in good condition. Little Paul ate several mouthfuls of egg yolk, much to Joyce's amazement and relief. Laurel mixed the white of Paul's egg and the other two eggs in with the rice to stretch them so all could share in the unexpected treat.

Later Rick Gordon shouted, "Look over there." All eyes followed his pointing finger. On a low birch branch perched two hens surveying the campers and muttering to each other.

"God is surely good to us," Dorothy said.

Laurel couldn't respond for the lump in her throat. She looked at her mother, who was wiping away a tear.

"How did they get up here?" Jill asked.

"God sent them," her father replied.

With the meal finished, Joyce decided to wash some diapers. She went downstream a ways, and, using a large rock as a washboard, pounded and twisted until her hands were too numb from the icy water to wring out another diaper. Then she spread them out on bushes to dry.

"I wouldn't spread them out like that," her husband cautioned. "They're too conspicuous from the air."

"In this warm sun they'll dry in minutes. If any plane or helicopter comes near, I'll hide them quickly."

"Too bad you didn't bring disposable ones."

She stared at him. "Are you serious? Imagine bringing a two-year supply of diapers along! We'd need a truck just for them."

"With the pounding you were giving them they'll do well to last two months. Doesn't that one on the low bush have a tear in it?''

His wife glanced at it. "Yes. The rock had two or three jagged spots. I'll look for a smoother one tomorrow."

"Tomorrow?"

"At least every other day." She laughed. "That is, unless you're willing to let your son adopt a more primitive mode of dress."

Rick had been appointed official lookout for planes and helicopters. Suddenly, with typical eight-year-old excitement, he pointed straight up and shrieked, "There's a plane!"

So high that they could scarcely hear the engine noise circled a small single-engine plane. Joyce and Larry simultaneously grabbed diapers off the bushes. Everyone else scrambled under a tree or bush.

When the plane had vanished, Larry helped Joyce hang the diapers on branches at the base of a large tree. "This method of drying may take longer, but I'm sure it doesn't advertise our position so loudly," he said. "Let's hope that plane wasn't spying on fugitives."

About midafternoon angry black clouds seemed to rise out of nowhere. They quickly obliterated the sun as though an unseen hand pulled a blanket over the earth. The clouds clashed against each other while the roll of thunder caused the earth to tremble. Rick, Kathy, and Chucky screamed as the others watched the scene in terrified silence. The darkness of midnight settled over the earth.

Soon they heard an ominous roar, followed by an earthquake that shook Boundary Bald Mountain so violently that boulders flew in all directions. No one could remain standing. Some, crying to God audibly and others silently, clutched bushes and roots to avoid being hurled down the careening slope. Cooking utensils, food supplies, sleeping bags, all rolled, slid, or bounced on their downward chase. The stream that had been their water supply changed its course on the drastically altered landscape and flowed in another direction.

Meanwhile the morning of the fifteenth found Duane on his knees when Rocky brought him his daily ration. "I brought less than usual because they'll be coming for you today, you know."

"Yes, I know," Duane said slowly.

"It might not be too late to save yourself."

" 'Whosoever will save his life shall lose it: and whosoever will lose his life for my sake shall find it.' "

The guard went away shaking his head, wondering whether anxiety had driven his prisoner insane.

That evening two policemen with handcuffs came to get Duane. He offered no resistance as they linked his wrists with theirs. They led him out to a small enclosed courtyard, where they placed him facing a recently constructed brick wall with his hands cuffed together on the opposite side of a large post. He noticed two other similar posts.

"I understand there are two more," one of the policemen commented. "Let's bring them and get this over with."

Duane heard their footsteps retreating and the courtyard door open and close. He did not know if he was alone in the courtyard or not. The fresh air of the spring evening smelled wonderful after his two-week confinement in the reeking cell. But his knees were so weak that he sank to the ground. For a second he wondered whether he would have any warning, then hoped he would not.

Soon the policemen returned with Keith. They attached him to the post next to Duane's. When they were gone Keith looked over at him and said, "They told me you had renounced your beliefs. I was sorry I hadn't been of greater encouragement."

Duane shook his head. "They had me in solitary confinement."

"Well, I guess in their way they were doing all they knew

how to change our minds and thus save our lives.''

"They probably don't relish this execution either,''
Duane agreed.

The policemen returned with Dwight. As they were
preparing to handcuff him to his post the warm sun suddenly
ceased to shine. A crash of lightning snapped off the post.
The policeman dropped the key to the handcuffs. Dwight
leaned over and picked up the key, which he attempted to
return to the officer, who was trembling too violently to
accept it.

Then there came a roar like that of a locomotive, followed by such heavings of the earth that the brick walls
enclosing the courtyard toppled in seconds. The policemen
fled, screaming. Calmly Dwight took the key still in his hand
and unlocked Keith's handcuffs, then Duane's. Duane felt
strength return to his weak knees. The three men looked
around the courtyard and noted two pistols lying beside an
upturned table. They left the weapons undisturbed and
climbed out of the enclosure over a wall of rubble.

The sky grew blacker. The streetlights came on, only to
vanish moments later in flashes and sparks as another quake
snapped their wires. Lampposts, telephone poles, trees, and
buildings reeled and toppled. Cars slid sideways as the streets
pitched violently.

Screams and prayers of the terrified, injured, and dying
competed with the roll of thunder that rose in a crescendo till
the earth throbbed.

Suddenly a shaft of glory pierced the clouds, and all was
still. Then a sound like rushing water came from the heavens
and echoed and reechoed through the earth. "It is the voice of
God,'' Dwight whispered.

Earlier that day, in Boston, Alexander glanced at the
morning paper while drinking his orange juice and waiting

for the toaster to deliver his customary two slices. Gina was still in bed. The headlines dealt with the progress of the peace talks. Farther down the page another caption caught his eye: "Doomsday for Dissenters."

"Oh, yes. This is the fifteenth," he mused aloud. "Think I'll check on my way to the hospital to see whether Laurel and Chucky have been found. They'll no doubt be sending Chucky to me, as they aren't planning to intentionally execute any minors." Then he turned to the sports section to see how the Red Sox were standing in the American League.

On the way to the hospital he stopped at the police station. "Could you check to see if a certain Adventist was captured?" he asked the sergeant on duty. "I was married to her once."

"What's her name and number?"

The sergeant punched out Laurel's name and identification number on a computer terminal. Shortly there appeared on the screen the following information: "Laurel Lambert Robertson Manning. Female. Age 27. Divorced from Alexander Robertson. Son, Charles Robertson, age four. Recently married to Duane Manning. Last seen in area of Brassua Lake, Maine."

"Good!" Alexander thought.

He went through the same procedure for Duane and learned that he was awaiting execution in the jail at Skowhegan, Maine.

Soon Alexander was busy visiting patients at the hospital and caring for emergencies. On his evening rounds he stopped in to tell old Mrs. Jobe her X ray looked good and she could leave the hospital the next day.

"Oh, thank you, Dr. Robertson. I can hardly wait to see my new granddaughter."

He smiled. "This isn't the first, surely."

"Oh, no. I have twelve other grandchildren. But this one is special. They say she looks just like *me*." Her face beamed as she squirmed with embarrassment.

Alexander patted her shoulder. "Well, you take good care of her. If she looks like you, she must be a mighty pretty baby."

Just then a crash of lightning startled both of them. A roar, and the building began to sway. Patients screamed. He hurried to the window and watched as an adjoining wing jackknifed and collapsed in a cloud of dust.

In terror he watched the Charles River boil up to cover Storrow Drive. He felt the floor slant toward the river. Mrs. Jobe screamed as her bed started to roll. It crashed into the wall at the same moment that her roommate's bed smashed into hers.

Alexander felt himself falling. Excruciating pain convulsed his body. He opened his eyes but could see nothing. Then cold water engulfed him.

"O God——" He opened his mouth to say the words, but the water filling his throat stifled his voice.

Chapter 36

FREEDOM

Duane, Keith, and Dwight looked around in disbelief. The wall of the jail on the courtyard side had collapsed, and the moans of the injured rose from the rubble. The frame office building connected to the jail hadn't suffered badly.

In the darkness—broken by the flames of nearby burning structures—the trio searched the abandoned office building for their clothes. In a closet Duane found his wedding suitcase intact with his wallet and the clothes he had worn at the time of his capture. Keith and Dwight also found usable clothing. In the guards' bathroom they hurriedly cleaned up as much as possible without seeing. Duane had not shaved for ten days, and his beard was long enough to pass as intentional, though it badly needed trimming.

"Shall we stay together?" asked Keith, who really had no place to go.

"I'd like to check on my wife," Dwight said.

"Do you have far to go?"

"Just about six miles. I can walk. So long, and God be with you." Dwight shook hands with Duane and Keith and hurried off in the darkness.

"We can stay together if you wish, Keith, but I, too, want to check on my wife. We were married just before my capture."

"Yes, I know." Sadness fleeted across his face, but only

238

momentarily. "I don't blame you. You go on by yourself. I'll make out fine—Jesus will soon be here to take us all home."

He shook Duane's hand with a firm brick-mason grip. As Duane hurried away he glanced over his shoulder and saw the man standing alone in the dimness.

Frequent lightning flashes revealed gaping chasms in the road that made walking hazardous. Duane knew he would have to cover the fifteen miles to Bingham on foot, but the faintness he had felt earlier in the day had vanished. Carefully he crept along feeling his way. He wondered as he went if he had made everything right with his Lord. He couldn't think of any sin left unforgiven, but still he searched his mind.

An eerie wail, as of a hurricane, almost drowned out the cries of the injured and dying. The ground continued to heave and swell. Suddenly huge hailstones began to fall. Duane took shelter in an abandoned automobile. The hail soon turned the shatterproof windshield into a crazed screen diffusing the lightning flashes. It pounded the car in deafening blows that flattened the hood and dented the roof.

Almost as abruptly as it had begun, the storm ceased. The clouds rolled back, revealing a setting sun. He made use of the waning daylight to hurry on his way. Practically every house along the route had suffered earthquake and hail damage, and the owners frantically tried to make temporary repairs before nightfall. Pedestrians scurrying toward home, wondering what they would find, crowded the highway.

Duane had covered only a few miles when the darkness made further travel unsafe. In front of a small church he found another abandoned car, and after trying three doors that were too battered to open, he managed to enter by the fourth. He lay down on the back seat and quickly fell asleep.

Sometime during the night screaming awakened him. He could not see through the shattered glass, so he climbed out of the car. Black, angry clouds jostled each other everywhere except at the zenith, where a cloud tunnel revealed the glories of the starry heavens. People stood everywhere, their eyes riveted on the opening in the sky.

A hand appeared, holding two stone tablets, which everyone recognized, though they were closed. Slowly the tablets opened, revealing in letters of fire large enough for all to read the ten precepts written by the hand of God at Sinai.

Women fainted, men dropped to the earth and buried their heads in their arms in an attempt to eradicate the image still blazing on their retinas, while children screamed and hid their faces in their mothers' skirts.

The scene faded from the sky, and the angry clouds crashed back together. Someone dragged a silver-haired man in clerical attire from his prostrate position on the ground to the steps of the church. He raised his hands to quiet the crowd, when suddenly a rock hurtled past him. A voice shouted, "False shepherd." Others immediately picked up the taunt, and it soon swelled into a chant. More rocks began to fly as the mob rushed in fury upon one who had neglected to proclaim God's character as revealed through the transcript of His law.

Duane withdrew from the crowd and returned to the car. He tried to sleep, but the chant of the murderous mob continued to echo in his ears. At the first graying of the sky, he resumed his journey.

When he arrived in Bingham he saw a barbershop that appeared to be open. He entered, and the stooped barber peered over his reading glasses and laid down his day-old newspaper. "Can I help ya?" he inquired in a nasal twang.

"Are you open for business?"

"I'll do what I can. Power's off."

"I need a haircut, shave, and shampoo."

The man eyed him. "Ya sure do, Son. Been camping?"

"Off and on."

While lathering Duane's face the barber asked, "What d'ya make of all that's been happening the last coupla days?"

"Jesus is coming."

"Could be. Even nature seems to be agin us. Didn't get the Waterville *Sentinel* today. Probably the quake smashed the presses. Or maybe they just couldn't deliver it."

"I don't suppose you've gotten any news over the radio or TV either," Duane said from under the lather.

"Nope. Where were you during the quake?"

"Skowhegan."

The barber began sharpening his razor. "Was the damage as bad there?"

"Worse, much worse."

"You're a stranger here, ain't ya?"

"Yes. I'm looking for a Laurel Manning, who recently moved here. How can I locate her?"

The old man thought a moment. "Tried the post office?"

"No."

"Well, they should know her. It's just the next block." He pointed with his razor.

At the post office no one had heard of Laurel Manning.

"She's recently been married," Duane persisted. "Have you perhaps heard of Laurel Robertson?" No one had. The postmaster showed him how to get to the police station. When he entered he noted one wall was cracked open and the floor tilted noticeably. "May I help you?" the officer on duty asked.

"Do you have a register of the Adventists in this town?"

"I have a computer printout for the whole state, but it's not up to date. Who is it you're looking for?"

"Laurel Robertson Manning."

The officer scratched his chin in thought. "Name sounds familiar. Isn't she the girl who came to Reverend Kleppinger to be married a couple of weeks ago?''

"That's right."

"Yes, that one. They caught her husband and were holding him in the county jail. I guess they finished him off yesterday. The girl escaped. I've heard rumors she's camping with some others near Brassua Lake. By the way, what do you want with her?''

"I've been told she has given up her religion and is living in town. I'm an old friend and want to learn if that's the case.''

"We have names and addresses of everybody in town. It's illegal to rent to anyone without supplying this information to the police. Here's the book. Check for yourself.''

Duane looked up Laurel Robertson, Sue Robertson, Laurel Manning, Sue Manning, Laurel Lambert, and found nothing.

Somehow he felt a bit happier as he left the police station. A thought occurred to him for the first time. If Laurel had really capitulated and wanted him to do likewise, why hadn't she put a return address on her letter? And why didn't she come to the jail in person to persuade him to follow her example?

Chapter 37

CAREER'S END

Rasmussen paced back and forth in President McGrath's office, tightly clenched fists punctuating his remarks. "I can't understand what has gone wrong. The Adventists were all supposed to die yesterday. If any lost their lives, it hasn't come to my attention. But look at the millions of law-abiding citizens who did perish in the earthquakes and tidal wave. No doubt if I hadn't pleaded with our spirit leader, the city of Washington, too, would have been destroyed."

"Well, do you have any more suggestions, or do you intend to resign as my chief adviser?" she demanded, her faith in him severely shaken.

He turned toward her. "I keep trying to look into the future but never can get beyond this week. The spirits won't cooperate with me."

"Have you contacted your Spiritualist friends in other countries?"

Rasmussen shook his head. "Yesterday we couldn't get any signals through. Must be solar flares or something like that. I'll report to you when we're successful."

Rasmussen left the President's office and went to the radio room, where Jackson had already made contact with someone. As Rasmussen entered and closed the door Jackson spoke into the microphone, "He just came in. I'll let you talk to him."

243

"Who is it?" Rasmussen asked as he took the mike.

"Joe in Tel Aviv."

"Joe, what have you found out?"

The man's voice crackled and hissed through the speaker. "I don't know what's going on. I've never heard of earthquakes shaking the entire globe before. Most of Tel Aviv sank into the Mediterranean yesterday. Today I tried to drive to the station, but the road was so broken up I had to walk part of the way. I took a shortcut through a cemetery. The quake had thrown bodies everywhere."

"Listen. It's hard to hear you over the static. Have the spirits told you anything?"

"Nothing. Frankly, I'm terrified," Joe exclaimed.

"Yes, I know how you feel. Have you contacted anyone else?"

"I talked earlier today with Cardoni from Rome, which—as you probably know—has been in darkness for three days now. The power grid for that whole section of the country failed. The clouds are so black and thick no lamplight will penetrate very far."

The static drowned everything out for several moments, then it ebbed. "How did Cardoni radio you if the power's out?"

"He radioed from Naples. Said it took twice the normal time to drive down because the roads were impassable in many places. He said not to be surprised if I learn he has committed suicide."

"What!"

"Says the spirits have been tormenting him. He's afraid he'll go mad."

"Well, I plan to hang on a little longer. Things have got to get better."

Joe's voice sounded doubtful. "I hope so. Don't know how much more I can take."

Rasmussen slumped into a leather armchair and sighed. "Jackson, I really think we've had it."

The other man looked surprised. "But—but, only two months ago you said on TV that you expected Jesus to return in a matter of weeks to rebuild the Temple in Jerusalem and reign there a thousand years. Do you still expect that to happen?"

Rasmussen shrugged. "It could."

"What does your spirit guide say?" Jackson persisted.

"He seems to have lost interest in us." Rasmussen seemed to shrink within himself.

Jackson flipped off the radio transmitter. "Why don't you try again? It can't hurt anything."

"You're right." The spiritist stood up to go to his private suite. "I'll be back soon."

When three hours later he had not returned, Jackson attempted to call him. No response. Concerned, he called the White House guards to learn whether Rasmussen had left. No one had seen him since the old man had entered his suite. When President McGrath phoned Jackson in an attempt to locate Rasmussen, he told her what he knew.

A guard went to Rasmussen's suite and knocked. No one answered. He tried the door and found it locked. Producing a skeleton key, he unlocked the door and swung it open. The conference room was dark, as the heavy scarlet draperies covered the window. The guard located the light switch and flipped it.

Rasmussen sprawled on the floor, a splintered chair scattered around him, his face in a pool of blood. Cautiously the guard touched Rasmussen's cold face, then went for a doctor, who pronounced the spiritist dead. A preliminary investigation led to the conclusion that strangulation and a blow on the head from the chair had caused Rasmussen's death.

It seemed impossible that anyone could have entered the

room unnoticed by the guards or undetected by the security devices. The key to the room lay on the table beside Rasmussen's body. The windows were locked, and police found no fingerprints other than Rasmussen's on the body, key, or chair.

Eventually Jackson recalled that Joe had mentioned earlier in the day that the spirits had been tormenting Cardoni. Perhaps Rasmussen had also offended them, he thought. Or maybe it was just that the man was no longer of use to them.

Chapter 38

FINIS

Though the global communications network had suffered severely from Tuesday's earthquake and tidal waves, which had annihilated many major relay and broadcasting stations, gradually engineers reestablished communications. The air force managed to orbit a couple extra communication satellites. Many governments set up emergency portable base units. By Thursday night Washington was in contact with most of the globe.

Around five o'clock Friday morning the phone by President McGrath's bed rang. She could hardly pull herself out of her drugged sleep, but she realized that Security Chief Van Huesen sounded excited. "Our contact with Tokyo has just been lost. An hour ago Sydney cut off abruptly. An hour and a half earlier we lost New Zealand."

"What do you think caused it?" she asked groggily, fumbling for the light switch.

"I've no idea. Our seismologists report an earth disturbance of such magnitude that their instruments cannot measure its intensity or extent. It must have knocked out the satellite ground stations. As you know, most of the sea cables were cut long ago."

"Then you do not believe we are about to experience an enemy attack?"

"That's correct. But let me point out that natural catastrophes can be even more destructive.''

"Are we in immediate danger?'' She rubbed her eyes,
tried breathing deeply to clear her mind.

Van Huesen's voice trembled. "I—I don't know. If I
were a foreign power I would be very tempted to attack after
all the damage we've had. But then he would probably be
hurting as bad as we are. All we can do is wait.''

The President hung up the receiver and tried to resume
her sleep.

At nine o'clock the phone rang again. Van Huesen informed her that the military had lost contact with everything
east of Sri Lanka.

"How about Sri Lanka itself?''

"We're still receiving them.''

"What do they observe?''

"They are feeling some tremors. But they did notice a
small black cloud in the distance that appears to be approaching with considerable speed. There's disagreement whether
it is an atmospheric phenomenon or something in space.''

She tried to fight down her rising sense of panic. "Do you
think we should alert the nation to the possibility of another
earthquake?''

"Let's wait a few hours and see what develops.''

By two o'clock all communication east of Paris had
ceased. President McGrath felt that the nation should be
warned of impending disaster and issued orders accordingly.

Television programming had not resumed since the
Tuesday quakes, but many radio stations broadcast to local
audiences. Baseball fans grumbled about the cancellation of
certain games and lack of TV coverage of others. Children
were at a loss as to how to entertain themselves without their
favorite TV programs. The day was beautiful, and many
homeowners were taking advantage of the fine weather and
absence of TV to repair the damage done three days before.

Within a few minutes after President McGrath's order, radio stations interrupted their broadcasting to announce, "Please turn your dial to your Civil Defense station for an important message. We repeat, turn your dial to your Civil Defense station for an important message. Other stations are now asked to discontinue broadcasting."

The few who heard the message and did as requested learned that an unclassified disaster of unknown magnitude would affect the United States, starting in the east and progressing westward. It would travel about the speed of the earth's rotation and would arrive around sunset at any point. Those hearing the message were asked to alert others and prepare for it by getting away from buildings, especially tall ones, and to take food and water supplies with them.

President McGrath, after issuing the warning, refused to leave the White House. She said that since the nature of the impending disaster was unknown, she intended to remain at her post of duty. She did insist, however, that the Vice-president and the cabinet members flee from the city.

Radio operator Jackson also elected to remain at the White House. With the President beside him, he tried to establish contact with various parts of the globe. At five o'clock Brasilia reported tremors and the small dark cloud.

"It appears black, about the size of a man's hand. It has grown from a scarcely perceptible speck in just a few moments. It seems to be getting . . . "

Silence. All attempts at reestablishing contact failed.

"Shall we try Trinidad?" Jackson suggested.

President McGrath was pale. She arose unsteadily and headed for the door of the radio room. "No. It's too late. I'm going to pray. Please escape while you have time to get out of the city."

On the eastern slope of Boundary Bald Mountain the

little group of Sabbathkeepers scanned the horizon. They had
watched intently since dawn, and it was now dusk. No one
had made any efforts to prepare a meal. "Do you really think
it will be today?" Jill asked once more.

"We all got the same impression from the Voice," her
mother assured her. "It could hardly have been a coinci-
dence."

"Let's sing some more," Joyce said.

"You go ahead, but don't expect me to lead," Laurel
commented. "My throat is hoarse from so much singing."

"So is mine," Zip added.

"I think praying would be appropriate," suggested
Larry. "Can we form a circle and hold hands while each one
offers a short prayer? Mother, we'll start with you and go
right around."

Ten prayers were said. Each one remembered Duane,
and most also included Kathy's parents and the Ramseys.
But the main burden of each prayer was a plea for favor in the
sight of a holy God through Christ's righteousness.

At the close of the prayers Larry led in singing:

> "Lift up the trumpet, and loud let it ring:
>   Jesus is coming again!
>   Cheer up, ye pilgrims, be joyful and sing;
>   Jesus is coming again!
>   Coming again, coming again,
>   Jesus is coming again!"

To the amazement of all, an echoing male voice answered with the same refrain. In a few moments some rus-
tling bushes parted, and out stepped a man. "Duane!"
everyone shouted as they ran to meet him.

"How did you ever find us?" Laurel cried, as she flung
her arms around him.

Laughing through tears of joy, Duane answered, "I followed the singing."

"But how did you know where to look for us?" Mrs. Lambert inquired.

"A pilot." Duane could hardly talk for laughing. "I overheard him say he'd seen diapers sunning on the mountain. I figured they must belong to Paul."

While everyone crowded around, questioning him about his imprisonment and escape, Jill started jumping up and down. "Look, look!" she shouted and pointed toward the eastern sky.

A black spot on the horizon was barely visible against the darkening sky. Laurel and Duane stood with their arms around each other as all gazed in awestruck silence. The object rapidly drew nearer, becoming lighter as it approached, until it appeared as a dazzlingly white cloud whose base was ablaze. A dull rumble, barely audible at first, swelled to a throbbing roar as mountains and valleys flattened to a plain beneath the cloud. As it approached, all heaven came alive with radiant creatures surrounding a Being whose brightness surpassed the sun.

The little group on the mountain turned pale as they tremblingly sank to their knees and cried out, "Who is able to stand in the presence of God?"

The suspense was dreadful till a Voice from the cloud proclaimed, "My grace is sufficient for you." Then all heaven rang with the singing of the angel hosts.

As the cloud filled the entire sky the earth reeled, and lightnings added their feeble illumination to the scene. The Voice, like the blast of many trumpets, called, "Awake! awake! awake! Ye that sleep in the dust, arise!"

The bowels of the earth convulsed. Mrs. Lambert noticed someone at her side. Then she recognized Turner, not as she had seen him last, but even handsomer than when

she had first known him before the years had grayed his hair
and stooped his shoulders. She reached out to embrace him
and felt the vigor of eternal youth filling her own being,
sharpening her vision, smoothing the furrows time had
etched. "Turner!" she cried as she threw herself into his
arms.

"Madeleine! How beautiful you look!"

There stood Kathy clutching a person on each side of her.
"Mommy, why did you and Daddy leave me so long? I
missed you a lot." Her mother squeezed her hand in reply.

The cloud continued to roll westward. As the Being
seated on the throne passed directly overhead, Boundary
Bald Mountain flattened out. The roar of earth's convulsing
elements faded, while peals from ten thousand trumpets
welcomed ten adults, four children, and baby Paul—along
with multitudes of others—to the celestial throng.

Other interesting, exciting Orion books with something for every member of the family.

UNBLESSED
by Berneice Lunday

Religious persecution is not a thing of the past, as Margaret finds when she decides to marry outside her Catholic faith and realizes that her wedding day is not to be the end of the unhappiness she has known since childhood. A story of the cruelty of prejudice and one woman's search for happiness and a religious faith that included a loving God. An unforgettable account of courage and love. 128 pages, US$1.95.

THE COMPLEAT MARRIAGE
by Nancy Van Pelt

A manual for happy marriage that teaches how to understand, accept, communicate with, have fun with, and sexually fulfill your mate. Companion volume to *The Compleat Parent*. 160 pages, US$2.95.

THE COMPLEAT PARENT
by Nancy Van Pelt

A bestselling book of easy-to-learn, easy-to-use methods to effectively discipline your children. Emphasizes the importance of training before age five but also explains how to effectively communicate with and discipline children of all ages. 160 pages, US$2.95.

WITNESSES THROUGH TRIAL
by Marvin Moore

Stories of Christians whose faith held firm despite prison, hunger, wild Indians, and firing squads. And of those who will someday be able to see how their witnessing affected others. 128 pages, US$1.95.

WHERE ARE WE RUNNING?
by June Strong

A collection of essays reflecting June's uncommon way of looking at everyday events. The wit and wisdom that have made her monthly column in *These Times* magazine a favorite shine through in her latest book as it did in her two other works—*Mindy* and *Journal of a Happy Woman*. 128 pages, US$1.95.

FLEE THE CAPTOR
by Herbert Ford

The gripping story of John Henry Weidner, hero of history's greatest holocaust. As a member of the Dutch-Paris underground, Weidner saved the lives of 800 Jews and over 100 Allied aviators and others trying to escape the terror of Nazism. 373 pages, US$2.95.

THE APPEARING
by Penny Estes Wheeler

The days before Christ's return are filled with emotional as well as physical struggles. *The Appearing* is the story of five of those who endured to the end. As told in their own words. Available September, 1979, US$2.95.

HANDY ORDER FORM

Qty	Title	*Price	Total
	The Appearing (Available September, 1979)	$2.95	
	The Compleat Marriage	$2.95	
	The Compleat Parent	$2.95	
	Flee the Captor	$2.95	
	Unblessed	$1.95	
	Where Are We Running?	$1.95	
	Witnesses Through Trial	$1.95	

Subtotal		
Shipping and handling (10% of the subtotal, 75¢ minimum)		
Local sales tax		
Total		

Send this coupon to
Southern Publishing Association
P.O. Box 59
Nashville, TN 37202

*Prices good through December 31, 1980.